"This can

"Reckless," [...] t comes to you, I will [...]

His head lowered and she pressed a hand to the center of his chest to back him up short. She felt his heart beating and froze. She absorbed the way his breath snagged and his shoulders lifted and fell in rapid succession. To know she still had this effect on him—it was potent. "You better not kiss me, you fool."

"Why not?" he asked, the flat of his brow coming to rest against hers.

Don't answer that. Don't you dare answer that, Luella. "Because..."

"Because?"

Her hands had fisted in his collar. Now, when had they done that? "Because I want you...to shut the hell up." And then she did something foolish and all other manner of mixed-up things she didn't understand.

She kissed him.

Dear Reader,

Welcome back to Eaton Edge! In this second installment of my Fuego, New Mexico trilogy, I'm excited to give you Ellis's story. (If you haven't read the story of his sister, Eveline, and her hero, Wolfe, no worries! Each book can be read as a stand-alone romance.)

No one ever forgets their first love. Add in all the heartache of the one who got away and you have the story of Ellis and his heroine, Luella. A long time ago, these two fell in love against the stunning backdrop of Eaton Edge and northeast New Mexico. Then secrets, lies and betrayal tore them apart. Over a decade later, things between them are more complicated than ever...but their feelings for each other never went away.

I love the idea of old love renewing itself and a place like Eaton Edge bringing people who need each other together. I also love how Ellis is determined to protect Luella and those most dear to her from everyone, even the killer who is determined to chase her out of Fuego for good.

I hope you enjoy Ellis and Luella. As always, dear reader, happy reading!

Sincerely,

Amber

OLLERO CREEK CONSPIRACY

Amber Leigh Williams

Recycling programs
for this product may
not exist in your area.

ISBN-13: 978-1-335-59385-6

Ollero Creek Conspiracy

Copyright © 2023 by Amber Leigh Williams

For questions and comments about the quality of this book, please contact us at CustomerService@Harlequin.com.

Harlequin Enterprises ULC
22 Adelaide St. West, 41st Floor
Toronto, Ontario M5H 4E3, Canada
www.Harlequin.com

Printed in U.S.A.

Amber Leigh Williams is an author, wife, mother of two and dog mom. She has been writing sexy small-town romance with memorable characters since 2006. She lives on the Alabama Gulf Coast, where she loves being outdoors with her family and a good book. Visit her on the web at amberleighwilliams.com!

Books by Amber Leigh Williams

Harlequin Romantic Suspense

Hunted on the Bay

Fuego, New Mexico

Coldero Ridge Cowboy
Ollero Creek Conspiracy

Harlequin Superromance

Navy SEAL's Match
Navy SEAL Promise
Wooing the Wedding Planner
His Rebel Heart
Married One Night
A Place with Briar

Visit the Author Profile page at Harlequin.com for more titles.

To rescue animals. Thank you for helping to quiet the noise in our heads just by being.

Chapter 1

Luella Decker knew the devil never went down to Georgia. He had set up camp in her hometown of Fuego, New Mexico, for the better part of sixty years.

Now that he was dead, Luella couldn't wait to leave. Fuego was home to more tumult than security—more heartbreak than love—because the devil, Jace "Whip" Decker, had been her father. She'd come home after a six-month sentence in county lock-up long enough to sell her house, pack her things, load up her animals and hit the road.

Soon, she'd leave Fuego in the dust. She knew now never to retrace her steps.

"Turn here," she told the Uber driver.

"Okay," he said obediently. He'd been pretty leery since realizing he wasn't picking up a visitor to Fuego County Jail but a released prisoner. He glanced around. "You, ah, live pretty far outside of town."

"Yes." It's what she'd liked most about the Ollero Creek property. It was on the outskirts, far from prying eyes. She looked across the expanse. The landscape was the only thing Fuego had going for it. In early December, the red sand hills of her youth were dusted white. She could hear the car's tires sluicing over snowmelt that would morph into a muddy mess soon. In the distance, she could see the buttes and mesas that marked the high desert country for the jaw-dropping vista it was. The climate was hot and harsh in summer, but due to its position near the Colorado Plateau, it was cold and snowy in winter.

The driver cleared his throat as they rolled and bumped up the unpaved lane. "What, uh…what'd you do time for—if you don't mind me asking?"

She avoided meeting his eyes in the rearview mirror and chose not to answer. He was likely from somewhere inside the bounds of Fuego County…which meant he'd heard about her father abducting the daughter of a local cattle baron. The daughter, Eveline Eaton, happened to be something of a national celebrity.

That wasn't the only reason Luella's case was newsworthy. Alone, she was no one. When she wasn't working her day job as a trauma nurse at Fuego County Hospital, she lived on the fringes of society. Her father was supposed to have died after killing the Eatons' mother and stepsister in a land dispute seven and a half years ago. He'd disappeared into high desert country. Police had blamed his supposed demise on mountain lions.

It was the promise of living in Fuego without her father that lured Luella back to the town after an extended absence. She'd escaped after high school with her mother to San Gabriel—a clean-cut city far enough away from Fuego for peace of mind.

It wasn't long after she moved back that Luella learned the truth. Her father was very much alive and hiding out in the multitude of caves at Coldero Ridge. He'd come to her over the last seven years in search of food and weapons.

Luella had given him what he'd needed. She'd done whatever it'd taken to survive because nothing scared her more than being at Whip Decker's mercy. Long before he'd taken the lives of Josephine and Angel Eaton in cold blood, he'd knocked her and her mother around the double-wide that had been their home. He drank every afternoon until he was mean with it and condemned both her mother and Luella with words and the brunt of his hand, leaving scars on the surface and deep.

Some of her scars had faded. Others were permanent residents on Luella's skin and mind.

Seven years she'd lived in fear he'd come for her in the night and finish the job he liked to remind her he should've ended the night she was born. He'd brought her into the world. She'd known at some point he'd take her out of it.

That was why she'd been saving. For years, she'd put money away—determined to have enough to escape—from Whip Decker, from Fuego, from the dumpster fire that was her life there.

He hadn't taken her out of the world. He was gone for good this time, and she'd plead guilty to aiding and abetting him. The defense lawyer had argued coercion and self-defense so she'd only served six months but had lost the job she'd had for almost a decade and what little was left of her reputation.

The Uber driver whistled low as he made the turn into the driveway. "That's some house."

Luella's heart gave a tug. She'd painted it white so that it stood stark against the dry, red-stained landscape like the salvation it had been for her seven years ago. It was the first thing that had ever truly been hers.

It was three stories high, box-shaped, with a wide porch braced high above the dry creek bed. There had been no creek at Ollero Creek for half a century but a preserved waterwheel stood as its testament.

What she'd never told anyone—not a soul—was that she'd bought the house because it was ideal for stargazing. As a girl, she'd been obsessed with the cosmos—mapping them, understanding their pieces and their mysteries...

"Home sweet home, huh?" the driver asked.

She realized he'd parked and she was staring wistfully out the window. She frowned and shifted toward the door. "Thanks for the lift." She started to open it. "Oh," she said, hesitating. "I guess I need to pay you."

"The bill was prepaid."

"Pre..." She narrowed her eyes. "Who paid you?"

He drummed his fingers on the steering wheel, impatient to leave. "Uh, the app didn't say. It just gave me an address. And instructions to be there at ten."

Luella didn't like the idea of owing anyone anything. She opened the door and stepped out. No sooner had she shut it than the tires skidded and the car sped away, fishtailing across the icy, wet road.

She probably should've told the driver she wasn't a hard-core killer—that she'd never harmed another human being in her life. Then again, she thought, this was more fun.

The smile stopped before it started when she heard the restless sounds of her chickens. She took off across the drive and around the side of the house.

The rooster, Caesar, greeted her with a bob of his head and a hoarse croak. As her steps picked up pace, he flapped his wings and skittered out of her path. His grumblings sent the rest of the flock into shrieks and cackles. Inside their coop, wings beat and feathers flew.

She'd check in with them in a minute. First things first: she'd waited six months to see her man and she wasn't going to wait a moment longer.

"Mama's home!" she called as she swung into the barn. There were two stalls. The one on the left had held her sow and its piglets. She'd given them to her neighbor Naleen Altaha and her family in exchange for feeding the others while she was gone.

The stall on the right should have been occupied. Her heart sank like a stone when she saw that the gate was ajar. "Sheridan?" Her panicked call echoed back to her from the rough-hewn rafters.

There was no horse, no hay, no manure—no sign that anything had lived there.

"Oh, my God." Her stomach cramped and she pressed her hand to it.

Her horse was gone.

Her cheeks heated as panic escalated. She kicked the gate farther open so she could pass through it. She trudged back to the house, Caesar squawking irritably at her heels. She reached around the last step on the porch stairs and moved the smooth river rock she'd left there. Grabbing the key underneath, she ran up the stairs, shoved it into the lock of the front door, cranked the knob and flew into the living room.

The phone was mounted to the wall. She pulled down the receiver and dialed Naleen's number.

As it rang, she gave up trying to tamp down the heat

in her cheeks. She was a redhead and her horse wasn't where she'd left him.

"Hello?"

"Where's Sheridan?" she said. She did her best to ungnash her teeth but wasn't very successful there, either. "He's not here. Where *is* he, Naleen?"

"Calm down, Luella, okay?"

"Don't tell me to calm down!" Luella all but shouted. "Where *the hell* is my horse?"

"I'm trying to tell you!" Naleen said. "Three weeks ago, I saw him favoring his back right leg. I couldn't get the equine vet out there. He didn't want to come unless he knew you were available to pay for the home visit. So I thought about my ex-father-in-law."

"Griff Mackay? But he works at..." Luella trailed off. *No. She didn't.*

"It was the best I could come up with, under the circumstances," Naleen explained. "You have to admit, Griff is the best with horses."

Luella laid her head back against the wall and raised her eyes to the ceiling. "Why didn't you consult me first?"

"I thought something was really wrong with him," Naleen continued. "And I know how much you rely on that horse. So I didn't hesitate. Once Griff took a look, he said it was a small infection. Nothing major. And he offered to keep an eye on him until you came to pick him up."

Didn't Naleen know what it cost to board a horse? It was why Luella had come up with the arrangement she had with the woman and her husband, Terrence—to drop in twice a day to take care of her animals.

"I hope you're not too upset with me."

Luella braced a hand on her hip as she looked out

the window at the empty barn. She swallowed what she wanted to say. "I've got to go get him," she said.

"Hey, Luella?" Naleen said before she could hang up. "Welcome home."

"Thanks," Luella said emptily. She replaced the receiver in the cradle then raked her hands through her hair before heading up the stairs to the second floor.

Her bedroom was on the right—with her bed. She'd desperately wanted to come home, greet Sheridan, check on the chickens, locate her wandering cats then shower under the hot spray in her bathroom tub and crash in her own sheets for a week.

She bypassed the door for the second set of steps. The stairwell narrowed at the top as it spun up and to the left. There was one door on the landing.

She went through it into the dim attic. She took the flashlight off the wall next to the door and turned it on.

The floor was broken up. The boards had fallen away in the middle. The house was old, after all. She'd laid a single two-by-four across the hole to bridge the gap. Putting one foot in front of the other, she slowly made her way across the board to the other side.

There was a loose section of flooring near the end of the attic room. She went down on her hands and knees, removing the rug she'd placed there. She pried away the loose flooring and aimed the beam of light down into the space beneath.

Her money was there, just as she'd left it in even stacks. She breathed a sigh. With the sale of the house, it would be enough.

She had her ticket out of Fuego.

Reaching in, she grabbed the first stack of hundreds.

She removed the rubber band from the center and counted out several thousand dollars.

It would have to be enough. If Griff or anyone else at the stable he managed on the other side of Fuego had anything to say to the contrary, her cash stack would dwindle below what she needed. And that was unacceptable.

She'd sworn to herself she'd never go back to Fuego's largest working cattle ranch, Eaton Edge. But she needed her horse. She needed him badly enough she was willing to go against every part of her that told her not to return there.

Eaton Edge was nothing short of spectacular. There were those who claimed The RC Resort, a glamorous guest ranch owned by the Claymore family, was better. But Luella knew there was nothing more special than the Edge.

Maybe because she'd once thought she would be a part of it.

She passed the sign with the entwined *E*'s. It had been a girl's dream, one that had come crashing down around her ears along with all the others.

It was better not to dream, she'd learned, turning her Jeep under the naked cottonwood tree with its long, lonely wooden swing. She pulled in next to a line of dirty work trucks.

She ground the shifter into Park and gripped the wheel, letting the heat pump out of the vents. She stared at the hacienda-style ranch house with its long, low porch. In the spring and summer, geraniums hung in baskets along the front. The men hung any shed antlers they found from the eaves. The smells from the kitchen were welcoming, no matter the season.

There had once been a wooden ladder that led from the second-floor balcony up to the flat roof. She'd spent several nights there, flat on her back with the heavens open above her. She'd found planets and traced constellations. She'd witnessed meteor showers and comets.

She'd wanted to go to college to become an astronomer, thanks to endless nights on the Eaton House roof with…

Luella forced herself to look away from the roofline. There was a row of tiny icicles there, drip-drip-dripping. They'd melted down to spikes. When they fell, they'd be razor thin and deadly.

She shut off the ignition and opened the door. She made sure the cash roll was still in her back pocket and hopped down from the cab.

She thought of knocking on the front door. Then she chickened out. Astronomy and life in some capacity at Eaton Edge may have been her dream, but a lot had happened in the seventeen years since. Her father had killed Josephine, the Eatons' mother, and Angel. He'd recently abducted Eveline Eaton. Whip Decker met his end at the end of an Eaton scope. She'd been sent to jail for her part in it, however unwilling.

She doubted any of the Eatons had bought the coercion defense.

Luella was no more welcome here than she was at Sunday service.

She pulled her hat low over her brow and moved around the house. Trying to stay out of sight of the windows of the house, she wound her way through the empty vegetable patch. *I'm not trespassing*, she told herself. Although that's exactly what she felt like—a trespasser.

Undulating hills rolled into the distance. They were

blanketed in timid white. Grass peppered the snow. Icy puddles shined blue green, like mirrors in the valleys. Beyond the hills, she could make out the buttes to the northeast and the cliffs in the northwest. A river, interwoven with thin, broken sheets of ice, ran down the center like a ribbon.

The buildings were all white so they stood stark against the grass and sagebrush in every other season. The barns, the stable, the bunkhouses and workshops…they all followed the same Spanish-style architectural pattern.

She watched a plume of air escape her mouth in a wispy puff. Eaton Edge was the stuff of dreams, all right. She'd reached for them…and had fallen hard in the attempt.

Hunching her shoulders, she approached the stables. Maybe she'd be able to locate Griff without running into anyone else. Especially—

"Lu?"

She came up short of the stable door. She told herself to be strong and cold—like those icicles. Turning on her heel, she faced him—the man she hadn't wanted to face.

Ellis Eaton looked far too good under the clean white brim of his Stetson. He was tall, over six feet, with long legs encased in working-blue Wranglers and a thick buff-colored jacket.

He'd let his hair grow, she saw, like he used to. Needle straight, the hay-colored strands fingered the lids of his eyes. There was a freckle on one of the lids. It'd once driven her to distraction. His face was still tan from being out in the harsh sun day after day. *Honey-toned*, she'd thought.

Every inch of him was lean and long and honey-toned.

She shook herself. She'd learned not to dwell on how good he looked, always, or how a life outdoors had hewn him into the solid butte of a man he was now. She knew not to think how he was the only one of his siblings with a perfect dimple in his chin or how, like his father, Hammond, and older brother, Everett, he'd developed his fair share of laugh lines early.

He carried a saddle over one shoulder. He was wearing work gloves, handy against the cold.

He looked at her like she was as celestial as the moon, stars and planets they'd once marveled at from the roof of his father's house.

Unbidden, the subtle, earthy musk he carried on his skin hit her. He wasn't close enough to smell, or taste. But some memories were so consuming, they came at her like a battering ram whether it was in the middle of the night in her bed at Ollero Creek or the jail yard surrounded by dozens of inmates.

Ellis Eaton had never let her alone, whether he intended to or not.

He stopped staring long enough to set the saddle at his feet. He started taking off his gloves, one finger at a time, as he walked around it, his dark eyes passing from her red waves to her sherpa-lined flannel vest, her thighs in faded, fleece-lined Levis, down to her booted toes. The assessment was thorough. It nearly stopped her heart. "You're home," he said.

She frowned. *You're home.* He couldn't know how the words hurt. And yet…she felt anger and bitterness welling from the deep where they lived—where she'd built them to protect herself. "I'm out," she corrected.

"Today, right? It was supposed to be today." He started to smile.

She dropped her gaze to her boots because she couldn't

fight that—his smile. It was sun-kissed and sweet and his eyes…they grabbed. "I came for my horse," she stated.

His chin tipped up. "Ah." He bit down on the middle finger of the first glove as he went to work prying off the other. When he was done, he shoved them both into the pocket of his jacket. "Sheridan?"

She nodded, jerkily. "Naleen said she brought him here. I never asked her to do that. That isn't what I wanted."

He tilted his head. "We were happy to keep him."

"I can't imagine that's true."

"But it is," he told her. "He needed care—a place to recoup. And I think he's enjoyed the company."

"Sheridan doesn't like anybody's company."

A slow smile did creep over Ellis's face and, damn it, her heart missed a whole beat. "Come here," he said, holding out a hand.

She stared at that wide hand with its long fingers and hard-set calluses. She hugged her vest tighter around her, pressing her hands under her elbows when her palms tingled in reaction.

The smile faded by degrees. His eyes tipped down at the corners. It was a shame to watch them turn as sad as they'd been over the last year—a year that had been hell on him, too. He'd lost his father to a third and final heart attack and had gone from second-in-command at the Edge to acting chief of operations after Everett had been shot and nearly killed in the skirmish with her father.

If the rumors were true…and Luella had never asked directly, not wanting to know the answer…it was Ellis who had shot her father, ending his life.

Did he think about it, she wondered, when he laid his head down at night? Had there been any hesitation that day in the box canyon at Coldero Ridge when he'd sighted Whip Decker in the scope of his gun? Had there been time to think about how messed up their lives had all become?

Whose call had that been—for Ellis, with his puppy dog eyes and never an unkind word for anyone, of all people to be the one to kill her father?

Once, he'd had dreams, too—dreams that had lived in lockstep with hers. He'd wanted to be a pediatrician. While he'd gotten closer to realizing his dreams, completing his degree and accepting a residency in Taos, he'd given all that up to be by his father's side through the hard times, to be the dutiful son he was and live the life of a wrangler and cowhand.

As she followed him to the large stable yard, she scanned the horses along the fence. Several hands were there, saddling up. She avoided their bald stares and squinted for recognition among the barebacked mounts.

Ellis slowed, dropping back to stand next to her. He pointed into the near distance, lowering his head toward hers. "That's him over there, I think."

Luella raised her hand to block the angle of the sun. Near the corner of the paddock, she saw the shape of her roan. Light spilled freely inside her. It nearly split her clean through. She broke into a half trot, raising her hand to wave. "Sheridan!" she called. "Here, boy!"

She stopped when she saw two small figures. One wore a powder blue hat, the other fire-engine red. Their mittened hands reached through the slats of the fence toward her horse. "No," she said. She started running. "Stop!"

Fingers wrapped taut around her upper arm, bringing her up short. Ellis leaned in, his warmth burning clean through her clothes. "Hang on," he said. "Just watch."

"He's a biter," she protested.

"Watch, Lu," he murmured, his gold-stubbled cheek dangerously close to hers.

She shivered—from unwanted arousal, from twisted fear…a dizzy cocktail of the two. She moaned as she watched Sheridan lower his nose to those outstretched hands. He nibbled, but not the girls' fingers. He took what he was given, a treat of some kind. The girls broke into giggles. The smallest girl—the one in the red hat—clapped and pet him on the breast.

"I…" She shook her head. "I've never seen him… How long…?"

"Since week two," Ellis said. She could tell by his voice he was smiling again. "It gave me a scare, the first time I saw Ingrid reaching into his stall. But he took to the pair of them. So much so I thought about putting Isla up on his back. I needed your okay first. Is he around other kids often?"

She swallowed the lump in her throat. She watched the girls with their angel faces, their dark eyes like Hershey's Kisses… They were Ellis's and they were perfect. "Sheridan's never been around children," she managed.

Ellis shook his head. "Well," he said as he straightened, "you're welcome to bring him by whenever he needs a refill on treats. Isla and Ingrid are nothing if not generous."

Luella checked the urge to give herself a hard pinch. "They're sweet kids, Ellis. But Sheridan and I won't be coming back."

His head snatched sideways. After a moment, he said, "You're welcome to."

"We'll pretend that's true."

"Lu—"

Please, stop calling me that. She wanted to scream it. Instead, she said, "I appreciate what Griff has done. And what the girls have clearly been doing for Sheridan. But it's time he and I went home." She pulled the cash out of her pocket.

He grimaced when she extended it to him. "C'mon. Don't do that."

"I'm paying for his feed and board," she stated.

"It's not necessary."

"Don't be ridiculous," she dismissed, pushing the money at him again. "Take the money, Ellis!"

"Keep your money," he said, firm now, too. "He earned his keep by keeping my girls in smiles. I won't be forgettin' that."

She wished he would forget. Why wasn't it easier to forget? They'd lived their lives apart. He'd been married to another woman, for Christ's sake. And she'd made an effort—*such* an effort—to forget what had been.

Fuego was a small town. Run-ins were impossible to avoid. She'd run into him plenty since returning to Fuego seven years ago—and his wife, Liberty, and their sweet, perfect girls with their eyes so like his…too much like his.

It had been impossible to forget. It was one of the reasons she had to get out—leave—never come back. Because how else was she ever supposed to move on?

"Why don't you hate me?" she demanded to know.

"Hate you?" he asked, stricken. "Why would I hate you?"

"He tried to kill her," she said. "Your sister. He almost did kill Everett, just like he killed your mother and Angel And I helped him. I kept him alive the years that he hid."

"He made you do it."

"You don't know that."

"But I do," he said, softly. Her knees almost gave way when his tone gentled to match the look. "I *know* you. You wouldn't have helped him if he hadn't made you afraid, like he did when you were young." His gaze touched on the hook-shaped scar just visible under the knob of her chin.

"What if you don't know me anymore?" she asked. "What if I'm different? I went to jail, Ellis."

"Doesn't matter."

"It matters to everybody else," she reminded him.

"To hell with everybody else."

Her lips parted. She pressed them together until they numbed. "Do they still talk about us—in town? Do they still talk about our affair?"

"We didn't have an affair," he said, his teeth coming together.

"But she told them we did," she reminded him. "Liberty. And you never told them anything to the contrary."

"It was ugly gossip," he said, "with not one lick of substance. I don't hold by that."

"She's using it, isn't she?" she asked. "In your divorce. Adultery."

"She can say what she wants," Ellis told her. "Doesn't change the truth. Which is that you and I...we never..."

But they had. Just not after Liberty Ferris entered the picture. They'd had one another...on the rooftop...in the cab of his first truck...in his bed...in those spectacular hills that spread out around them. She'd been his.

There was so much water under that bridge, it had swept her away, drowned her, and baptized her as the version of herself she'd had to forge in the aftermath.

Had she drowned—or just been treading water all this time? That could account for why she was so damn tired.

"I'm leaving," she told him. "I'm selling my house and leaving Fuego." Before he could say anything, she went on. "I've made up my mind. There's nothing for me here anymore."

He searched her, and she hardened herself against the torrent of emotions that crossed his features. He began to shake his head. Then, a whistle cut across the yard and he looked around.

Griff was standing outside the barn, motioning him over.

"You've gotta go," she said. "I'll get my horse."

Before she could make a clean break of it, he stopped her again with the same hand.

She closed her eyes. "Let me go."

She heard his long inhale. Then his whisper. "It's that easy for you—goodbye?"

"Why shouldn't it be?" she asked, afraid of the answer—afraid to look at him anymore. It was like staring directly into the sun.

He hesitated for the longest time. Her pulse went off the rails. She stopped breathing. *Don't say it. Don't you dare say it...*

"You can leave," he said, low. "You can go as far away as you like. But a piece of you…it'll always be back here…"

With me. He didn't finish. But she heard it regardless. "It was never enough. That's why I never…we never…"

"Lu."

"Stop saying my name," she snapped. "Stop *saying* it like that. I'm not yours. And I need to be free. I need to be free of you, Ellis! Why can't you just *let me go*?"

His grip loosened.

She jerked herself upright. Rod-backed, she walked away.

The girls had their hands outstretched with more offerings that Sheridan hungrily accepted.

Luella laid her hand on his quarter. True to form, the horse swung his head sideways and sent her a measuring look.

"Hey, boy," she murmured. "Mama's here."

The smaller girl, Ingrid, gasped. "Your hair!"

The older one, Isla, sent her a scandalized look. "Shh, don't be rude! That's Miss Luella, the nurse. Remember?"

"I'm not being rude," Ingrid snapped back. "I love it! It's like fire!"

Luella stared at the wonder in Ingrid's eyes. Her heart gave a tug she couldn't lock down. "Thank you," she replied. "I always hated it."

"Why?" Ingrid asked. She reached up for her own chin-length curls that stuck out from underneath a red knit ski cap. "If I had hair like that, everybody would look at me."

The corners of Luella's mouth quivered. It wasn't quite a smile. But it may have been dangerously close. "That's what troubled me," she said. "Everybody always made such a fuss about it."

Isla studied the waves closely. "I like the curls," she said gingerly. Her face was so serious, and she picked her words carefully. This one was every bit her father's daughter. "Ingrid got the curly hair. Mine's too straight."

Luella sighed. She slid her palm down the length of Sheridan's spine. He nickered, turning his muzzle into her upturned hand, looking for more treats. "I would've sold my soul for straight blond hair like yours. I guess the grass is always greener." Unable to help herself, she pressed her cheek to Sheridan's neck, breathing in his smell. He had the power to quiet the noise in her head. She needed that now, more than ever.

"Is this *your* horse?" Ingrid asked.

"He is," Luella murmured. "And now I have to take him home."

"Aw," the girls said as one. Isla bit her lip and reached up to give his face another rub. "We'll miss you, boy."

Ingrid's face brightened. "Maybe we can come visit him?" she chirped. "Do you live close?"

Luella stared, blank, at their faces. "I…" She looked away, quickly. "Sheridan and I will be leaving Fuego soon."

"Oh, no," Ingrid said. Her pout was both pretty and devastating.

Isla let her hand fall away from Sheridan's face. "Come on, Ingrid. We should go back inside."

"Goodbye, Sheridan," Ingrid said as her sister tugged her off her perch on the bottom rung of the fence. "I'll miss you."

Luella watched them go, the most precious duo in the world. Then she turned to Sheridan, into him, burying her face in his mane and forcing herself to breathe.

They weren't going to be able to get away from Fuego fast enough.

Chapter 2

Ellis found it difficult to concentrate on cattle, getting them each their winter protein supplement and making sure they were dry and warm in this latest burst of plateau weather. He was distracted enough that he nearly found himself between the horns of two rival bulls the green new ranch hand, Lucas, his brother had taken on had forgotten to separate.

Let me go.

"Goddamn it," he muttered. The conversation with Luella was on a loop in his head. She was leaving Fuego...what, forever?

She'd disappeared once before, after high school. He'd gone early to Taos to settle into his college dorm and to try scoping out a place for her to live, too. They'd planned to attend university together. They'd planned a lot of things.

The sky was onyx, heavy with stars. It looked more inviting than the thick blanket he'd spread across the grass next to the riverbed where they lay in companionable silence. It was so quiet, he swore he could hear her heart beating.

Their hands were joined, his fingers playing through hers. He felt the band on her finger, the one he'd placed there with promises for always…

Always had lasted two months. The engagement had been so hush-hush neither of their families had known about it. They hadn't wanted to hear how foolish they were.

He hadn't felt foolish. With Luella, Ellis had felt a desperate kind of urgency. It'd been so strong, he'd thought not being with her would gut him.

It had. God, had it ever, however much he'd learned to live with it.

She doesn't want to be found, her mother had told him when, after six months, he'd finally gotten the woman on the phone. *Can't you take a hint, boy? She's moved on. It's about time you did, too.*

"Ellis."

Ellis's head snapped up, alarmed he'd been caught daydreaming again—not by a pair of bulls but by his sister, Eveline. She was a long way from her modeling days in New York and Paris with no makeup and windswept hair. But with her engagement to his friend Wolfe Coldero and her new job as stable manager at the Edge, he'd never seen her more herself.

She closed the distance to him. "Liberty's here."

"What?" he asked, setting aside the pitchfork he'd been using to freshen the hay. "She's not supposed to pick up the girls until tomorrow."

Eveline lifted a shoulder. "She won't say much—only that she needs to speak with you. Sounds serious."

With Liberty, it was always serious—like a self-guided missile. He looked down at himself. He looked like the well-worn cattleman he was—the kind Liberty had made it very clear she hadn't wanted him to be.

She'd wanted to be the doctor's wife. She'd wanted a life in the city. He'd come close to giving her both. But then his father's health went into sharp decline and he'd given that up to be by Hammond's side. He'd brought Liberty along to Fuego, thinking...*hoping* she'd adjust.

Their marriage had gone sour. Her complaints about small-town life and his work hours had been incessant. He'd done his best to bear it. There hadn't been an alternative. His father had been ill, and Everett had needed his help holding up the family business.

The girls had been his saving grace. They loved the Edge. They took to the land, the animals and riding as he and his siblings had as kids.

How could Liberty object so bitterly to something Isla and Ingrid loved with every measure of themselves? Her request for divorce had shocked him to the bone, especially when she'd left the house they'd bought together in Fuego and taken the girls to Taos.

More shocking had been her allegations of adultery, which she'd spread through town like wildfire. The claim that he and Luella had been having an affair...it was nasty and salacious.

She'd hurt him, and by extension, she'd hurt Luella. Why else would Luella be leaving town, too?

I need to be free of you.

Ellis pulled off his hat, turning the band in his hands as he and Eveline approached the house. He felt a scowl on his mouth. It dug deep at the corners. As they climbed the steps of the porch to the back door, kicking the snow off their boots, he glanced up and stopped.

Night had come early, as it did this side of the year. The stars winked.

He released a breath. It clouded in front of him, curling away as he stood and stared at the heavens.

He could see Gemini holding hands on Orion's upper left shoulder.

He hadn't known the names of the stars until Luella. He'd stayed awake so many nights, listening to her tell their stories…

"Ellis?"

He lowered his head, blinking at Eveline.

Her hand was on the doorknob and there was a crease between her eyes. "You okay?"

He was crushing the hat in his hands. Frowning, he dropped them to his sides and tapped the hat against his leg. "Fine."

Her gaze swept across his face, knowing. "You'll tell me the truth later."

No one needed to know what was going on in his head. The best part about being the family counselor was that he rarely had to confess his own thoughts or feelings.

They went through the door, wiping their boots on the mudroom mat. They hung up their hats and shrugged out of their coats, placing them on the pegs lining the wall. The kitchen was to the left. The housekeeper, Paloma Coldero, fed the family and the hands three meals a day. A place at her table was not to be taken lightly.

Ellis smelled chili con carne and his stomach twisted greedily. It was his favorite of all her meals. Regrettably, they bypassed the kitchen for the living room and entry hall where Liberty was waiting.

Ellis stopped when he found Everett there, too. He stood, all six feet five inches of him, his arms crossed, feet shoulder-width apart and his three cow dogs sitting at attention, flanking him. With his hair overlong and the full growth of a beard that had grown unruly over the lower half of his face over the months of his recovery, he looked untamed and intimidating and he knew it.

Liberty faced him, her hands clenched at her sides. Her long, pencil-straight brown hair fell sleek over the shoulders of her blazer. Her chin came to a sharp point and it was jutting out in defiance. Her back was straight as an arrow, her posture impeccable, and her foot tapped on the floor. As Ellis and Eveline entered the room, her gaze snatched to the pair of them. Not an ounce of warmth touched her features. "You kept me waiting long enough."

"I was in the barn," Ellis explained. "Everett, you can call off the dogs."

"Can I?" Everett asked. He didn't take his eyes off Liberty. There was a dark gleam to them—one that promised hurt.

"I got this," Ellis told him. "Take the dogs. Smells like chili's on."

Everett didn't move. "I'll stay," he said evenly. "You turn your back for a second and something goes missing."

"What would I take, exactly?" Liberty took a scathing look around. "There's not much, is there?"

Everett's lips turned inward. He rubbed them together, carefully. They all knew their father had liked keeping the decor simple on the home front. Since his death six months ago, the family had kept things as he'd liked them. Redecorating wasn't on anyone's agenda. "You've stolen plenty already, haven't you, princess?" Everett asked her. "You've stolen my brother's reputation. You've practically stolen my nieces out from under him…"

"Everett," Ellis said. He wasn't afraid of Liberty, but angering her any more than she already was wasn't wise. Not when the terms of their divorce were still in dispute—primarily custody of Isla and Ingrid. "Let her come in."

The standoff lasted another minute…two. Then Everett eased back, ever so slightly. He gave her a baneful once-over. "Keep the dogs with you," he said to Ellis as he moved away. "Just in case she bites."

"Is he freaking serious?" Liberty muttered as Everett and Eveline moved off.

Ellis looked down at the dogs. Their eyes were on him, waiting for his command. "Lie down," he murmured and waited for them to relax and sprawl across the area rug. "We weren't expecting you until tomorrow. You know Paloma likes taking me and the girls to church on Sunday morning."

She hitched her purse higher on her shoulder. "Change of plans. I'm taking the girls to the children's museum in Taos tomorrow. I promised them we'd go."

"Tomorrow's Sunday."

"So?"

"The museum's closed on Sunday." He spread his hands. "I know enough about city life to remember that."

She glowered at him.

He dipped his head, staring at the points of her shiny black boots. They weren't working boots. They were fancy, soft and buttery—best built for sidewalks. "What do you want?" he galvanized himself enough to ask. "You want to take the girls home early?"

"Yes," she admitted. "But first, we should talk."

He felt a muscle in his jaw twitch as he glanced up the

stairs. He could hear giggling. The girls were there, in their room, probably invested in their collection of plush horses or dollies. He was going to have to say goodbye to them sixteen hours early and it was going to hurt.

Easy, he told himself. "Let's talk in Everett's office."

The dogs followed him, obediently. He didn't wait for her to enter before pouring himself a tall shot of whiskey at the sideboard. At the sound of her pointy-toed boots, he knocked the whiskey back, swallowing fire. He was normally slow to anger. He'd always prided himself on that—the glacial slide between his cool and his temper. Since summer, however, circumstances surrounding his family and his divorce had gotten harder and messier. Holding it all together, including his composure, had been almost impossible. He was bound to lose his grip on something eventually and he feared very much that that something was going to be his anger.

"Isn't it your office now?" she asked, shutting the door behind her. "Though, hasn't it been long enough for Everett to recover?"

"He took a bullet to the chest and nearly bled out before they could get him to the OR." He dropped the glass back to the sideboard with a clack. "You don't come back from that. Not whole."

"Some say he's a shadow of himself."

"Talk's preferable to truth for some," he drawled.

"There you go insinuating things again." She paused. "Let's see it."

"See what?"

Gesturing to the chair behind the desk, she said, "You. In the seat of power."

"No."

Her eyes were practically glittering as she walked

around the desk, her fingers tracing the wood. "Is it not what you wanted, all these years? To be closer to your father? 'It's my destiny.' That was your excuse for making us leave our life in Taos."

"It's my destiny to be here," he granted. "It's my destiny to work in the family cattle business. But that was my father's chair. Now it's Everett's. Not mine."

"So you're not enjoying any of it?" she asked. "Being in charge. Taking his place."

"It's not about being in charge. It never was."

She lifted her chin. "Then this next part shouldn't be too painful for you."

His jaw had been so tense. He only noticed when it went slack. Unease slithered through him, alongside suspicion. "What do you mean?"

"You should sit," she said and planted herself in his father's chair.

"I like where I'm at," he replied.

"Suit yourself," she said, scooting the chair up an inch. She planted her palms on the desk. "I've spoken to my attorney."

"Greasy."

"His name is Grisi."

"Same thing," he weighed.

"It is not…" She trailed off, catching her command slipping. "I've decided the terms of our divorce."

He tucked his tongue against his cheek and made a noise. "I thought that was something we were supposed to do together."

"You and I don't do anything together anymore," she reminded him.

"Then what is it you want from me?"

She licked her lips, caught herself and firmed them

together. "You own twenty percent of shares in Eaton Edge."

"Yeah. And the girls have ten each, to be transferred to them on their twenty-first birthdays, respectively."

"My sources tell me," she said slowly, "that the Edge is worth upwards of around two hundred twenty-four million, easy."

He shifted his feet. He didn't know exactly what the Edge was worth. He'd never been inclined to ask. "What's your point?"

"That means that you yourself are worth somewhere in the neighborhood of forty-four million dollars."

"You want a payout?"

Her hands folded neatly, one on top of the other. "I want the shares. Twenty percent of Eaton Edge and your seat on the board."

He stared for a full ten seconds. Then he barked a loud laugh.

Liberty jerked. "Jesus," she muttered. "*Why're* you laughing?"

"Because you did," he said. "You laughed until you were blue in the face when I told you I was moving back here. Then you spent the next several years letting me know exactly how much you hated everything about Fuego and the Edge, so much so that you pulled up stakes and hightailed it back for the city. And now, after dragging our divorce negotiations out for *eight* months, you're telling me you want my shares?" He laughed some more. "Hell, woman. You are a piece of work."

"I don't owe you anything, least of all an explanation."

"It's my birthright," he indicated. "I think I deserve one."

"It's Isla and Ingrid's birthright, too."

"You wish it wasn't," he said. "You pulled them out of Fuego Elementary and enrolled them in private school fifty miles away." He shook his head. "No. This is about something else."

"What's that?" she asked, tightly.

"You want to hurt me any way you haven't already done," he told her. "You like hurting me."

"You hurt me first," she stated.

"How exactly?" he asked. "I'm still confused on that point."

Her eyes darkened so fast, the flash of blue dimmed and the pupils damn near took over. "You said her name."

Ellis closed his eyes. Leaning back against the sideboard, he lifted his face to the ceiling, doing his best not to take himself back there. But there was truth here—the one truth there was in all of this. "I said her name," he acknowledged. "Once. Doesn't mean I had an affair with her or even thought about doing so."

"You said another woman's name when you were in bed with me," Liberty hissed. She was quiet, deadly so. "That's all the evidence I need."

"It didn't mean anything," he said, more heatedly. He couldn't help it. They'd gone over this ground—a thousand times before. "It meant nothing."

"You say that," she said, nodding, "knowing what I can take. What I'm *going* to take."

"You can't take from me what my father gave. There're previsions. Protections. It's in his will."

"I don't expect to settle this in front of a judge," she admitted. "You're going to give it to me, nicely."

"I'm starting to believe you're not thinking clearly."

"You'll do it," she said. The point of her chin came up again. She smoothed the blazer over her hips as she rose from the desk. "If you expect to get more than a few week-ends with the girls."

His head snatched back, as if she'd struck him. "You can't be serious."

"You know me," she said, stepping to him. She smoothed her hand over the collar of his work shirt. She traced the stubble along his jaw with her eyes. Her lip curled. She'd always demanded he be clean-shaven if he expected to share her bed. Anything else was unkempt, unappealing. "I'm never not serious." She hitched her purse onto her shoulder. "I'll go get the girls ready. Come kiss them goodbye and make them your little promises and let's all hope you decide to keep them this time."

As she left the office, Ellis found he couldn't move. Her devastation spread through every part of him, going beyond what her petty gossip and threats had done to this point.

She was determined to ruin him altogether.

Chapter 3

Luella did sleep in her bed. Exhausted, she'd collapsed on the hand-spun quilt after making Sheridan comfortable in the barn and indulging in that hot shower she'd been dreaming about.

She slept twenty hours and woke, as groggy and muddle-headed as she'd felt when she'd closed her eyes.

She hadn't dreamed. That was something. If she had, she was afraid of what she'd see: the back of her father's hand—her jail cell—Ellis's face when she told him she was leaving?

He'd looked like a whipped dog.

She wasn't going to sit around thinking about it any more than she had to. She wasn't responsible for however much her leaving hurt him. She had to leave for her own sake.

She called the Realtor, scheduled a walk-through and appraisal. She sorted her mail, which Naleen had tried and failed to stack neatly on the kitchen table. As her Balinese cat, Sphinx, twined figure eights between her legs, rubbing a long, satisfactory greeting around her ankles, and her American bobtail, Nyx, reclined in the sunny windowsill above the sink, she unsealed billing statements, threw out junk mail and puzzled over a handful of postcards from San Gabriel…

Luella fanned the postcards out, clueless. San Gabriel was two counties over. Her mother, Riane, still lived there with Luella's aunt, Mabel. Luella, too, had lived there for a time—after her relationship with Ellis had gone belly-up.

The postcards were addressed to her. She recognized the disordered script of Aunt Mabel. There were strange one-to-two-line missives on the back of each one:

Baby.
Mother.
Father.
W.J.
S.G.W.C.
S.9.06.
Nightstand.

Luella scratched the center of her forehead with the tip of her pen. Mabel, an artist, was known for her eccentricities. Luella wondered if her mother, a rigid, unhappy woman who liked to parcel her unhappiness onto others, knew about the messages.

Doubtful. Mabel had been bedridden for the last year. Luella had visited San Gabriel enough to know her mother was taking care of her properly. But she ran a tight ship and did her best to pretend her life in Fuego had never happened by marrying a man from her church and permitting no more than a few cursory visits from Luella, preferably when her new husband, Solomon, was not at home.

Luella contemplated visiting anyway to check in with Mabel and ask about the messages. Yes, it meant a dreaded run-in with her mother. But she had nothing but free time now that the nursing director at Fuego County Hospital had made it very clear she shouldn't return to her nursing job there.

It shouldn't feel like this much of a loss. But it was a sore spot. Going to school in San Gabriel after leaving Fuego and Ellis had saved her from the wells of depression. It'd given her a purpose.

It didn't matter that that purpose had lured her back to Fuego with the promise of a job at the nearby hospital. Neither did it matter that working the COVID unit at the height of the pandemic had pushed her to the brink of despair and burnout. Being a nurse had saved her. It wasn't astronomy, but it had given her a life when she'd thought her life was over.

Wherever she did wind up going this time, there wouldn't be many people who'd hire her with a record.

To avoid thinking about that, she gathered her cleaning supplies and began to dust. She'd left her house tidy. Because she'd lived in the mess and stench of Whip Decker's double-wide, she liked things tidy. Yet being away for so long, there were the cursory cobwebs and dust motes. She scrubbed floors over-hard and washed windows until her arms ached, stopping only long enough to let Nyx out when he roused himself from his respite and yowled.

She wiped the thick wooden beams that crisscrossed over her living area from the top of a rickety ladder and nearly fell off when a knock clattered against the door. She felt the ladder tip and grabbed onto the beam above her for dear life.

The ladder settled back on four legs. She breathed a sigh, loosening her grip on the beam.

The knock came again.

She ground her teeth. Coming down the ladder, she contemplated how long she'd been cleaning. Had she had lunch? Her stomach growled a telltale no. Sweeping her hands over her hair, she dropped her cleaning rag and snatched open the door…

…and nearly shut it again in Ellis's face.

He planted his hand on the door, bracing it open. He didn't look happy.

That made two of them, she thought. "Last time you were here, I tried to shoot you," she reminded him.

"You could have shot me," he remembered. "You chose not to."

"You find encouragement in the damnedest places." She put her weight against the door when he pushed. "Don't. I don't want you in here."

"Don't shut the door in my face."

"Why're you here?" she demanded. "I asked you to let me go."

"You're not gone yet," he said.

She wished she was. Then they wouldn't be doing this. She'd thought she'd said goodbye—the hardest goodbye. "What do you want?"

He reached into his back pocket and pulled out the wad of money.

She cursed.

"You left this on the desk in the office. Take it. I know you need it."

"I don't want to owe you."

"Take the money and we'll call it even."

She wanted to bare her teeth...but she was aching everywhere. Somehow, sleeping hadn't taken the ache away.

He sighed when she didn't reach out. Shifting his feet, he fit his shoulder to the frame of her door and he looked at her, good and long. "What do you want me to do?"

"Go away?" she suggested. Hadn't they established this?

"I can't do that."

"Why not?" she asked.

"Because you don't deserve to be run out of town like this. It's my fault."

She rolled her eyes. "Not everything is about you, Ellis."

"I said your name," he said. "Okay? I said your name once. In bed. With my wife. That's how she got it in her head that you and me had an affair. And now the damn gossips are runnin' you off."

"I'm sorry. Back up." She held up her hands, forgetting to brace the door closed against him. "You did *what*?"

His puppy dog eyes were on full display. He stared plaintively at her until she was forced to look away.

He swung the door farther in. "You got some bread or cheese or something?"

Her mouth fumbled. "Why?"

Ellis stepped inside, unbidden. He veered into the kitchen. "I missed lunch and I'm feeling peckish."

As his boots clomped toward her refrigerator, she lifted her hand in an empty gesture. "Are you really just letting yourself in?"

"Looks that way, doesn't it?"

She stood rooted to the spot. Ellis—in her house... This was inconceivable. Still, her mind circled around

one point and one point only. "You…said my name…
when exactly?"

His head was in her refrigerator. His voice floated to
her, miserable. "It was months ago. In the spring. Liberty
and I…we were already having trouble. She hated Fuego.
Everything about the place." He straightened, lifting a
carton of orange juice. "Is this any good?"

"Sure?" She hadn't exactly gotten around to the shop-
ping since coming home but said nothing of it. *"And?"*

"We talked. I suggested we go to therapy. I couldn't
let the marriage break down. The girls deserved a unit.
I didn't want to be like my parents. Divorced. Distant.
That's *awful* on the kids." He unscrewed the cap and
lifted the juice, drinking straight from the jug. He lowered it, smacked his lips. "Ah…that's…that's not right."
He capped the bottle and tossed it into her trash. Then he
bent into the fridge again. "She countered. She wanted to
try for another baby." He stood, a jar of pickles in hand.
Turning it around, he looked for the sell-by date. Then he
unscrewed the lid and sniffed. "If we were ever happy, it
was just after each of the girls were born."

She watched him shut the fridge, open several kitchen
drawers until he located a fork. Then he leaned back
against the counter and probed the inside of the jar. She
reached up for her head, unable to keep up with the on-
slaught of information. "I'm not sure why all this has to
live in my head, too."

"I'm getting to it," he said, biting into a pickle. He
chewed, hummed, nodded and took another bite. He offered the jar to her.

Winding her hand, she said, "Get to the point, *please*."
And then get out. Why had she let him in? Now he was

here—in her space—her sacred space where no one else—but especially not *he*—belonged.

"Fine," he said, finishing off the pickle. He peered into the jar, looking for another. "We started trying. We even began talking names. It all went to hell, though, after the spring festival. You remember the festival."

She squinted. It seemed like a lifetime ago. "Do I?"

He stopped moving, his eyes coming to rest on her. "You don't remember?"

"Remember *what*, Ellis?"

"You were there, outside the first aid booth. You were wearing a blue dress. Your hair was down, around your shoulders. You left it free, the way I used to…" He trailed off, looking back at his… *her* pickles. "Anyway… Ingrid needed a Band-Aid. She'd tripped and skinned her knee and Liberty didn't have any in her purse. You doctored her up, the way you do, and we all talked for a minute. Just small talk. Nothing out of the ordinary. Like all the other ordinary conversations we've had since you came back from wherever it was you went after high school. I didn't think I thought much of it—except how goddamn pretty you looked."

Her face was burning—because she did remember. She remembered how she'd thought he'd looked at her. Like he used to. She'd thought it was her imagination. And how could she dwell on it and what it did to her when Liberty had been standing right next to him, her arm through his, her hand in the smaller girl's—Ingrid— while his had been in the other girl's—Isla.

They'd looked like a catalog cover—the all-American family. He'd felt so far away from her… It'd hurt, more than it normally did.

"Liberty wanted to try again that night," Ellis went

on. "We put the girls to bed. She lit some candles, put on some lingerie—"

"The finer points you can keep to yourself," Luella ventured.

"Sorry," he said and took another bite. He chewed until he could talk again. "We were going at it. I didn't even know you were a thought in my head. But then your name…it was just out there. Right out in the open. And she looked at me like I'd stabbed her."

"Well, yeah," Luella said with a nod. Any woman could understand that.

"It didn't mean anything," he stated.

"Ugh." She plopped down in a chair around the table. *"Why* are you telling me this?"

"Because if you're leaving town because of the things Liberty has been saying about you and me…" he began, kicking out a chair for him, too. He lowered to it. "It's because of what I did. I said your name and that led her to believe that you and I had been…intimate."

"To say the least," she growled. "According to townsfolk, you and I've been doing it like rabbits."

He grimaced. "It's not right."

"So why didn't you fight it? Why didn't you try to stop the talk?"

"Because I thought people in Fuego—people I've lived near and a good many of whom I've worked with most of my life—would see through it. They know me. They know what kind of man I am."

She paused. "The kind that says another woman's name in bed with his wife?"

He balked.

She did what she'd told herself she wouldn't do—she took pity on him. She knew what kind of man he was—

one with integrity. He was a man who settled arguments. He didn't start them. Ellis never started them. He was the one who normally made everything better. His standing in Fuego had been unimpeachable...until Liberty's claims about the two of them. "Your strategy backfired."

"It crashed and burned," he agreed. He pushed the jar away. It slid into Mabel's postcards. "And I wasn't the only one who suffered for it. I came here to say I'm sorry, Lu, for whatever pain and grief this whole mess has caused you."

He reached for the hand she'd laid on the table. She lifted it before he could touch it. Her heart knelled against the wall of her chest at the thought of him touching her.

He made a noise in his throat— one of frustration or longing. She couldn't tell and couldn't dwell on it.

He reached into his pocket and pulled out the money again. When she hissed at him, he held up a hand. "I know there's something you need help with around here. Even if it's getting the house ready to sell...I'll do it. I'll do whatever it takes to settle things with you because I can't leave it like this. You deserve better, however things ended between us all those years ago."

"What do you mean by that?"

"Now, that you have to remember."

"I don't want to remember."

"You remember leaving," he wagered.

She felt a small knot of bile building at the back of her throat and refused to answer.

"You...disappeared. I proposed to you. You said yes. And then, you disappeared."

"It wasn't that simple," she muttered.

"Wasn't it?" he asked. "I meant what I said. I wanted to marry you."

"You don't think I meant yes?" she challenged.

He treaded carefully. "I think you got scared."

She wanted to throw the jar of pickles at him. "You need to leave." She got up, scraping the chair back. "I'll be going to the bank tomorrow morning. If you're not going to leave me be until I give you something to do then you can come back then and fix the chicken coop. The wire fencing is starting to come loose, and I can't have the hens running around all over the place."

"Show me." He beat her to the door, opening it wide for her. "Christ!" he cursed when Nyx greeted him with a startled screech and darted between his legs.

The cat leaped at Luella. She caught him in midair. He hissed, back arched high. One paw curled over a row of translucent claws and swiped.

"Ah!" Luella cried, cupping a hand under her chin where it stung.

Nyx kicked off her with his back legs and went tearing off under the couch.

Luella turned sideways, away from Ellis, as she lowered her hand. There was a thin stripe of blood across her palm.

Ellis's hand lifted to the back of hers. It hovered, barely there, but it burned more than the scratch. His fingers closed around her wrist and he turned her to him. "Let me see."

"I'm fine." He smelled like nights on the plain and spring rain and shiny golden dreams right where they'd fallen. When his touch rose to her jaw, she torqued her chin away. She pressed it into the soft flannel of her shoulder, closing her eyes tight. "*I'm fine*, okay?"

Her pulse was high in her ears and the ache was back, full-force.

Stop it, she told herself. *Just stop*.

"We should clean that." His fingertips feathered across her cheek. "Where's your peroxide?"

"Ellis." She took several steps back from the warm line of his body. "I worked in an ER for years. I know how to take care of a scratch."

"'Course, I know you're capable, but it's a bad spot."

"I've got it."

"Does that cat act like that all the time?"

"He was just scared," she said. "Animals react differently to fear."

Words brushed softly across the tip of her ear. "I know some humans who behave that way, too."

She flushed hot and red. Breathless, she backpedaled, desperate for air. "Get out, please."

"Exactly," he said. "You still want to show me that coop?"

She heard his boots retreat to the door. She forced herself not to watch the way he fit his hat over his head, dipping his crown low instead of bringing the hat up to it. It'd always been Ellis's way—to open doors, to bow from his height to put on a hat or a shirt or...

She used to love watching him dress. She'd loved watching him piece together what she'd unraveled, always with the lazy, satisfied smile that came from their loving. It had been enough to take her breath away.

He still was.

He'd said her name—with Liberty?

"Close the door," she said.

"What?" he asked, pausing on the stoop.

"Just..." She planted her hand against his jacket shoulder and pushed him farther out. Then she yanked the door from him and shut it.

With him safely on the other side, she took a leveled breath. She planted her hands on the door, closed her eyes again and worked to knit the pieces of herself back together. She'd done it so many times, she only had to close her eyes to imagine them weaving their broken selves back together—like Mary Shelley's *Frankenstein*. Not pretty but functional.

When she was certain-ish that she was okay, she opened the door.

He stood on the porch with his hands on his hips, confusion all over his face.

She moved around him.

"You forgot your coat," he said, chasing her with it.

She snatched it, aware of the fact that the cold was slapping her in the face. Her teeth were chattering by the time she punched her arms through the thing. When he stepped up to help her zip, she waved him off. Her Frankenstein seams were starting to tear already. "I don't need you."

He lifted his hands. "Sorry," he said. "I don't want you to catch anything."

"The chickens are back this way."

"Lu?"

He was so close at her back, she could practically feel her name rolling off his tongue. She hugged herself.

He touched her, his hand on her arm like yesterday.

She kept her back to him but found her feet stopping in the sludge of ice and snow on the ground.

She felt his breath cascading across the hair. "I want you to be okay," he said.

"I'm okay," she said defensively.

"So why're you leaving?"

"I have to," she told him. "I moved back here because

I got hired at the hospital. Now that that job's gone, I've got nothing to keep me. And you should've fought what Liberty said—what everyone in town said. You should've fought for—" The words *me* and *us* battled for dominance on her tongue and she swallowed them. "You should've fought. Period."

"I'm sorry."

"Ellis," she said, exasperated, "it's not just about the gossip. I'm leaving because I'm a Decker. No matter what I do, people will always see me as Whip Decker's daughter. I can't live with that legacy."

He came around her front. She tried taking a step back but his touch held and she was forced to stare at his shirtfront. "He's gone this time. He doesn't have power over you anymore."

"His name does," she said. "I'll never not be Luella Decker to these people."

"You were always Lu Decker," he murmured. "And it meant something different. You made it mean something different. You built a life here. Why can't you do that again? Why do you have to leave?"

"Because…" She shook her head and turned her face upward. It was daytime—no stars. But she could see the moon. She closed her eyes to it, too. "I'm tired of hurting. Whether it's from you or his legacy, I'm just tired, Ellis." She tried to throw him off. "You always had to be there, didn't you—with your puppy dog eyes and your white hat? You've always been there, everywhere I look. How is anyone supposed to move on—to just learn to *be*—when you're *everywhere*?"

"I know," he breathed.

"Do you?" she asked, derisively.

"I do," he said. "You're everywhere for me. Waiting

in line at the Tractor Supply. Or buying a watermelon at the roadside stand. Whether you were in your blue dress or your blue jeans…it didn't seem to matter. I looked and I wanted."

"Too far," she said, accusingly. "You've taken it too far."

"Yeah," he said with a small nod. His whisper-soft gaze passed from her left eye to her right. He was down to a whisper. "With you, I've always done that, haven't I?"

When his feet shifted toward hers and his front nearly buffered her, she pulled in a strangled breath. "This can't be happening. It's—"

"Crazy," he said. "Stupid. Reckless. Just like before. When it comes to you, I will never not be crazy, stupid, reckless."

His head lowered and she pressed a hand to the center of his chest to back him up short. She felt his heart beating and froze. For a moment, she counted the beats. She absorbed the way his breath snagged and his shoulders lifted and fell in rapid succession. To know she still had this effect on him—it was potent. "You better not kiss me, you fool."

"Why not?" he asked, the flat of his brow coming to rest against hers.

Don't answer that. Don't you dare answer that, Luella. "Because…"

"Because?"

Her hands had fisted in his collar. Now, when had they done that? "Because I want you…to shut the hell up." And then she did something crazy, stupid, reckless and all other manner of mixed-up things she didn't understand.

She kissed *him*.

Ellis stumbled back a step. "Lu."

"I said shut up," she demanded, dragging him back to her. She raised her mouth to clash with his.

Hell, she was leaving, wasn't she? She'd never get the chance to kiss Ellis Eaton again. She'd dreamed about it for so long…him—his kisses. Why not one last sip for the road?

"Mmm," he groaned, eyes seamed tight. There was a burrowing line between them. "You taste so good."

"No talking." She grabbed him by the ear. "Just kiss me, once, and never again."

"The hell I can." He spread his hands over her hips as his mouth swooped to hers. The fool man licked and teased, fumbled and smoothed. He breathed into her.

It was like an electric current, from him to her. She'd felt dead for so long. Depression had come back to bite over the course of her sentence. She'd started sinking back into the tangled net of numbness that was as familiar as it was discomfiting. It'd been ready when the bars rolled into place, locking her in her cell. She'd been flirting with it long enough, thanks to her time in the COVID unit and her father's ugly secrets.

She'd been numb for six months. So why all of a sudden did she feel electrified, from her head to her toes?

Shocked, she stumbled over her own feet and the soles of her boots skidded on the icy drive.

He yanked her up by the forearms like she was weightless. When she still couldn't catch her footing, he backed her up to a point near the house where the snow was packed. When her boots gained traction finally, she realized her back was up against a trellis with bare, dry vines and there was nothing in front of her but him.

He planted his palms on her face, framing it gingerly.

He kissed her, lovingly, then again in the same indulgent fashion until she didn't know which way was down and which way was Ellis. And all the while, that current sang up and down her body. She felt every nerve dance, every jet flame of her pulse... She'd wondered if this part of her had shriveled up and died.

She wondered if being struck by lightning would be as devastating...

He broke away so they could catch their breath but he didn't back down. "It's still there," he said in disbelief. "It's all still right here."

She shook her head automatically.

"Yes," he argued.

"No." Did he not realize it was too much—too much for a body to handle?

"Do I need to prove it?" He touched his lips to hers, just barely—enough. He nibbled and sipped and her legs were jelly. She had to hang on to keep from losing her footing again.

"I don't want it." Her voice shook. She couldn't stop the trembling. She felt so much, tears punched through and threatened to spill.

He raised his head enough to gauge her expression. He smiled, slowly—a crooked smile that was real and sexy and had lived inside her head for years. "Now that's something *you're* going to have to prove."

"I will," she pledged. "Just as soon as you back off."

"Honey, you grabbed ahold of me. You *still* haven't turned me loose."

Studiously, she untangled her arms from around him. They fell to either side of his hips before flailing in reaction and she was able to drop them away. "Back off, Ellis."

He waited a beat, licked his lips. Her blood sluiced, slow and molten. She'd lost it—lost herself all over again. *Son of a bitch.*

The sound of a whinny broke through the quiet. It was the high-pitched, distressed kind of whinny that brought Luella to attention. "Sheridan," she said, pushing Ellis back and sprinting around the house for the barn...

She stopped in her tracks. Her momentum nearly carried her topside over and she wavered over the spot.

The yard was littered with hens. They lay, limp, on the frozen ground. Feathers lifted on the breeze but otherwise there was no movement.

Luella pressed her hand over her mouth to hold back a scream. Every single one of them was dead.

Chapter 4

Ellis stared at the scene. The hair on the nape of his neck and arms lifted. As his gut tightened, he grabbed Luella before she could take a step forward. "Stay back."

"They were fine." The way she said it wasn't right. Her voice was too flat, almost a monotone. "I fed them, changed their water… They were laying."

"Lu," he said, planting himself in front of her. "Go back inside."

"They were fine," she said again, her gaze level with his sternum. She didn't blink. Her voice, again, didn't sound like her own.

What the hell? "Lu, honey," he said evenly. "Their necks are broken."

She blinked, finally. Her gaze, glassy, lifted to his. "What…?"

"They didn't just keel over," he explained. "Somebody did this."

"Somebody." The first grasp of understanding broke through. The first emotion bubbled behind it. Her breathing hitched. "Who would…?"

"Go on inside," he urged, walking her backward. He couldn't let her study them any closer. "I need to look around."

"Sheridan," she said. "He's in the barn. I have to—"

"I'll check on him," Ellis assured her. Her face was perfectly heart-shaped. The skin of her cheeks was like ice when he touched them. Moments before, they'd been red as cherries. "Lock the dead bolt and don't let anybody in but me."

She panted over several breaths then closed her eyes. She gave a quick, jerky nod.

"Go," he said. When she broke away, he added, "Run."

He was pleased to see that she did. As soon as he heard her feet clatter up the stairs, he went to his truck and pulled the rifle down from the rack behind the cab. Glancing out over the landscape, he broke it down. Then he loaded several shells and reassembled it. He strapped it across his shoulders and took the safety off.

None of the hens lay together. Their bodies didn't overlap. There was a perfect halo of snow around every one of them. He trod carefully around the edges, trying not to disturb any footprints. Moving to the barn, he could hear the roan kicking the gate. He pushed the door open, swinging the rifle up.

It was a small building—just big enough for two stalls and a short hayloft.

Sheridan's ears were back and the whites of his eyes were showing. His tail, too, was high, and his hooves danced in the hay Luella had freshened for him only hours ago, from the look of it. "You see something?" Ellis asked him.

The horse showed his teeth in answer. He snorted and kicked the gate again.

Ellis peered into the shadows of the other stall. Taking several steps back, he swung the barrel up and tried to get a look in the loft.

Luella was low on hay, which made it easy to see that there was nobody hiding out here.

A loud bang brought him up to his toes as he swiveled the rifle toward Sheridan's stall.

The feed bucket knocked against the metal gate once then again. The horse knocked it off its hook in a show of displeasure. It fell to the ground.

Ellis blew a breath out sharply and lowered the gun. "What's with your mama and crazy animals, huh?" he asked.

Sheridan braced his neck upward. He looked tough, but Ellis could see him quivering. He wanted to soothe the horse but knew he'd lose his fingers if he reached over the gate.

Ellis moved out of the barn and did two turns around the perimeter. He edged around the workshop then tiptoed through it. There were several deer hides hanging from the low rafters that had been cleaned, tanned and dried. He shifted through them slowly, making sure every hiding place was empty.

He frowned as he made his way around the house, inspecting the shadows of the large waterwheel closely. The benefit of Ollero Creek was that it was flatlands as far as the shining cliffs to the north—miles of open country impossible to hide in.

At least, it was that way to the north. To the south was town. Ellis knew neighbors were sparse out this way.

How long had he been inside? Was it long enough for someone to sneak in by truck, break two dozen chicken necks, position them just so in the yard then make a clean getaway?

Ellis went up the stairs to Luella's porch.

She was waiting outside the door. "What'd you find?" Her shotgun was in her hands. "Is Sheridan okay?"

"I asked you to wait inside," he said warily.

She eyed his gun. "Sheridan," she said again, plainly.

He put the safety on the rifle. "Your horse is all right. Just spooked."

She studied his face before deciding the truth for herself. She lifted her chin though he saw little relief. The glassy note was back in her eyes.

He didn't like it. "Let's get inside," he urged. "Come on." He placed a hand on the small of her back.

It was only after the door closed and it was bolted that Ellis laid the rifle down on the kitchen counter. He then leaned over the sink to get a good look out of the window. The cat lounging on the sill flicked its tail but didn't try to take a swipe at him.

"Did you see anything?" she asked. "Anyone?"

"No." Her windows faced north. Prairie grass peeped through snow, dotting the landscape as far as the cliffs. Nothing spoiled that view but shadows from passing clouds.

"Who would do this?" she asked in the same even tone from before.

He rounded to see that she had lowered to the couch. The shotgun was across her lap. "They didn't leave a calling card, other than maybe footprints and tire tracks."

She frowned. "Someone from town then."

"I think it's most likely."

She turned the disconcerting, dead-eyed stare to the window close by, eyes roving over the terrain.

He walked to her. "Are you okay?"

"Fine," she said, too quickly. "What do I do?"

Stop looking like that, he thought. He needed that odd mannequin stare to stop. "You're not going to like it."

"Say it anyway."

"We need to get the police here."

"No," she said decisively.

Her eyes were too blue in her face. She was white as snow. Lowering to the space next to her on the couch, he didn't touch her. He was afraid to. She was so still, he was afraid she'd fracture. "Lu, I can't do anything about tracks. But they can."

"I don't want them here."

Ellis scouted for patience. It was the sheriff who'd hauled her to jail shortly after they'd found her tied up on the edge of a road. She'd been hogtied by her father, the same man that Sheriff Jones had claimed she'd aided and abetted. As a result, she'd spent the last several months behind bars. Ellis couldn't blame her for not wanting the police involved. "You don't trust Jones," he said.

"You're damn right I don't."

There was some heat behind the words. He latched onto it. *There you are, Lu.* "What about his deputy, Kaya Altaha?"

"What about 'no police' don't you understand?"

"When Jones wanted to haul you in after we'd found you on the road that night," Ellis remembered, "Altaha was the one who told him you needed medical attention. She was the reason you were treated first. I don't think she believed you could have been involved with your father. She's a friend. I can call her, personally, and have her come out on her own to check out the scene."

Her spine was straight. Her posture hadn't caved, and her jaw was strong and set. She pressed her lips inward. "You really think it's going to do any good?"

"Yeah, maybe," he said. "Somebody's got to know someone's hurt you."

"They hurt my chickens."

"They hurt you!" As her eyes swung to his, he heard the words echoing back to him. He didn't try to take them back or the agitation that had escaped with them. "They hurt you," he said, more quietly. "And they're going to pay for it. That's why we need to get Altaha down here, so she can help us catch 'em."

She scanned his face. When her eyes settled on his lips and hers parted, he felt the warm feeling around his navel that was always present around her heat to a torch.

"You better be sure about this," she whispered. She placed her hands on her weapon. They wrapped around it, white-knuckled.

She'd withdrawn into herself again. Ellis cursed and dug the phone out of his coat pocket to place the call.

Ellis owed the deputy a lot. Not only had she become a personal friend—she'd practically saved his brother's life. When Everett had been shot by Whip Decker at Coldero Ridge during the man's last stand, Kaya Altaha had been the one to administer triage on scene and call in a rescue helicopter.

His brother had come too close to dying. The surgeons at Fuego County Hospital may have saved him from the brink of death, but it was Altaha who'd been responsible for his getting on the operating table to begin with.

The Jicarilla Apache Native thought fast on her feet. Not much got past her, from what Ellis had seen. Her work wasn't swayed by personal judgment or local politics. As she peered from underneath the wide brim of her deputy's hat at the chicken-strewn yard, her full mouth turned down at one corner. Her dark eyes were narrowed to slits. "How long did you say you were inside?"

"Twenty to thirty minutes, max," Ellis answered.

"And you didn't hear anything?" Altaha asked, kneeling in the sleet to examine the closest hen.

"Only the horse when we were outside," Ellis said. "He's been spooked by something."

"That horse acts strangely in the best of times."

"He stayed with us for a while at the Edge. I never saw him like this."

They both could hear Sheridan kicking the gate again and Luella's soothing tones from inside the barn.

"You're right about them," Altaha said about the chickens. "Looks like their necks have been broken. Luella was in the house with you the whole time?"

Ellis weighed the question then sent a sideways scowl to Altaha. "Don't do that."

"It's just a question."

"The kind that made her nearly talk me out of calling anyone out here," he noted. "She thinks everybody's out to get her."

"Answer the question, Ellis," she said, standing again.

"Yes, I was with her."

"The whole time?"

"The whole time!"

"Doing what exactly?" When he didn't answer immediately, she added, "I can't put the pieces together without knowing the whole picture. What's your business with Luella Decker?"

"She's leaving Fuego," he answered reluctantly. "I had to know why."

"Luella's leaving Fuego?" she asked. "When?"

"She didn't say exactly."

"Did she give you a reason why?" Altaha wanted to know, picking up the bag she'd set nearby. She took out a digital camera and checked the lens.

"She doesn't feel that she's welcome," he replied.

"One could argue that, as the town villain's daughter, she's never felt particularly welcome," Altaha considered. "People have made certain of that." She raised the camera to her face, angled herself over the first hen and snapped a picture. "Why leave now?"

Ellis surveyed the dead. "Guess she's had enough."

"Sounds like some part of you wants her to stay," Altaha muttered, leaning over the next hen for another shot.

"That doesn't sound like a deputy," he observed.

She raised herself to her full height. With the hat, she was no more than five-two. "No. But I hope it sounds like a friend."

He contemplated that as she went about taking pictures of the entire scene. He trusted Altaha. But he'd never admitted his feelings about Luella—to anyone. His family had speculated about his relationship with her, he knew. But they'd never openly discussed it.

"When the snow's melted like this, it's difficult to get anything solid from tracks," she observed.

He knew she'd parked at the mailbox and walked to the house from there. "What about tire treads?"

"I took some pictures," she replied. "I'll need to take photos of yours and Luella's so we can compare."

"She didn't do this, Kaya."

At the sound of her name, Altaha straightened from a crouch. "It's good you called me. Whip Decker snuck around in plain sight for years. Jones didn't see it. It's made him look bad."

"Now he's got it out for Lu?" Ellis asked.

"When he got word of her return yesterday, he didn't have much good to say about it." She shifted her weight. "And he's not the only one."

"Who else?" Ellis asked thoughtfully.

"I'll make a note," Altaha assured him. "Cross-reference it with whoever lives on this side of town. See what comes back."

"Thanks," Ellis said, "for coming out."

"Can't say it's my pleasure," she said, tilting her head over the sleek black feathers of a plump hen. "This doesn't feel impulsive or random. It's calculated…"

"Planned," Ellis agreed. "Some sick bastard planned this."

The rooster made hoarse croaking noises as he peered at one of his prone ladies. Altaha made a noise. "You got lucky, didn't you, Big Bird? Say cheese." She raised the camera and took the rooster's picture, too.

"His name's Caesar."

Ellis looked up and saw Luella. She was still a shade too pale. Her mouth was drawn in a grim line.

Altaha examined Luella, doing well not to make it obvious. "Did they all have names?"

Luella stared across the debris field. Ellis could see the shaded half circles under her eyes. "Yes. I bought half of them as chicks and raised the others from hatchlings."

"I'm sorry," Altaha said, sincerely.

Luella studied her with a neutral expression. Then she gave a nod.

"Do you hunt?" Altaha questioned.

"A nurse's salary doesn't always cut it. Times get lean. I hunt in season."

"So do you have any game cameras?" Altaha wondered.

Luella looked toward the eaves of the house. "I do… but they've been off since I was away. I never turned them back on."

Ellis saw the game camera high above them. It had been mounted underneath the eaves of the house. "You should turn them back on," he told her.

"Can you think of anyone who knows of your return?" Altaha asked.

Luella glanced at Ellis then quickly away. "This one, obviously."

Altaha took her notebook from her back pocket. She made sure the camera was strapped around her neck and started to jot Ellis's name. "He give you any trouble?"

"Usually," Luella replied.

Ellis tilted his head in return but kept his mouth shut. He'd seen the flash of emotion on her face. Even if it meant she was annoyed or angry at him, he'd take anything above the hollow shell she'd disappeared into.

"Other than that," Luella went on, "the Uber driver who dropped me off. He said somebody had prepaid." She asked him, "You didn't do that, did you?"

Ellis shook his head.

"Somebody else anticipated your release," Altaha decided aloud, making quick notes. "Anyone else?"

"Naleen," Luella said, "your sister."

Altaha nodded. "Have you been to town? To the market or feed store?"

"No," Luella said. "But I did go to Eaton Edge yesterday."

"Anybody see you there?"

"I did," Ellis noted. "I saw her."

Luella held his stare, brooding.

Altaha frowned. "Anyone other than Romeo?"

"The girls," he said. "You talked to the girls."

"I did talk to them." The line of Luella's mouth softened. "They were precious."

"Hard to believe they're Liberty's kids." Altaha stopped and checked herself. "That was uncalled for."

"Not entirely," Ellis muttered. "Griff saw her, too."

"I called Ms. Breslin at the realty company, too," Luella said, "to see about putting the house on the market. Other than that, I can't think of anyone."

Altaha tapped her pencil against her pad. "This'll make a start." She flipped the cover down then tucked it into her pocket. "I'll make some calls, get these pictures back to the office and call if I need to know anything else. Is that okay?"

Ellis fought a smile. The question was simple, but it would mean something to Luella.

"Yes." Luella paused. "Thank you, Deputy."

"Of course," Altaha said. "I'll need to take two or three hens, for autopsy so we can confirm how they died. Do you need help—taking care of the rest?"

"I'll see to that," Ellis told her.

"No," Luella argued. "I will."

"Lu—"

"They're my chickens, Ellis," she said. "I'll bury them."

"You need protection," he noted.

"You've got a ranch to run, as I recall."

"I'd keep my doors locked," Altaha advised. "And cameras on in case whoever did this comes back."

Luella's brow furrowed. "It's Sheridan I'm worried most about."

"I can come back for him," Ellis said. "I can bring him to the Edge."

She scanned him for a long time, considering. Then she shook her head. "I can bolt the barn door, same as I can bolt my own. We're both better off here."

Ellis wasn't so sure about that. But she was right. He was still chief of operations at Eaton Edge as long as Everett was in recovery. He didn't think that had changed since he'd left an hour ago. It put a foul taste in his mouth, leaving her. But he didn't see as he had much of a choice. "I'd like to help you bury them, Lu," he said quietly.

Altaha tucked her pen into her breast pocket. "Hell, bring me a shovel. I'll help, too."

Chapter 5

Luella had to leave the house again. She wished there was someone she could call. For the first time in a long time, she wished she had friends—not just neighbors like Naleen and Terrence.

She couldn't get the scene out of her mind—her hens dead in the yard—or how she, Ellis and Altaha had had to fight to dig a hole deep and wide enough in the hard-packed ground they'd uncovered beneath melted snow to bury the lot. The morning after, there was nothing but scattered feathers and Caesar wandering dolefully around an empty coop.

It'd been frightening—how quickly the numbness had grabbed hold of her again. She'd hidden behind it. The shock, the anger, the grief…they were emotions too big to handle shoulder to shoulder.

There were times she had to admit she turned to the numbness for consolation. She'd had to do that after she escaped Fuego the first time for San Gabriel. She'd gotten far too comfortable in the numbness. She'd sought it more recently during her time working in the COVID unit...

The worst of it was that he'd seen it —Ellis. He'd seen what the numbness did to her once it had a chance to grab hold.

A part of her hadn't wanted him to leave. After they'd buried her chickens and she'd watched him drive off, she'd been afraid to go back inside her own house without the warmth of him beside her.

That was something else she'd had to contemplate as she lay next to her shotgun all night long.

She set her game cameras back up to stream and alert her to any movement around Ollero Creek. If she, Sheridan, Caesar and the cats were going to get away, she had things to take care of in town first.

She stopped by the feed store for hay. Rowdy Conway had come out of his auto repair store to gawk at her and even lifted two fingers to his brow to salute her. She stared at him hard until he crawled back to where he came from.

Had he done it? Had the lewd town mechanic killed her chickens?

She looked around the parking lot and saw that she'd drawn attention. People were looking and talking in small clusters.

She's back. Luella Decker's back.

She slammed the tailgate of her truck and went around to the driver's door to get inside. She shut it with a hard yank.

She was pulling into the bank when she saw the sheriff and the deputy coming down the sidewalk toward her.

Luella put the truck in park and wondered briefly what would happen if she simply bypassed the two of them.

The sheriff's hard expression brought her hand up short of reaching for the jacket on the passenger seat. As they made a beeline, she rolled down her window. "Sheriff," she greeted.

Sheriff Jones had a heavy brow, a muscled jaw and clear blue eyes that cleaved. Next to Altaha, he looked ridiculously tall. There was a settled paunch around his middle, just large enough to rest on his gun belt. When he swept off his hat, his head was shiny and hairless. "Ms. Decker."

She didn't flinch at the way he said her last name. It took a lot. She moved her eyes to Altaha. "Deputy."

"Luella," Altaha returned. "How are things?"

"Busy," she noted. "I should really get back to—"

"We'll only take up a moment of your time, Ms. Decker," Jones said, widening his stance.

When he refused to elaborate, she knew he was waiting for her to get out of the truck. She set her mouth carefully in a neutral line, shut off the ignition and opened the driver's door. Stepping down to the pavement, she faced them, weaving her arms across her chest in what she damn well knew was a defensive stance.

Jones spoke first. "My deputy tells me you're on your way out of town."

"That's the plan," Luella admitted.

"There's been trouble at Ollero Creek."

"Yes. Someone murdered my hens."

He ran his tongue over his teeth. "No leads."

Luella looked to Altaha, who rushed to clarify, "Not yet. The vet had a chance to look at them, though. Their necks were broken, for certain."

Luella grimaced. "What about the tire treads? You said you took pictures."

"We're still going over those," Altaha said. "I canvassed your closest neighbors and questioned everyone on the list you gave us. We have a pretty clear understanding now of who knew of your return."

"Ellis Eaton was with you when the incident occurred." Luella scowled at Jones's statement. "He was."

"So you've got yourself an alibi," he surmised.

She nearly rolled her eyes but stopped just in time. "Whoever did this, Sheriff, snapped the necks of twenty-three chickens. *Snapped* them. In a very short period of time. You may think I'm capable of that, but I find that kind of violence toward animals abhorrent."

He raised a brow. "You'd like that on the record, wouldn't you, Ms. Decker?"

"All right," Altaha intervened. "We just wanted to drop by and update you on the case."

"Sure," Luella said, not breaking Jones's stare.

"You got business at the bank?" Jones asked.

"No," Luella lied. "Just casing the joint."

If she wasn't mistaken, she saw Altaha's mouth curve just before the deputy cleared her throat and shifted her feet.

"We're watching you, Ms. Decker," Jones warned.

"I'm sure, Sheriff," Luella replied as the two took off across the street. As soon as they disappeared into the pawnshop, she opened the truck door again. Reaching over the driver's seat and console, she pulled the jacket off the passenger seat and grabbed the handle of the duffel bag she'd hidden underneath. She locked the truck then went into the bank.

And was nearly mowed down by Paloma Coldero.

"Luella Belle Decker."

Panic struck Luella like a high-speed train. She felt

her feet moving back toward the door. Paloma was a formidable figure. How else could she run the house at Eaton Edge and keep Everett in check as she had for the better part of his life?

The woman had cared for him, Ellis and Eveline when their mother, Jo, ran off with Paloma's brother, Santiago, to Coldero Ridge. The scandal had rivaled Luella's own family's. Paloma was practically Ellis's adopted mother and was one of the few who knew how deep his attachment for Luella had gone.

Paloma had caught her once, Luella remembered— sneaking downstairs just after dawn from Ellis's bed, mussed and carrying her own boots.

Nobody intimidated her quite like Paloma.

Bracing her hands around the duffel strap, Luella tried to read the woman's face. "Ms. Coldero."

Paloma made an unfavorable noise. "It's Paloma to you and always has been. Let's not pretend otherwise."

Luella's mouth fumbled. "Thank you?"

"No trouble," Paloma said. She had painted brows, wide hips and a swinging walk. She was either the warmest person in the world or the most discerning. There was no in-between. "I'm pleased to see you've returned. I knew about it, of course. You know Ellis. He can't keep a secret to save his life."

Luella opened her mouth then carefully shut it, unsure what to say to that exactly. She and Ellis had many secrets.

"I hear Ellis came to see you yesterday," Paloma said.

"Well, sure," Luella said for lack of anything better. Who *hadn't* heard Ellis had been at her place?

"Tell me, Luella Belle," Paloma said, "*did* the man behave himself?"

Kissing. Kissing entered her mind like a solar flare. She'd kissed Ellis. He'd kissed her. They'd decidedly not behaved themselves together.

Her mouth worked around several explanations in the space of a moment but none of them made it out.

Paloma lifted her chin, knowing. "I see. Well...you tell me if he should be punished and I'll see to it."

"Him?" Luella heard the word eject. She closed her eyes. "I mean...that's... No, you don't need to... We both..."

Paloma surprised her by laughing. It was deep and rolling. "I'm teasing you, *niña*. I hope the rumors about you leaving Fuego aren't true. You're a good girl, despite the talk. It's a shame so many people choose not to see it— see *you*."

Luella gaped at the woman.

"I see you," Paloma said, leaning forward slightly. "You know that. Keep it with you. Know you got somebody in your corner."

Luella blinked several times. Shocked by the sudden rush of kindness, she shook her head quickly. "I..."

Paloma's warm hand covered her cold, fisted one. "Don't let them chase you off. Not unless it's what you want, deep down. Know what you want, Luella Belle. And you take it."

Luella could say nothing as Paloma replaced her bank card in her wallet. "Is leaving what you really want?"

Luella looked away quickly. "Um... I'm unable to really justify an alternative." Her voice wavered. It shocked her, almost as much as the line of questioning. "I'm trying to..." She milled her hand, fishing for answers that weren't there. "Trying to figure things out..."

"You let me know if you need help moving, if that's the answer. I know a few good-ish men. You come to the Edge sometime. I'll feed you. You need some more meat on your bones."

Luella braced her hands on her hips and did her best to breathe through the kindness. More meat on her bones? She'd always been on the round end of pear-shaped. The stress of the last few years hadn't helped. "Okay," she said weakly.

"Take care."

"Mmm-hmm," Luella offered. When the bells over the entrance tinkered and the door closed behind Paloma, she let out a shuddering breath.

Why did kind words hurt as much as an open-handed slap? Luella had never understood it. But she was just as powerless against unexpected words like Paloma's as she'd ever been.

She hadn't cried after losing her hens. Not because it didn't matter. Crying meant opening herself up and opening up was a terrible, horrible idea she couldn't afford any more than kissing Paloma Coldero's adopted son's sultry mouth.

Her stomach hurt from holding everything—*too much*—in. She didn't grieve—her animals, the dregs of her family or her childhood, her first love…anything anymore. Life had given her far too much to grieve. It was impossible to do it without unraveling. Maybe that was why she welcomed the numbness sometimes, even if it scared her.

She slapped her forehead with her palm—one good, hard slap. Then, thinking again, breathing carefully, she went about stitching herself together once more. She counted the threads, made those stitches nice and tight so they'd hold for more than a few hours at a time. *Maybe? Please.*

Go back to Eaton Edge? Was the woman crazy?

She caught the wave of the bank teller. She walked to the little window at the counter. "Hello, Mrs. Whiting. How are you?"

"Luella," Mrs. Whiting said. She didn't smile or offer near as warm a greeting as Paloma had. "It seems talk's true and you have returned."

"Yes." Luella cleared her throat, tightening her grip on the handle of her bag. "I was hoping to speak to Mr. Monday. I'd like to open an account."

"What kind of account?"

"A savings account," Luella said.

"I'm afraid Mr. Monday retired this October," Mrs. Whiting said. "You wouldn't have heard that. Not while you were in prison."

Luella fought the urge to sigh. "I wasn't in prison."

"I beg your pardon?"

Luella raised her voice. "I wasn't in prison, Mrs. Whiting. I served my time in the county jail."

"It's apples and oranges, isn't it?" Mrs. Whiting asked, tightly.

"For some," Luella said wearily. "Who can I speak to about opening an account?"

"You'll have to make an appointment with the new bank manager," Mrs. Whiting stated. "Jedidiah Gravely."

"Jed," Luella said, fighting the urge to curl her lip in distaste. "Fine."

"How's your mama doin'?" Mrs. Whiting asked as she consulted her computer screen about that appointment.

"Fine, I guess," Luella said. "We haven't really spoken."

"Your own mother," Mrs. Whiting admonished, looking down the sharp blade of her nose.

"My own mother," Luella said back.

"She's a good woman, your mother," Mrs. Whiting said, writing something down on a bank card. "Despite who she married the first time."

"Despite that," Luella echoed emptily.

Ms. Whiting handed the card over. "Come back tomorrow morning. Mr. Gravely will see you then."

"Thanks a lot," Luella said as she turned away from Mrs. Whiting.

"You have a nice day," Mrs. Whiting returned, emptily.

Luella stuffed the card into the back pocket of her jeans and began to walk back to the doors.

Something hit the floor behind her. Someone cried out in alarm. She glanced around and froze when she saw the man spilled out on the black and white tiles and the woman bent over him, cloaked in worry. "He's not breathing!" she cried. "Somebody call 911!"

Luella dropped the duffel. She crossed the lobby. She put her fingers to the man's neck, felt for a pulse. There wasn't one.

She took off her coat. "Ma'am, is this your husband?"

"Yes," she said, frantic. "Ben. Benjamin Tate."

"Was Mr. Tate having any trouble this morning?" Luella asked, working quickly to unbutton the man's jacket over his chest. His torso lay still. No respirations. Luella positioned him until he was flat on his back. She tipped his chin up, made sure his mouth was open, checked for obstructions. "Shortness of breath, chest pain?"

"He said it was indigestion," Mrs. Tate said, crying freely now. "He took some Pepcid. That's it."

Luella glanced around, saw that Mrs. Whiting was on the phone with the emergency dispatcher. She had to work quickly to give the ambulance time. Placing both hands just below Mr. Tate's breastbone, she interlocked them then straightened her arms and began chest compressions. She kept them coming, hard and fast, counting under her breath. When she got to one hundred and ten, she stopped to do several rescue breaths.

Mrs. Tate was sobbing now. Mrs. Whiting and the other tellers were crowded around her, doing their best to console her.

Come on, Luella thought when Mr. Tate's ribs didn't rise. She quickly switched back to chest compressions, making sure to press in a full five centimeters with each one. Sweat began to roll down her hairline. She heard a rib break, but she kept going, repeating the process even after Jones and Altaha rushed in.

She saw Mr. Tate's ribs rise after another set of rescue breaths.

"Ben!" Mrs. Tate shrieked. "Oh, Ben, come back, sugar!"

"Paramedics are here," Altaha said, placing her hand on Luella's shoulder.

Luella looked around to see them rushing in with the stretcher. "Code blue," she said, stepping back and giving them free rein over the situation. They asked quick questions, she gave quick answers. Then she followed them out with Mrs. Tate to the ambulance.

Once husband and wife were loaded and the doors shut, Luella watched the ambulance disappear.

The sirens faded. Only then did Luella see that the crowd had thickened. Not only was everyone from the bank on the street with her. Everyone from the laundromat, the pawnshop, the bakery and barber shop was there, too.

She cleared her throat. It was a raw. Pushing her hair back from her face, she felt the dew on her skin.

"You did good," Altaha said on her right. "You may have saved his life."

Luella took a breath. "We'll see."

"Did you lose this?"

She looked around to find Sheriff Jones with her duffel. She took it. "Thank you."

His gaze wasn't any friendlier than before. She looked around and found discerning looks. She hugged the duffel to her. "Excuse me," she said as she picked her way through the bystanders to her truck.

Eveline Eaton stood in her way. Luella felt the collective breath of the crowd and heard the whispering as she stood toe to toe with her father's last victim.

"Luella," Eveline greeted. "I was hoping to run into you."

Did Luella hear that right? She was tired now and there was ringing in her ears.

"I'm glad the Tates found you before I did," Eveline said. She was blonde, polished even in snow-and-dirt-encrusted boots. She was slim and leggy, every bit the model she'd once been. "We should have lunch sometime."

Luella stared at her for what she was sure was a full minute. "If you say so."

"I do," Eveline said with a smile. It was genuine, with a flash of straight white teeth. "It was me, by the way."

"You who?"

"Who paid for the Uber," Eveline revealed.

Luella shook her head. She shook herself. *She did?* "Why would you do that?"

"That's a talk for another time," Eveline told her.

"Preferably, when the entire town isn't eavesdropping on us."

Luella glanced around. No one had moved. On cue, Altaha raised her voice. "What is this, a block party? Back to your business, people!"

Luella watched them scatter like roaches when the light comes on. "You think they'd have better things to do."

"It's been six months," Eveline said with a shake of her head. "I figure another six years and they'll start talking about something else."

Luella almost snorted a laugh but stopped.

Altaha approached them. "I'll let you know about Mr. Tate," she told Luella. "They'll notify us of his status at some point this afternoon."

Luella nodded. "I appreciate it."

Altaha looked to Eveline. "And I guess I'll see you and Wolfe later."

"Maybe," Eveline said. At Luella's cautious frown, she explained, "It's poker night at the Edge. You could join us."

Luella shook her head. "I best be getting back to my animals."

"Any more trouble at Ollero Creek?" Altaha wondered.

"Not that I know of."

"Give me a call if anything changes. Normally, we ask people to call the station but Jones is real sensitive about you, for some reason."

"For some reason," Luella muttered, frowning.

"He saw the money in the bag."

Luella swore out loud. "After my crack about casing the joint, I guess he thinks I robbed the bank."

"Mmm," Altaha said. "I know you're not liable to

put a foot wrong, but I'd be extra careful. There wasn't anybody happier to hear that you're skipping town than the sheriff."

"You're leaving town?" Eveline asked. "Why?"

Luella thought about answering, but she settled for: "A conversation for another time."

Eveline gave a slow nod. "Give me a call, too, when you're up for a lunch date."

Luella lied, "I will." Then she retreated into the safety of her truck and locked the door.

Chapter 6

Ellis felt as if he were juggling bulls, hcifers, calves, tractors, one touchy ATV that didn't get up and go like it used to, and a stack of paperwork he desperately wanted to set fire to. Still, he stayed ensconced in his father's office long after he'd left the barn. Night pressed against the windows. There was a nice fire crackling in the hearth. Paloma had brought him a plate of enchiladas verdes and sat with him while he ate.

Now Ellis pressed the office phone between his ear and shoulder while he filled out pay stubs, checking off the names of their winter team as he went. He took a sip of water from the glass Paloma had brought him, swallowed, adjusted the phone again and said, "So when you add to one side of the equation, what do you have to do to the other addend?"

There was a slight pause. Then Isla said, uncertain, "Add the same number to the other side, too?"

"Almost there," Ellis said. His pen hovered over the checks as he thought about it. He sat back in the chair, giving his back a stretch. Who knew sitting for hours at a desk could cause just as many aches and pains as being on a horse all day? "You know Lady Justice and her scales? One side can't level with the other until they balance each other out."

"Uh-huh," Isla said. He heard a wet sniffle.

Ellis's heart ripped. Isla was a marvel at so many things. She was an accomplished rider on her horse, Boon. Her nimble fingers could race across piano keys like they were made to do so. She liked to write poems and songs.

The enemy was math. If not for math, Isla would have nothing to weigh her down. "It's okay, baby. We're going to get this," he said.

"It's so hard, Daddy," she cried. It was as soft as a mouse—not the lion's roar he knew it was inside her.

"I know," he murmured. "But I want you to think about those scales and the best way to even them out. When you make one number bigger, you have to make the other..."

Another pause. "Smaller?"

He closed his eyes and gave into a proud papa smile. "And how do you do that?"

"By subtracting the other addend by the same number?"

"Yes," he said, beaming as he sat up. He grinned at the room at large, then stopped when he saw there was no one to share his pride with. "Baby, you got it."

"Daddy?"

"Yes?"

"Ingrid got in trouble at school today."

Oh, boy, he thought. Where Isla's weakness was math, Ingrid's was curiosity. A scientist trapped in a child's body, she'd snuck small animals into her bedroom for study. She'd given up on piano in favor of deep cloud contemplation. She liked nothing better than lying in the grass of the park outside the studio where Isla practiced once a week, watching the clouds shift or trying to find insects.

She didn't suffer fools, either. She could charm just about anybody with a grin but one foul word from someone at school was cause for retaliation. And it'd only gotten worse since the separation. While Isla never complained about her new school in Taos, Ingrid did so regularly and with increasing volume. She wanted to come back to Fuego. She wanted to ride, too. While form and hands were paramount to Isla, Ingrid just wanted to clamber up on her pony, Dander, and go. She would ride all day if Ellis let her.

He braced himself and asked, "Do I need to talk to her?"

"I don't know," Isla said, rife with anxiety. Isla carried too many worries—far more than a seven-year-old should. Her voice dropped to a whisper. "You know those tiny ketchup packets?"

"Yeah," Ellis said, apprehensively.

"She squirted one in a boy's eye."

Don't smile, Daddy, Ellis told himself, tipping the receiver away from his mouth. He worked to keep his facial muscles at half-mast. There was pride here, too, but... *Straight face.* "Well...did he do something to her first?"

"Yes. He said a bad word at her."

Ellis squinted. "He's in kindergarten, too?"

"Yes."

"Jesus," he muttered, pulling the phone away from his ear and gathering a steadying breath. Bringing the phone up once more, he asked, "What does Mama say?"

"Oh, she's mad," Isla said, still in hushed tones. "She

says if she gets called to school one more time, she's going to…"

When she trailed off, Ellis dipped his chin. "Isla?"

Liberty's voice cut across the line. "It's time for bed, Ellis. You've kept her awake long enough."

Ellis checked his watch. "She needed help with her homework. And since when do they go to bed at seven thirty?"

"Since Ingrid started dozing off in Bible school," Liberty said.

"That's because she's bored and she wants to run around outside," Ellis said. "What's this about Ingrid being in trouble? You're not going to punish her?"

"Why shouldn't I?"

"Because the kid cussed at her," Ellis said. "You can't blame her for—"

"I *can* blame her for behaving like a—"

"An Eaton?" he finished for her.

Liberty sighed. "I've been called to the principal's office three times this semester."

"Maybe if you brought her here more," he said, "she could run and play and be with the animals. She could get her energy out. You've got them wrapped up so tight with music and Bible school and homework, she doesn't have a chance to get it all out. It builds up. Maybe this accounts for some of her negative behavior."

"You want more time with them?" Liberty asked. "Okay. Sign those shares over to me first."

Ellis dropped his face into his hand. He scrubbed. "There's got to be something else you want—"

"Not if you want shared custody."

He checked the urge to throw the receiver across the room. "This is extortion and you know it."

"Maybe next time try not sleeping with someone else."

"I never…" He rubbed his teeth together. If he yelled, it was only more ammunition for her. If he yelled, she'd hang up and her feelings for him would tank further, if possible. He released a long breath. "I need you to reconsider. Please."

"You need more time," she surmised. "You take all the time you need. In the meantime, the girls will remain in Taos with me."

"You can't—"

"Do you want to tell the girls good night or not?" she asked pointedly.

A knock on the door brought his head up. It opened and the Edge's head wrangler, Javier Rivera, peered in. "You're missing all the fun, *amigo*. The deputy's robbing us blind. She and Everett just went all in. They're the last ones standing."

Ellis nodded mutely. He waited until Javier shut the door. Then he told Liberty, "Put them on."

"Good night, Daddy," Isla said.

Louder, Ingrid called, "'Night, Daddy! I love you! Give Dander a kiss for me!"

"Will do." A smile stretched across his mouth. "I love you, too. Both of you. Okay?"

"Okay!"

"Okay, Daddy."

"Good night," Liberty said, then the line went dead and Ellis stared into the fire, feeling burned like kindling.

"You play like you used to race cars," Altaha said as she and Everett slapped cards onto the table one after the other.

"Yeah?" Everett asked. Ellis had found them alone

at the kitchen table. The others had left. The game had been won by the deputy, apparently, and now she and Everett were engaged in an intense, late-night round of War. "How's that?"

"Badly." Altaha whooped when she won a set. She scooped his cards and her cards her way. "Thank you!"

"Woman's a goddamn con artist," Everett said to Ellis. "Why do we invite her?"

"Because you Eatons," Altaha said, stacking her side of the deck, "you don't back down from a challenge. Right?" she asked Ellis.

Ellis thought of Liberty's demands and badly wanted a stiff drink. "Even if it kills us." He focused on his brother. There was color in him tonight. Maybe a little light in his eyes and it was good to see, Ellis had to admit. Everett needed a challenge other than the one he'd been fighting with himself. PTSD had been a hard battle. Trucks and tractors backfiring sent him right back to summer and the box canyon and the shot that had shattered his sternum and nearly put him in the ground.

His brother was leaner, harder and had been lost for the better part of six months. Ellis had said nothing out loud about working late on those pay stubs and the rest of it because his brother needed this: this simple interaction with others to bring the light back—the fight back. His brother, who'd always thought on his feet and juggled cows, papers, ranch responsibilities like a king and now was fighting something bigger than himself. Not physically, anymore, but a mental battle that was just as treacherous.

I can't punch something I can't see, he'd told Ellis one particularly bad night a few months back.

Ellis and Paloma had fought to get him into therapy.

He'd dug in his heels, but after confining himself to the ranch for weeks at a time watching reruns of *Yellowstone*, avoiding town and people in general, he'd finally broke. He was now seeing a therapist once a week in San Gabriel. Paloma and Ellis took turns driving him. They'd both watched Hammond Eaton let his health slide away. They weren't going to do the same with him.

Poker nights helped, too, Ellis thought. Paloma hated gambling but even she had to admit these bimonthly gatherings were good for Everett.

"Ah!" Everett cried when Altaha took half the deck in another close battle. "You're a card sharp, sweetheart."

Altaha raised a brow and sent him a deputy's glance.

"Deputy," he quickly amended. Then fumbled again. "Sweetheart. Deputy sweetheart."

She stared at him for several seconds. Ellis counted them, watching his brother sweat it out and enjoying it. There weren't many people who could make Everett perspire with a look. A slow smile worked its way across Altaha's mouth. She slid her eyes over Everett's form. "You didn't eat. Paloma wasn't pleased."

"She lives to complain in my ear," he muttered, tossing his cards onto the table—what was left of them. "I gotta give her something."

"I'm starting to understand why a rancher like you has remained decidedly single," she said, lifting her glass from the table. It was half-full of beer that was no longer frothy. "You're a perfect ass."

"Thank you," he said with a tip of his hat. "It's been a while since I've gotten a remark like that."

She snorted. "Oh, they make hats for asses like you. You know that, right?"

"I've got plenty of hats," he drawled. "You wanna see 'em?"

Altaha laughed. It sounded remarkably like a giggle and Ellis froze. Was this… Were they…flirting? She waved her hand. "I'm going to take a pass on that. Maybe some other time."

"I'll hold you to it," Everett said. There was a smile on his face. It was sly, as it'd once been. Around the edges it was soft as it never was.

Ellis was inexplicably starting to feel like a third wheel. "Any updates on the case at Ollero Creek?" he inquired.

Altaha made a noise. "Nothing solid. Tire treads are pretty common. They were newer, though. Definitely a four-by-four."

"Everybody's got a four-by," Everett commented, re-assembling the deck.

"That's true," Ellis said. "So it's a dead end?"

"The case isn't cold," Altaha said. "I'm not giving up on it, Eaton. A little faith, huh?"

Faith had been hard to come by. He was still raw from the phone call. Picking up an abandoned beer glass, he took a gulp of the lukewarm contents. He winced, set it down with a clack and tried not to stew over the idea of Isla going to bed sad or Ingrid in trouble with her mother or Luella alone at Ollero Creek. "Has Luella reported anything?"

"No," Altaha replied. "I checked in with her this afternoon. She saved Ben Tate's life at the bank. He's in stable condition."

"I heard," Ellis said quietly. He'd also wondered over the enormous sense of pride he'd felt when he had. Not surprise. Of course, she'd saved a man's life. Just a strange well of pride in the woman that hadn't been his in seventeen years. He looked around for the Bluetooth speaker that was blaring country music out in deafening waves. "You should turn that down."

"I like this one," Everett opined. He'd been watching Ellis closely in the talk of Ollero Creek. "Who doesn't love a good ditty about a man pining after some girl he left behind?"

Altaha made a gimme motion with her hand. "May I?"

Everett eyed her once then unlocked the screen of his phone and slid it her way.

"Thank you," she said, hands busy scrolling. She grinned. "This one," she said when the country music cut off, "is for you, sad boy."

"Me?" Everett asked as a piano intro flooded the room.

Altaha stood, pushing back her chair. As Gloria Gaynor started crooning, she started to spin.

Everett leaned into Ellis. "What's happening here?"

"I think…" Ellis raised the beer to his mouth again "…the good deputy is dancing."

Everett's jaw loosened as Altaha's braid went flying and her hips started to move. "I feel like I'm seeing Darth Vader without his mask."

Ellis found himself smiling at the display. "She's got moves. Maybe as many as you used to. Oh," he added when Altaha crooked her finger. "I think you're being summoned."

Everett raised his hands. "Ah, no. I don't think so."

Altaha rolled her eyes. "Come on! I hear Everett Eaton used to tear up the floor at Grady's Saloon."

"Before he was banned," Ellis mentioned.

"Banned," Everett said with a decisive nod. "For life."

"Then you're past due," Altaha insisted. "Get your boots over here before I sit on you!"

Everett pursed his lips. "That's not a threat, sweetheart."

"Now!" Altaha said, grabbing him by the hands and yanking him to his feet.

Next to her, Everett looked as tall as a tree and just as awkward. "You do know hootin' leads to hollerin'?"

Altaha beamed. "That's what I'm counting on, cowboy."

As Ellis saw the good deputy out to her truck some time later, he said, "I can't remember the last time Everett smiled."

"Your big brother's going to be fine," Altaha assured him. "He just needs to remember who he is. That guy who used to race cars and cut a rug at Grady's. The same guy who punched True Claymore in the teeth at my sister's wedding."

Ellis laughed. "Yeah. We're still paying for that one. You know the Claymores tried to sue? Even when he was recovering from his gunshot wound."

"Annette and True Claymore are a pox on this town," Altaha said. "If not for True's brother, the reverend, I'd say run them all off. But you didn't hear that from me."

Ellis raised his hands to show he wasn't listening.

Altaha stopped moving toward her truck. "I heard a rumor."

He crossed his arms. "We love those around here."

"If this one's true, I've got something to say about it. Word is your ex is asking for your shares in Eaton Edge in exchange for custody."

He sunk his hands into the pockets of his jeans. The night was cold. He blew clouds into the cutting wind. "Where do you get your sources? They're uncanny."

"As a matter of fact, it was Annette Claymore bragging at the barber shop," Altaha said. "Every chair was full. Four cosmetologists, one barber and eight customers heard every bit of it. Now it's spreading like a virus." She paused. "You're saying it's true?"

Ellis sighed. "Yes."

"May I speak as your friend now, not your deputy?"

"After all that hootin' and hollerin' in there, it's hard to see you as anything else," he remarked.

"Fight her," Altaha said. "Fight her to the teeth."

He groaned. "I can't lose my girls, Kaya."

"You can't lose your birthright either," she said. "If not for your sake, then for your father and your brothers. It'd kill them both. And if you are willing to fight, I've got someone you ought to speak to."

"You know a good divorce lawyer?"

"No, but I do know the man your wife was having an affair with."

He took that. It went down like a serrated pill. "You... What?"

"Walker Sullivan," Altaha supplied.

"The...bronc buster?" Ellis had a laugh. "I thought that was just..."

"Careful, moon-eyed looks and talk over the last seven years like you and Luella Decker?" Altaha asked. "No. It was more than that."

"Do you have proof of this?" he asked, trying not to wince at how much she'd been able to discern about him and Luella. "Of Liberty and Walker?"

"They were screwing in the bed he shared with his wife, not yours, if that makes you feel any better."

Was any of this supposed to make him feel better?

"You recall they separated, too. Last Christmas."

Ellis shook his head. "Hang on. Liberty hates cowboys. The whole lifestyle, everything about them. Why would she want another one?"

"There are some forces greater than all of us. It doesn't need to make sense. It just is. Or was. Seeing as Liberty's living in Taos now, I'd say the affair's over."

"Jesus. Did you learn all this at the barber shop?"

"No. Walker's ex, Rosalie, is friends with Naleen. They talk. Naleen passes on pertinent information. She was in the shop the day Annette told everyone about Liberty's evil plans for you. I think she told me about Liberty and Walker so I'd pass it along to you. Not everybody sided with Liberty during the separation. I hope you see that now. And I hope you fight fire with fire."

He studied her. She was angry. Maybe as angry as he was. He gave a slow nod.

"Does your family know what she's trying to do?" Altaha asked.

Ellis shook his head. "Everett's got enough on his mind. Eveline and Wolfe are planning a wedding. And Paloma worries enough already."

"They need to know," she advised. "Here." She dug into her small, battered handbag and pulled out a card. "This guy—he lives an hour away but he helped Naleen get primary custody of Nova in her divorce from Ryan Mackay. There was infidelity involved in that case, too." He hesitated. "On both sides. It was ugly but this guy helped."

Ellis took the card with some reluctance, read the name and practice and realized he was in this now, all in.

"Call Rosalie, too," Altaha added. "She still lives in that house by the Tractor Supply. Even if she did burn that mattress."

"I guess I should say thank you."

She patted him firmly on the shoulder. "Do it later when you feel less like a man scorned. Oh, and somebody needs to say it. Spending your free time with Luella Decker might not be the best look for you if you're going to tell the judge you didn't sleep with her."

Ellis's brow furrowed. "But I didn't sleep with her."

"I believe you. But a judge may not if you're sleeping with her now."

"We're *not* sleeping together."

She flicked the strap of her purse over her shoulder. "Tell me right here and now if the opportunity presents itself you won't touch her for the next twelve months."

Unbidden, Luella's mouth entered his mind. Her sweet mouth in her heart-shaped face. Her taste—like muscadines ripening on the vine.

He had touched her. He'd chased her across her yard and touched her and now he was burdened by the knowledge that all that'd been between them before was still there. It was right there—ready and waiting like fruit on the vine.

When his mouth opened and stayed that way, she pointed at it. "You see that right there? That's trouble."

"It doesn't mean I'm going to sleep with her," he claimed. But the words sounded unconvincing in his own ears.

"Hell, Ellis," she said, walking backward to her truck, "I'd have jumped on your brother tonight to cheer him up if you hadn't been here after everybody else went. And he and I have a lot less history."

The idea of Everett and the deputy together alone long enough to make these decisions for themselves made Ellis's head hurt a little. "You mean well, I guess. Good night, Deputy."

Chapter 7

Luella frowned at the postmark on the large manila envelope in her mailbox. She lifted it to the light.

San Gabriel.

Luella stared at the writing—her name, her address.

Aunt Mabel's handwriting again.

Luella carefully tore the top of the envelope. What had her aunt sent her now? Would it make more sense than the short-worded postcards still sitting on her kitchen table?

She reached in and pulled out a photograph.

Confused, she opened the envelope wider. It was empty. Turning the five-by-ten over, she frowned at the faces on it.

She didn't recognize either one.

Luella leaned back against Sheridan's warmth. She'd saddled him for a ride around her property where she'd surveyed fences and looked for signs of entry around the perimeter. She'd found nothing out of place.

Luella studied the photograph in closer detail. She did recognize something. The sign for the Fuego Horse Arena was in the background. The couple, embracing around the waist and smiling for the camera, was in the foreground. In the middle ground were various people, out of focus, milling here and there in hats and chaps.

The rodeo, she discerned. The man was wearing chaps, too. No hat. He had a full head of dark, shaggy hair and he was tall. Stupid tall. Very *Smoky and the Bandit*.

The woman wasn't dressed for an event like he was but she was sporting boots and a flat-brimmed hat as well as a printed blouse that looked like something made in the eighties.

There was a date in the bottom right corner of the photograph. Luella squinted because it was a bit smudged. *03-11-87*.

"Eighty-seven," Luella mused. She offered the photo for Sheridan to have a look. "Year before I was born. Fifteen years before you, handsome." She kissed him above the nose.

He chuffed, turning his nose against her torso to blow his breath across her.

She ran her fingers through his forelock. The woman had red hair, she saw upon closer inspection.

Red hair.

Luella's fingers tangled in Sheridan's mane. She studied the face of the woman again, hard. It was heart-shaped, like her own.

Her jaw dropped. "Mom?" she said out loud. Then she shook her head, unable to relate the smiling woman in the photograph to the bitter woman in San Gabriel who answered by the same name.

Luella flipped the photo over again. Nothing but blank

space on the other side. No message. "What the hell, Mabel?" she asked. The man in the photograph might be a mystery, but it was most definitely not her father. Too tall, dark and good-tempered. "What are you trying to tell me?"

The sound of a truck approaching had Sheridan's hooves dancing back on the driveway. Luella grabbed his bridle as she looked in the direction of the highway.

It was one of the trucks from Eaton Edge. She braced herself, stuffing the picture back in its envelope and tucking it under her arm. The truck slowed and the window rolled down.

Luella balked at the face of Eveline Eaton in the driver's seat. "Hell."

Eveline laughed. Her breath plumed out the window from the warm cab. "I think you meant hel*lo*. A little out of practice?"

"Yeah, sure," Luella said. "What are you doing here?"

"I don't expect you to call me about that lunch you said we'd arrange. And I've got something to say to you."

"You want me to invite you into my house?" Luella asked, doubtfully.

"That is the way to do things," Eveline considered. "Maybe we could even do something crazy like have a cup of coffee together."

"I don't have anything to go with coffee."

"Then we'll just have to starve," Eveline drawled. She eyed Sheridan. "Hey, big boy. We've sure missed you at the Edge."

Luella covered his nose in defense. "I'll let you in," she said, resigned.

It *was* odd, leading Eveline inside after stabling Sheridan. Luella took her time supplying him with fresh water and bolting the door. She checked on Caesar. He'd taken to lingering in the coop. She pretended it didn't break her heart. As she mounted the steps to the porch, she jumped at Nyx as he chased her feet across the boards. "Scoundrel," she hissed when his claws sank into the jeans over her calf and he worked his way up her leg. She shook him off. "Go on, now!" Digging her keys out of her pocket, she shoved one into the first dead bolt. "Watch him. He strikes without warning."

"Oh, most men do," Eveline gauged. She eyed the key going into the second dead bolt but didn't say a word about the strong security measures.

Finally, Luella shoved her way into the house, letting Eveline come in, too. She shrugged out of her jacket, hung it and her keys on the peg and made a beeline for the coffeepot.

"Aw," Eveline cooed. "What's this one's name?"

Eveline saw her take off one soft leather glove to raise her hand to Sphinx's back. The feline was reclining on the back of the couch. "Sphinx. She won't swipe."

Sphinx purred at Eveline's attentions. Luella found two clean mugs and poured coffee. She set the mugs on the table, set out napkins with them then sat down. "What'd you want to talk about?"

"You don't believe in small talk?" Eveline asked, stroking the line of Sphinx's spine one last time before taking off her other glove. She pulled out a chair at the table and settled.

"As a rule," Luella decided.

Eveline nodded. "Talk's cheap when it's common." She lifted her mug and blew across the surface. "I think that's something we've both learned the hard way."

Luella frowned. If Eveline was trying to find common ground between the two of them, she'd need to keep searching. Eveline Eaton was a ball of sunlight who no doubt could still squeeze into those size two runway outfits she'd once dazzled the world in.

Next to her, Luella felt like a rock in comparison. Her cable-knit sweater was a neutral color and a bit drab. Her boots were battered and her size twelve jeans had wide tears around the knees. In contrast, Eveline wore a warm wool coat that looked new and Ariats that had barely been scuffed.

"Postcards," Eveline said, picking one of Mabel's messages off the top of the pile. "Someone has an admirer."

"Hardly," Luella murmured, taking a sip of her coffee. She held the mug in her hands because she'd forgotten her gloves on the ride. The heat soaked clean through her skin.

Eveline frowned at the message. "'W.J.'?" She made a face. "Whoever this is from has just as big a gift for gab as you."

"It's my aunt," Luella said, reaching out to take the postcard. She pulled the stack closer. "She lives in San Gabriel. My mom's been afraid her mind's been slipping for years. This seems to confirm it." She eyed the manila envelope she'd set on the side table by the door.

"Is she ill?" Eveline asked, unwrapping her scarf.

"Not that I've heard," Luella said. "I don't talk to my mom much anymore."

"Maybe you should go see for yourself."

"The last time I went, my mom and I couldn't sit in the same room for more than a few minutes at a time."

"Why not?" Eveline asked. "I remember your mother. Riane, right? She was always the nice lady at church who handed out peppermints."

Luella remembered the woman who'd hidden under that one. The one who'd take a beating from Jace Decker and make sure her daughter knew she was the one to blame for it. *Devil's spawn. Bad seed.* And later, *Hussy. Jezebel. Whore.* "She forgot how to be nice a long time ago."

"I'm sorry to hear that," Eveline said.

Luella shifted in her seat, uncomfortable. "Why did you pay for the Uber?"

Eveline lowered her eyes to the table. She traced a parting in the wood with a neat fingernail. "Because I met your father. Like my mother and half sister before me, I met him in the worst way. I survived where they didn't. And over the last few months, I've come to understand that you did, too. You survived that, somehow—as a girl and a woman. I survived one day with him. I can't imagine the strength it took for you to live through all that you did."

Luella stilled.

"Also," Eveline said, bringing her hands together on the table, "you tried to warn me about him this summer. You said whoever was stalking me didn't want to be found and I should leave it be. I get what you were trying to do. You were trying, in your way, to save me from him because you knew what he was capable of. If I had listened to you, Everett might not have been shot and you might not have gone to jail."

"And my father would still be out there," Luella stated. "He'd be alive. In a way, I owe you and yours for taking care of him."

"It wasn't me," Eveline said. "Not directly."

"But you didn't quit and he's dead and we're both here alive to talk about it, apparently."

Eveline offered her something of a smile. "If you *are* going to leave Fuego, I wanted you to take my gratitude with you, and I wanted you to know how much I admire you."

Luella closed her eyes. She shook herself slightly. Was she dreaming? Ellis's sister...admired *her*? "Did...did Ellis put you up to this?"

Eveline's expression went blank. "What does Ellis have to do with anything?"

"Nothing. Never mind." Luella pushed herself up from the table. "Thank you... I think."

"Likewise," Eveline said, rising. She reached for her gloves and scarf. Her brow knitted as she pulled them on, one finger at a time. "I was sorry to hear about your chickens. What a horrible thing. They think it was someone from town?"

"That's the working theory, I believe," Luella said, leading Eveline to the door. "Someone who wants to make it known that I'm no longer welcome here, most likely."

"And you're all alone out here?" Eveline said, looking around.

Luella's gaze fell on the cat stretching itself as it walked lazily across the back of the couch. "I have Nyx and Sphinx and Sheridan. Caesar the rooster, too, even if he is downhearted."

Eveline laid her hand on Luella's arm. "This is rough country to be a woman alone in. I know that now."

"I have a gun," Luella told her. "How's Wolfe? I haven't seen him."

Eveline's grin blazed. "He's fine. Busy. He's wanted to visit but we just finished the house. He's been trying to get Santiago's wing ready so he and his caretaker can move in."

"It's nice that you're bringing him home to Fuego," Luella commented.

"It'll be good for everyone," Eveline said. "Wolfe hated him being so far away in the mental facility. Paloma can visit him whenever she likes, and he'll be able to see the desert and the mountains he loves."

"When is the wedding?" Luella asked, a bit awkwardly, surprised she wanted to make the effort. Something had eased between her and Eveline, however, which made it easier.

"March," Eveline said. "A spring wedding at the Edge. With Wolfe and Everett's feud finally over, it'll be perfect. It's the place that brought Wolfe into my life."

Luella hissed when a bracing wind laced across the porch. She'd forgotten her jacket inside.

If Ellis were here, he'd be chasing her with it.

She nearly smiled. It made her stop and scowl. "There's a storm coming. Another blizzard. Drive careful."

"Sure." Eveline's teeth flashed. She fit her sunglasses into place. "You do know my brother's in love with you. Don't you?"

Luella's pulse skittered. She felt her breath hitch. From far away, she heard her voice. "Which one?"

Eveline's laugh tittered into the air. As she waved and went back to her truck, Luella stood frozen at the top of the steps, glad of the cold snapping her cheeks.

When Eveline drove off, Luella beat feet down the steps, needing the cold a bit longer to pipe down some of the heat inside her.

My brother's in love with you.

Ellis, young and smiling—carefree and golden— filled Luella's mind. The star-shaped diamond ring he'd given her, missing for over a decade now, was an itch at the base of her finger.

"I wish this could last forever," she told him as they sat underneath the shadows of their horses. The clouds were passing fast. She could hear thunder on the horizon. They'd have to ride soon—ride hard for the ranch house or the nearest shelter. The need to linger, to stretch time so that his shoulder pillowed her cheek and the circle of his arms remained unbroken, was too much for her to give up, even for a storm.

"Who says it won't?" he asked, turning his lips against her temple for a brushing glide.

There was a smile in his voice. She could tell. Hers faded by gradual degrees as thunder knelled again. It was too perfect to last—the moment. This. Some part of her knew. She'd known from the moment he smiled at her in class over a chemistry book. She'd known the second he'd asked her out under the guise of stargazing on his roof.

She had known it from the moment she'd realized she loved him—how hard *she loved him—and when he'd told her he loved her in return.*

From their first dance—it was supposed to be at homecoming but he'd taken her into the hills after her father had knocked her around. And the first kiss, shortly thereafter. Their first time inside a sleeping bag near a crackling fire under the stars not long after spring thaw. And all the times after—she'd known she couldn't keep him. How could he be hers when he was so perfect?

She'd never had anything perfect—not until Ellis. If her mother was right and her father, too, she wasn't meant to.

She was so afraid of breaking his heart—in quiet mo-

ments like these where she felt the rush of time against the sweet, languid undercurrent of longing and love, it broke hers.

The moments were slowly, quietly breaking her heart, because she knew they were inevitably bringing her closer to when time won and everything fractured.

How could she keep him when she and her world were so imperfect?

She'd do anything, she realized, to be perfect for him...

She'd tried to be perfect. When he dropped down on one knee and proposed, she'd felt relief beyond measure. This would be her way of keeping him. No one could argue with a ring. It meant she belonged to Ellis and the Eatons, and she'd never have to go back to her father or her mother.

Luella stopped short, the memories falling fast at her feet as she faltered.

The chain she'd used to lock the barn door was lying in the mud. The bolt had been cut.

The door hung open and she didn't hear Sheridan inside.

Chapter 8

Ellis stomped on the gas. Visibility was growing worse by the minute. Snowflakes batted the windshield as the wind funneled them in at an angle. He put on his headlights and veered in the direction of Ollero Creek.

The phone call from Luella had been unexpected. It had also been hysterical. Sheridan was gone and he didn't have much hope that she'd done as he'd asked.

Wait, he'd told her. *Wait for me. Don't go looking for him yourself.*

He nearly took out her mailbox, cranking the wheel to the left when he finally saw her driveway creep up. The tires bounced in and out of ruts, but he didn't slow.

He braked in front of her house. Her truck was there. He ducked out into the weather, keeping his head low as he raced up the steps to her porch and knocked on her door.

No answer.

He peered through the window. The cat, Nyx, stared back at him, lifting its paw to bat at his face on the other side of the glass.

Ellis cursed, going back down the steps. He went around the house to the yard. The barn was just as she'd left it, closed and empty but for the rooster.

He studied the ground. There were tracks, but they were fading.

He ran back to his truck. The flakes were starting to grow fatter and fall faster.

He opened the door of the horse trailer behind his truck. "Come on," he urged to his horse, Shy. He was already saddled and ready to ride, as he had been at the Edge. Ellis zipped his jacket, put on his gloves, pulled his bandanna up over his nose and mounted. Then he set out around the yard to follow both the woman's and the horse's tracks.

They'd gone north, in the direction of the cliffs, across the long empty prairie. Because of the snowfall, he couldn't see the cliffs or anything more than ten feet in front of him. The house quickly faded behind him as the storm swallowed him and his mount.

He frowned when he noticed another set of tracks alongside Sheridan's. About fifty yards from the house, he saw the first signs of blood. He pulled on Shy's reins. His stomach hit the ground before his feet as he dismounted.

The blood trail was thin, but it traveled with Sheridan's hoofprints as far into the distance as he could discern. He followed on foot a ways, just to be sure.

The boot prints going forward were jumbled. Was there a confrontation? Or had Luella stumbled? Was she hurt?

The tracks grew lighter, barely discernable. Ellis stayed on foot, leading Shy one step at a time.

The blood trail was the only thing that remained consistent. "Son of a bitch," Ellis said as the prints nearly faded out altogether. He was about to lose them. Snow crusted the brim of his hat. It gathered on his shoulders. Squinting, he tried to pick shadows out of the white haze. "Lu!" he called, cupping his hands over his mouth. His voice was absorbed by the falling snow. There was no echo. When no sound came back, he raised his voice further, straining his vocal cords. "Luella!"

Panting, he laid a hand over the horn of Shy's saddle. Before he could lift his foot to the stirrup, he heard the distant sound of a whinny. Then, a woman's shout, followed closely by the sharp report of a gunshot.

He mounted fast. Bringing his rifle around to his front, he urged Shy forward at the gallop.

Shadows did take shape in front of him. The horse. Ellis grew closer and the red of Luella's hair broke through the snowscape. She was belly-down on the ground. For a split second, he thought she was hurt and he nearly lost his mind.

Then he saw her shotgun in her arms, aimed in the direction of the horse.

"Lu!" he called.

Her head swiveled. "Ellis, stop! He's armed!"

Before Ellis could react, another gunshot rang out, louder this time.

Shy bucked a split second before impact. Ellis felt the burn across his arm. Then he felt himself falling away as Shy bucked a second time. The reins fell from his hands.

The ground jarred him. He kept his head up. He tried sucking air into his lungs. They refused to work. The wind had been knocked out of them.

Stay calm, he told himself when the urge to panic

mushroomed. He did get his breath back, siphoning it in and out in steady puffs and thinking through the situation.

The rifle had fallen a few yards away. He tried to orient his surroundings. It was difficult with the wall of white around him. Shy. Rifle. Luella. Sheridan, fifteen feet away.

He crawled through the brush and snow to the rifle. He took off the safety then tilted his head, trying to sight. His arm screamed. He felt the warm wet growing inside his jacket. He breathed carefully, aware that his pulse was jacked up. If he could keep his breath steady…

He didn't wait in vain. The shadow of a man stepped out from behind the horse.

"Son of a bitch," Ellis breathed. Holding the rifle steady, he squeezed the trigger.

A cry flew out of the flurry, along with twin whinnies from the horses. Luella cried out, too.

Ellis lay very still, watching the shadow in his sights. It folded over. For a moment, he thought it would crumble to the ground.

It straightened instead and fled into the white wash.

Ellis got cautiously to his feet. "Lu?" he called, bringing the rifle up in front of him. He sidestepped to her, watching for the figure through his scope. "You all right?"

"Am *I* all right?" she called, getting cautiously to her knees. "You fell off your horse. Are you hit?"

He made a noise. The blood was running down the inside his sleeve. The wound was little fire torpedoes dancing up and down his arm. "I saw blood in the snow. Is that you or—"

"It's Sheridan," she said, urgent. "He's been hurt."

"Call him," Ellis said. "He doesn't look tethered."

"The bastard was using him for cover," Luella moaned.

"I know," he replied. "Call him. He won't come to me."

Luella lifted her fingers to her mouth and released a shrill whistle. "Here, boy! Come!"

Sheridan milled across the far point of their vision. Then his shadow grew stronger against the white.

"That's good!" Luella called. "Come here, boy! Come to mama!"

Ellis breathed a sigh of relief when Sheridan trotted the rest of the way to Luella. He kept himself between them and the last point he'd seen the man's shadow disappear into the storm.

"Oh, God, Ellis," Luella cried. "He's hurt. He's hurt real bad."

"It's all right," Ellis soothed, brushing his hand along the horse's flank. It was sticky with blood. "You can ride with me. We'll lead him back to the house and see if we can't get the doctor out to look."

Dr. Wilstead shook her head as she leaned over Sheridan's prone form. The horse lay sedated on the floor of the operating room at her office in Fuego. She patted the wound on Sheridan's croup with gauze. "This is a travesty," she muttered. "I hope they catch whoever did it."

Luella's hands were like ice even though she'd been indoors for over an hour now. Weariness was heavy in her bones.

Her baby was bleeding. Not to death. She knew that. Still, her mind went places she'd rather it didn't as she assisted Wilstead with the operation.

She swallowed. Her throat was bone dry. It was lucky Wilstead had agreed to let her into the OR. The doctor had needed an extra pair of hands and her regular assistants had all been snowed in. Lucky for Sheridan, Wilstead lived above stairs of her practice with her family. If not for her…what would she have done?

"We nearly did," Ellis said on Wilstead's far side. He was also assisting. "If it wasn't for this godforsaken storm, we'd have had him."

"I'm just going to sew Sheridan up now," Dr. Wilstead told them. She'd already located and extracted the bullet.

"It's small caliber," Luella said, studying the blood-stained slug in the petri dish at Wilstead's elbow.

"Nine millimeter," Ellis added.

"It's going to take a while for him to heal," Wilstead informed them. "But he's going to be all right."

"You'll keep him here," Luella surmised.

"I think that's best," Dr. Wilstead replied. She read Luella well. "He'll be safe. I promise."

Luella nodded, wishing she could believe just for a moment that either she or Sheridan could be safe again. "Thank you."

"There's water in the mini-fridge at the nurse's station," Wilstead revealed, stripping off her gloves. "You both look like you could use something to drink."

Luella felt fatigue pressing down on her eyelids. As she cleaned her hands in the sink in the corner of the room, she couldn't get the scent of Sheridan's blood from her nose.

She glanced back at him. His eyes were open, blank and staring.

Luella turned away when her stomach churned and nausea brimmed. She couldn't lose him. She just couldn't. Wilstead said he'd live, but Luella knew there was no going back to Ollero Creek. At least, not for Sheridan. And how was she supposed to face it without him?

She fled the operating room, wending through the halls of Wilstead's practice without direction. Everything ached—every muscle and joint.

She'd felt so alone out there. The storm had swept across Ollero Creek so quickly. She'd lost her way. If not for the blood in the snow...

But then the fear—the desperation, the despair. If anything happened to Sheridan...

Seeing Ellis come out of the whiteout like the fairytale knight he was had rocked her to her core.

He'd come for her—fighting cold and wind and snow. He'd come.

She tried to hold on to that feeling, the tidal wave of relief and faith and...well, she was very much afraid that the appropriate word was *love*. However, the fatigue crushed her. Her boots felt like they were lead-lined. Her head ached.

She felt like a soda can under a steel-toe boot, shrinking under pressure.

It was a familiar feeling. She remembered well how burnout had chased her through her graveyard shifts of the pandemic. This felt too close to that. And the numbness lurked, a blanket of shrink-wrap she knew she wouldn't be able to dislodge once it wrapped around her.

"You okay?"

She closed her eyes at the voice behind her at the nurse's station. Wilstead's practice was normally a hive of activity. Now there was no one in the hallway between the OR and the station.

Again, though, she found she wasn't alone.

His touch passed over her arm, then the other in long, soothing sweeps.

She felt her head tipping back to the warmth she knew

was there—the warmth he'd offer in a heartbeat. Her pulse quickened at the promise of something that wasn't numb or bleak.

Ellis. The promise of him. Would it ever not be there if she did the impossible and stayed in Fuego? Could she really give up the promise of him?

When she didn't move or answer, she felt him close in. She didn't step away. She didn't even think it. *Tired*, she thought. It was the fatigue.

She could almost believe that. But as his head tipped down to hers, she felt his lips in the nest of her hair, then his cheek. A shiver, infinitesimal, shimmered through her, lighting the way for him.

Closer, she thought.

It was inexplicable. But with Ellis came heat and she was so damn sick of being cold.

She wanted to feel. She wanted to feel him.

"He's okay," he murmured, mistaking her shiver for a sob. "Hey…" His hands trailed down her wrists until they found hers. He cupped her palms in his. "He's going to be okay."

She watched his long fingers twine with hers, interlocking. The texture of his skin was rough. She welcomed the friction. She felt her lashes flutter as his ribs pressed into the line of her shoulders on a long inhale.

He was breathing her in.

And, just like that, he flipped the switch and turned her on.

She didn't pull away like she should've. She didn't do anything like she should've.

My brother's in love with you, his sister had said just hours ago.

All this time? she wondered. Through it all—marriage, fatherhood, the life he'd lived apart from her?

He let go with one hand, tightened his grip on the other, bringing her around.

She was out of regrets and fresh out of excuses.

There was a contemplative bar between his eyes. He didn't quite meet hers, either. Instead, he studied their linked fingers, how they blended. How they fit.

She wanted to smooth that line. She wanted too much.

It didn't help at all when he raised her knuckles to his mouth. His eyes closed and the freckle on his eyelid flashed as he skimmed a kiss across them.

She felt so small and so full. The light of him pulsed in her blood. It choked out of the emptiness. It shined so brightly it burned.

Her breath left her in a scattered rush. She pulled her hand from his and waited until his eyes snapped open and he began to understand what she wanted from him. Her arms twined around his neck.

His lips covered hers. She demanded that vital body-to-body contact. She opened her mouth to his, tilting her head and amping the kiss up until she forgot about storms.

Hunger gnawed and twisted low in her belly. His hands cradled the back of her head and his lips turned against her cheek then her ear, into her hair.

She tipped her head when his mouth found the sensitive place on the side of her neck they both knew was there. Shuddering, she opened her eyes and let the fluorescent lights on the ceiling blind her. She was soft and weak, alive and undone. It felt *so good.*

He made a deep, sexy noise in his throat. "You still shiver when I do this," he breathed against her throat.

The words were hot against the damp circle his mouth left behind. "I can't… How am I supposed to *think* knowing you still shiver…?"

"Think?" she repeated. There was no thinking with Ellis—only churning, burning, aching…

He suckled that point on her throat.

Her nails dug into his shirt. If he didn't stop, he'd break her down. She'd be nothing—no strength left, no sense or pride.

She planted her hands on his shoulders and pushed.

He stumbled back a step. He was panting. A flush crawled up the length of his long, muscled throat. His open mouth closed, his lips turning inward as if to lock her taste in. His eyes were hooded and…

Oh, God. His eyes were the worst part. In them she saw everything he made her feel.

She told herself to look away. She didn't need to know what she did to him. She didn't need to know what he felt. As she touched her tingling mouth and watched him recover himself over the course of several ragged breaths, she realized she couldn't stop.

Later, she pledged. Later she'd blame it on the gunfight, and nearly losing her horse to a madman. But a smile bloomed, unbidden and absurd, on her lips.

His gaze tracked its progress. His eyes measured the wide curve of her mouth then the flush she felt on her cheeks. They circled her features then rolled back as he closed his eyes. "Oh hell," he cursed under his breath, bracing his hands on his hips as he turned a half circle away. "You're too much."

She'd seen his answering smile. It was shy and knowing, all in one.

Would he do this to her forever? She had to wonder.

Was the answer to all her bad days, her dark moods…was it always going to be the one she'd abandoned?

She thought about tracing that flush with her fingertips. Better, her lips. But she found the wet black stain on the elbow of his jacket. Her lips parted, once, then released a distressed sound when the scent of blood again washed across her senses. "Ellis…" She gripped his shoulder, accessing the area. "You're hurt?"

His eyes, still steeped in her, touched on his sleeve. "I'm fine," he said. Then he grinned. "Honey."

She shook her head, all the good feelings gone. "You've been bleeding. You've been bleeding for a *while*."

"It's nothing, Lu," he said. "Just a graze."

"Graze…" Her thoughts flew back to the snow-covered prairie. He'd fallen off Shy and hit the ground just after the second gunshot…

She began to tear at his jacket.

"What're you—"

"Uh-uh," she grunted, breaking off buttons and yanking down the zipper underneath to get to him. Her heart was in her throat. She yanked the collar loose over his shoulder, torqued it down his arm until she could get a decent look.

There was blood everywhere. It was hours old, but the smell of it and sweat stung her nostrils. Her stomach clutched. "Oh, *God*, Ellis! Why didn't you *say* something?"

"You were scared out of your mind about your horse. What was I supposed to say?"

"I don't know," she said with a sneer. "Maybe something like, 'Hey, you know what, honey? I've been *shot*!'"

He laughed and she checked the urge to deck him. When she tugged at the sleeve once more, trying to remove the jacket completely, he grimaced. "Easy, easy," he urged.

"Goddamn it," she growled. Grabbing him by the wrist, she trudged the rest of the way to the nurse's station, dragging him behind her. "Take off your damn clothes."

"The doc's in the next room," he warned. "I'm not sure we should—"

She whirled, planted her hands on his chest and knocked him back against the counter. "I'm not trying to get into your pants, you idiot! I'm trying to dress your wound! Take them off!" She started digging through cabinets and drawers, taking what she might need and muttering as she did.

"We need to have a conversation about your bedside manner," he considered.

"You really don't know when to shut up," she remarked, dumping her supplies on a tray. She washed her hands in the sink thoroughly before grabbing a pair of gloves from the open box next to it. She tugged the first one on, grabbing it by the wrist to fit it tight between her fingers as she turned back to him.

His jacket and shirt were gone. She saw the bloody mess of them on the floor. More, she saw the long line of his torso, the sprinkling of golden fuzz over the expanse of it, and the hard muscles under it, the wide, hard points of his shoulders and the stark line of his collarbone.

The wound was a few inches above the elbow. It glared red and was more than an inch in length.

She swallowed. "You've been carrying this. This whole time."

"It's fine," he said. There was no humor left on his face. "The blood makes it look worse than it is."

She glowered. "I'm a nurse, Ellis. I know what this is and it is *not* fine."

He blew out a breath and leaned his hips back against the counter she'd shoved him toward.

"Sit up there," she demanded, bringing the tray.

He hesitated, but at her approach, he eyed the tools and decided to comply. He pressed his hands down on the counter and boosted his hips over the edge, his triceps popping out at her as he did. His hair fell over his brow and she saw the pain contort his face. His eyes met hers, honest for the first time with the level of discomfort he was in.

Her irritation drained. Keeping her hands steady even when they wanted to shake, she starting mopping up the mess.

The corner of his mouth trembled in the upward position. "Be gentle with me," he whispered.

His breath washed over her cheek. She swabbed, daubed, discarded and repeated then angled his elbow so the lights shined on the gash. She cursed, long and dirty. "You need sutures."

"Bandage me up and I'll be—"

"If you say 'fine' one more time, Ellis, I swear to God—"

He lifted his free hand to stop her. "I get it. Sorry. Just…do what you've got to do, sweetheart. I trust you."

She glared at him for a handful of seconds before she went looking for more supplies.

It took a while to get him sewn up. He didn't make a sound, but she saw sweat beading on his brow and upper lip. The flush was gone, along with a good bit of his color, and his breathing was a touch labored.

When she was done, she stood back and studied her

work. She gave a satisfied nod even though the smell of his blood was still strong in her nose.

What if the killer's aim hadn't been off? What if Shy hadn't bucked at the last second? What if that nine millimeter had gone in above the sternum, the same place his brother had taken a bullet six months ago?

"Thank you," he said.

"Don't," she said, pulling off the other glove. Turning to the sink, she disposed of the gloves then cranked the tap to scrub her hands. "You know the drill. Keep them dry. You should probably talk to your doctor and get an antibiotic. You don't want infection. Give the sutures two weeks. And try not to use that arm." When she'd washed her hands thoroughly, she dropped her face to the sink and splashed water on it.

She felt his hand low on her back. It feathered over her spine before coming to rest just above her belt. "I'm all right, Lu. You did a good job."

She shut off the water and reached blindly for the paper towels.

He handed her a wad. She patted her face dry. "Don't you think too much Eaton blood has been spilled because of a Decker?"

"No more blood will be spilled on account of this guy. We're going to get him. I promise you."

"You've promised too much in the past," she reminded him. "It backfired. I don't want it to be that way again."

"I don't regret my promises," he stated. "I only regret letting you out of yours."

She straightened, wishing he'd step back, give her some room. "I shouldn't have called you tonight."

"God knows what would have happened to you out there if you hadn't."

"I should've called the deputy instead," she said. "I should've—"

"Do you know what it'd do to me," he asked, "to lose you like that?"

He sounded anguished. "You're the one who's hurt."

"Takes more than that to kill a man like me," he said, tugging her around to face him. "I think my brother's living proof of that."

"You may be an Eaton," she said cautiously. "But you're not imperishable."

He smiled once, a furtive movement that vanquished some of the trouble in his eyes. Then his gaze turned down over her mouth, following its curve.

She turned her face away. "Don't do that."

"What?"

"Kiss me again."

"You kissed me again, honey."

"Why did you let me?" she said, her voice rising enough to echo through the clinic halls.

He let out an unsteady laugh. His words dipped low. "Because it was worth it—*so* worth it."

"This is Fuego—where *everybody* talks."

"We're alone."

"People find things out. What if us kissing gets back to Liberty? What if she uses this to hurt you?"

His eyes darkened, growing troubled again. She hated it but did nothing to stop it. "One of us," she said heavily, "has to start thinking clearly again."

"Sure," he said with a small nod. He braced his hands on his hips. "You want me to apologize?"

"You're sorry?"

"You really want me to answer that?" he asked, hoarse.

No. Knowing exactly how un-sorry he was wouldn't be good for her at all. She sighed. "You have to stop."

"Stop what?"

She gathered her strength because his sexy drawl wasn't helping. "Stop kissing me back. Stop looking at me like… like you can't live without me—because we *both* know you can."

He stared, his gaze dark and conflicted.

"Just…stop," she finished with little breath or energy left. "Promise me that. Not for my sake…but for your own."

His eyes rolled up and around. They closed and he nodded, tipping his head to the side to ease the tension in his neck. "I promise," he returned.

She tried telling all the dark, downtrodden parts of herself that this was the way it had to be. This was the way things should have stayed between them. She'd let him shift the status quo. She'd let him move it a mile up the road and continue doing so until she lost every ounce of wherewithal she'd built. "Thank you."

"Just remember," he warned, his gaze coming back to hers with grim finality. "I keep my promises. You know that, Lu, better than anybody."

Her heart started to pound. She had to get out of here…

"You can't go home to Ollero Creek," he said. "We barely got out of your driveway to get here. I'd say it's a far sight worse now. The storm hasn't let up."

Her shoulders slumped. What was she supposed to do if she couldn't go back?

"Don't hit me," he asked of her.

She began to shake her head. "Why would I…"

"You need to come home," he said, "to the Edge. With me and Shy."

Automatically, she crossed her arms over her chest. Why did he have to say it like that? *Come home.* "I can't."

"Where else have you got to go?"

"The motel."

"Where's your wallet, Lu?" he asked. "Besides, I don't like the idea of you being alone someplace off the highway when the guy who took a shot at you and Sheridan is still out there. I called Altaha. She can't meet with us until tomorrow morning. She's trapped 'til morning on the rez visiting her mother. And I know damn good and well you don't want me calling Jones…"

She thought about that and shook her head.

"The road to the Edge will be clear. Everett and the hands will have made sure of it. They always do."

"Listen—"

"Sheridan's safe here with the doc and her family above stairs," he continued, unhindered.

"I know. I just—"

"I've promised not to kiss you or touch you or *look* at you. You know I'll hold by that."

"Ellis—"

"Come on home with me, Lu," he persisted, unrelenting. "I'll drive you back to Ollero Creek first thing in the morning. I promise."

When he broke down her excuses like that, what choice did she have?

Chapter 9

Ellis knew how painful it must be for Luella to enter Eaton House after so much time. She hesitated on the threshold, eyeing the room beyond him with a wariness that slayed him.

He held the door open wider. "Come on, honey," he murmured. "It's cold."

She remained on the doorstep. He could see her building her weaponized defenses, one by one. The stillness was taking over, bricklaying the panic until she started to look glassy, just as he'd seen her look before.

He reached for her, but Paloma swooped in. "Ellis, where have you been? We were worried sick. And shut that door. You're letting the cold in." Before she could close the door for him, she found the woman on the other side. "Oh." Her demeanor changed. "Oh, you poor thing."

Ellis watched Paloma throw a strong arm around

Luella's waist and guide her in, leaving her no choice but to enter. "Did you get snowed out instead of in, *niña*?" Paloma shut the door with a loud bang. Luella jumped. Ellis wanted to soothe her, but Paloma snapped her fingers at him. "Take her coat."

"Yes, ma'am." As Paloma rattled on about a warm meal and a hot bath, Ellis positioned himself behind Luella. He knew what he'd promised. What he wanted was to put his hands in the auburn waves of her hair. It'd fallen out of its strict braid and was messy and wet.

He made himself take her jacket by the shoulders as she unzipped and slipped her arms free. Paloma led her in the direction of the kitchen and Ellis hung her jacket on a rack on the wall next to his brother's. He was surprised to find both Eveline's and Wolfe's there as well. They had a full house.

Instead of slipping off his own jacket and joining his family in the kitchen, he went out the door again. Shoving his hands into the pockets of his jeans, he ducked his head low and trudged back to his truck. Shy needed to be stabled. He could do with a good grooming session and a blanket as well as his fair share of treats. He wished Isla and Ingrid were there to see to that. Shy ate up their attentions and they showered him with them, knowing he was Daddy's own horse.

He wondered what it would be like having them all at the table together—his girls and Luella. He unlatched the door on the horse trailer and walked Shy out onto snowy ground. As they came around the truck, a light hit his eyes. He raised his hand to block it.

Everett's voice came out of the dark, stringent. "I oughtta kill you."

Ellis blew out a breath. "After dinner. I'm starved."

"What the hell were you thinking?" Everett asked, dogging him step for step around the house. "I had to hear it from frickin' Wilstead that you tried to get yourself killed. Was this summer not enough? Has our family not lost enough?"

Ellis turned on him. "You think I don't know what this family's lost, Everett? I was there—waiting outside surgery for the doctors to tell us whether you lived or died. I was there beside you when Dad took his last breath. And I was there when Eveline was dragged into that frickin' hellhole. I have watched every remaining member of my family come up against death in the last year."

"So why'd you decide to go chasing it, too?" Everett wanted to know. "If I'd known you'd leave the ranch and run off to risk your life for that woman, I wouldn't have kept you in charge."

"Her name's Luella, you son of a bitch," Ellis snapped. "You *know* her name! And you want me out as acting chief, you say the word."

Everett glowered in the light from the porch. It crossed streams with the light from the stables, casting odd shadows in the thickening sludge around their boots. "You know what it feels like to almost lose a brother. Did you need me to know, too?"

"I didn't do this to scare you," Ellis said. "I did it because—"

"Oh, hell, Ellis, don't say you love her," Everett intervened. "There's no coming back from that stupidity."

"You're right," Ellis said, walking on with Shy. "There's not."

"Seventeen years," Everett said, on his heels. "Seventeen years and you still can't let go. Not if your life or your family depends on it."

Ellis was done with the conversation—so done.

"I know you tried to hide her here," Everett revealed. "When Whip beat her so bad, she couldn't go to school for two weeks. You hid her in the rooms above the stables. You took her food, soap, clothes and blankets."

Ellis didn't say anything. It was too hard a place to revisit, even if he did wonder how Everett had found out when no one else had.

"I know you looked for a place for her in Taos," Everett continued, dogging Ellis and Shy into the stable. Out of the wind, his voice grew louder. "Near your dorm where you two could be close to each other. Maybe even live together."

Ellis led Shy into his stall. He went about the process of uncinching and unsaddling.

Everett hung on the gate, his arm long over the top. "I know you gave her a ring."

Ellis's hands stopped for a second—only a second—before he recovered himself. He carried the saddle out of the stall when Everett opened the gate for him and walked it to the tack room.

"Whatever happened to that ring, anyway?" Everett asked. "A whole carat, right? Set you back around fifteen grand."

Ellis lifted the saddle into its place. "How the hell do you know that?"

"I have eyes," Everett said. "I have ears. More, I know you. I know how your mind works, and your heart. Where Luella's concerned, you've got too much of one and not enough of the other."

Ellis blew past him again, grabbing a grooming tote while he was at it.

"You don't think you need to ask my permission?" Everett asked. "To keep her here."

Ellis checked the urge to kick the gate open, but only just. "She's got nowhere else to go. And I own twenty percent of the Edge, same as you. You want me to get Eveline so her forty can stack up against you too?"

"She'll stack 'em against me on principle," Everett muttered. He spat in the hay. "Both of you. Thorns in my side. Liberty called, by the way."

That did stop Ellis. The brush in his hand fell to his side. He shuffled from Shy to the gate and reluctantly looked down the row of stalls at his brother's long form.

"When were you going to tell me?" Everett asked. "I might be looking across the table at her instead of you during board meetings next year."

"It's not going to happen."

"So you're giving up on your girls, then? Just like that?"

Ellis swung the gate open. The brush dropped to the ground. "Is that what you think of me?"

"Man's too much a fool to stay away from his mistress?" Everett questioned. "There's not much else he wouldn't do."

Ellis's strides quickened. "I don't care what kind of shape you're in. I'm going to kick your ass."

Everett pushed off the wall, shoulders high. He made a come-hither motion. "Come on, boo. I'm ready."

Ellis's hand curled into a fist, eyeing the smug line of Everett's mouth. Before he could do something about it, a loud whistle cut through the stables. Several horses startled. They stamped their feet. Ellis's feet came up short when he saw the figure of his future brother-in-law, Wolfe Coldero, in the doorway.

He frowned at the pair of them and raised a brow underneath the brim of his old black felt hat. Mute since childhood, he raised his hands in a question.

Everett sneered. His and Wolfe's feud had been long but had finally cooled when it had been Wolfe who had gone into the depths of the box canyon to rescue Eveline from Decker. Still, there was some lingering resentment on Everett's part that was unlikely to be put to bed anytime soon. "Always the frickin' hero," he muttered, backing away from Ellis. "Maybe you can talk some sense into him," he added as he passed Wolfe on the way out.

Ellis took several breaths to calm himself. He never came to blows with Everett. It was Ellis who deescalated things before they could get that far.

The pain in his arm gnawed at him. He relaxed his fist and avoided Wolfe's gaze as the man approached, patting each horse on the nose that stuck its head out to greet him. He had a way with horses and Ellis's sister that was uncanny.

Ellis picked up the brush and grabbed Shy by the bridle. He'd followed Ellis halfway out of his stall. Ellis steered him back in then went through the motions of grooming him.

Wolfe stopped at the gate, observing. He lifted his shoulders.

"Fine," Ellis responded. "On edge, is all."

Wolfe lifted his hand to his own arm.

Ellis recognized it as the place he'd been shot. "It's just a graze."

Wolfe tipped his chin up but stopped short of a reassured nod. His hands moved in a language both he and Ellis had made up as children and young adults. *Luella's shaken up.*

Ellis considered, picking the hair out of the brush

bristles. "Probably from being back here more than anything."

Wolfe nodded. *Were you really going to fight him?*

"I wanted to," Ellis said, truthfully. "What does that make me—kicking a man when he's down?"

Wasn't that what he was doing to you?

Ellis chose not to answer. "I'm not giving up my girls. He has to know that."

I know you won't.

"Liberty was having an affair," Ellis revealed. "A real one with Walker Sullivan. Did you know?"

I would have told you.

Wolfe would have told him, Ellis knew. "I can fight her. I don't have to give her anything, if I play my cards right."

We'll help.

Ellis nodded. "Thanks. How is she, other than shaken up?"

They both knew to whom he was referring. Wolfe had witnessed more of Ellis and Luella's relationship than others had. They'd even taught her a good deal of their sign language. Wolfe's hands moved to show him. *Settling some. Paloma's helping.*

Wolfe pushed his way into the stall. He clapped Shy on the chest a few times, ran his large hand along his withers. He held out his hand.

Ellis stopped and looked at the man's face.

It was broad-planed and maybe more familiar than his own. He eyed the brush.

"I can finish," Ellis protested.

Wolfe's hands milled in explanation. *You're dead on your feet. I'll finish up.*

Ellis blew out a breath. He *was* tired, damn it. The

events of this afternoon were catching up with him. It wasn't just his arm that hurt, he found, but the line of his shoulders and spine from being unseated. Blowing out a breath, he relinquished the brush to Wolfe. "Thanks."

Wolfe patted him on his uninjured arm then went about the chore of tucking Shy in for the night.

Luella stood by while Eveline and Paloma made her a pallet in front of the fire in the office. "I can just sleep on the couch."

"Nonsense," Paloma chided. "You need something better than that on nights like these. Especially after what you've been through."

Luella felt at a loss. It was an empty, aching feeling she couldn't suppress any more than her fatigue. "I don't have to sleep in the house. I know there's room above the stables."

"They're being renovated," Eveline revealed, patting a pillow to flatten it. "My father left the rooms to Paloma so she wouldn't have to commute from town anymore." She glanced up at Luella, tossing the hair out of her face. "Besides, Ellis wouldn't want you so far away as that."

Luella couldn't think about what Ellis wanted, any more than she could think about what she wanted. She'd seen the stairs. Did the eighth tread up still shriek like it had when she was younger? Did Ellis still sleep in the third bedroom on the right?

"I'll loan you some clothes," Eveline offered as she stood up. "I keep some things here for nights like this."

Luella bit her lip. Then she remembered herself and said, "Thank you." She looked to Paloma. "You've done too much."

"Think nothing of it," Paloma said, standing with

some help from Eveline. "We're just glad you're okay after that mess today."

Luella opened her mouth to respond but was interrupted by a knock on the door. When she saw Ellis at the door with his good arm raised against the jamb and his tired eyes, she closed it quickly. He hadn't had a chance to change, either, and he looked as ragged as she felt. His gaze skipped past his sister and Paloma and landed squarely on her. "You doing okay?"

"Fine," Luella said.

Ellis eyed the pallet. He stepped in. "I'll sleep here. You go upstairs."

"No!" she protested. "No, this is fine. There's nothing wrong with—"

"Lu," he said, quietly. "I am too tired to argue. I'm sleeping here. You take my room."

"I don't want—"

"It's one night," he said, near exasperation. "I won't be able to sleep if you don't."

Luella felt both Paloma's and Eveline's gazes. She wanted to turn away from all of them. *Sleep in Ellis's room?* How could she possibly?

Paloma decided for her. "Right this way, Luella Belle." She eyed Ellis after taking Luella's hand. "You need a shower."

Ellis's mouth quirked in a ghost of a grin. "You sweet thing."

As Luella followed Paloma out, she couldn't help herself. She raised her eyes to his. They held for one second— two too long. His gaze flickered briefly over her mouth before Paloma tugged her gently on.

The eighth tread didn't just shriek anymore. It screamed. On the landing, Paloma turned to the right.

One, Luella counted as she passed the first door. Her heart picked up pace, just as it had when following Ellis through the darkness when she was eighteen. *Two. Three.*

Paloma flipped on the light and went about tidying while Luella stood frozen in the doorway. "I just changed the sheets this morning. He hasn't slept in them."

"Slept in them?" Luella repeated numbly, eyeing the bed. Everything was just as it had been.

"You'll want a shower," Paloma said. "I'll get you that change of clothes from Eveline. You didn't eat much at dinner. Do you want me to bring something up? Some comfort food to help you settle?"

What was this, a luxury hotel? Luella shook her head faintly.

Paloma sighed over her. She trudged back to the door, took her by the hand and made her sit on the bed.

Luella watched Paloma take off her boots, as if from far away. Her head was floating. This couldn't be happening. She couldn't be back...

"It'll all be all right," Paloma said, patting and rubbing her hand. "Are you sure you don't need anything else?"

Luella stared at her. "I... I don't know what I'm doing here."

Paloma squeezed her hand. "You need sleep," she murmured. "That's what you're here for. Remember?"

Luella found herself nodding, latching onto the simplicity.

"You'll get yourself cleaned up," Paloma said, "because when your head hits that pillow, Luella Belle, you won't have to think about it. You'll just rest."

"Are you sure?" Luella asked, her voice wavering. She was shocked by the weakness.

"Absolutely," Paloma said with a smile. "And if you

don't believe me, I can send up something to help you do so."

Luella thought about it. Then she shook her head vigorously. "No. I'm... I'll be fine."

Paloma's smile turned into a full-fledged grin. "Thatta girl." She patted her hand some more like she was a child again. "Morning's the time for all those pestering thoughts."

"Right," Luella said, nodding. "You're right." She squeezed Paloma's hand back. "Thank you. You've been..." She didn't know how to finish without breaking down completely.

"We'll talk, if you like," Paloma said. "In the morning."

"In the morning," Luella parroted. When Paloma got up to start the shower in the adjoining bathroom, Luella released a long breath. She tried not to look at the pattern of the bedspread—blue and green striped—or the antlers over the door—Ellis's first buck. She tried not to look at the bookshelf with the medical journals or textbooks... or the shirts hanging inside the open closet.

She did her best not to see or smell anything. Because too much of it would force her back into all the tender, loving memories she'd tried so desperately to suppress.

Paloma had been right, thank God. Luella slept a hard, dreamless sleep that put her out of her misery. When she woke, groggy and wondering briefly if she'd been drugged at some point, she felt a familiar weight on her chest. Opening her eyes, she stared into a set of unblinking yellow ones and frowned. "Sphinx?"

She sat up in bed. Sphinx shrank to her belly at the sudden movement. Her purring ceased.

Luella let out a shuddering breath, scooping the cat into her arms. "Where did you come from?" she asked, bringing Sphinx's cheek to her own.

The cat's purring set off again with a vengeance. She bumped her head against Luella's hand and arched her back under the glide of a stroke.

Luella looked around. She was in Ellis's room. The sun was gleaming through the slight parting in the curtains. Cradling Sphinx, she swung her legs over the side of the bed. In the bathroom, she brushed her teeth with the toothbrush and toothpaste Paloma had loaned her. She tried finger-combing the curly mass on top of her head but gave up.

She was stunned to find her clothes from yesterday clean and folded on Ellis's dresser. As she dressed, letting Sphinx twine around her ankles, she studied the two hand-drawn illustrations taped to the mirror. The one signed *Isla* in tidy cursive was a sweet rendering of three cartoonish figures on horseback. The other signed *Ingrid* in uneven print letters was what appeared to be a picture of three dragons. The largest dragon with its wings wrapped around the two smaller ones was labeled *Dadee*.

Luella blinked several times. She shoved her feet into her boots. Then she picked up Sphinx and opened the door.

Three large dogs waited outside. They were belly-down on the floor, having had their noses pressed to the parting between it and the hardwood. As one, they jumped to their feet when she appeared.

"Now, now," she warned when they lifted their noses toward the cat for a curious sniff. She felt Sphinx tense. "Stay back."

One did a small bunny hop onto its back legs, getting

far too close for comfort. Sphinx hissed and Luella took a step back into the room.

"Down," called a voice from down the hall.

Luella peered around the jamb. She felt her stomach clutch at the sight of Everett. He closed the door of his room smartly as the dogs came to greet him with a scritchity-scratch of claws. His hand reached down to pat each of their heads. "Outside?" he asked and they quickened, ruffing in whispers from their long throats. He finished buttoning the cuffs of his shirt as he led them to the stairs. "Should've figured you for a cat person," he muttered as he passed.

Luella narrowed her eyes but said nothing as his steps and those of his furry companions clattered down the stairs together. Tucking Sphinx under her chin, she gave him time to get all the way down before starting downstairs, too.

She followed the smells of breakfast into the kitchen. There she found Wolfe, Eveline and Everett, having just let his dogs out the back door, around a large butcher-block table and Paloma hovering over all of them.

Luella felt like an imposter.

"Lu."

She closed her eyes briefly as the low word trickled down the length of her neck. Turning, she found Ellis. He was already dressed, clean-shaven and smelling of aftershave. "Good morning," he offered.

His dark eyes shined in such a way that made her warm and toasty. "Morning," she returned. She thought of his arm. "How are you?"

"Riding high on Mexican coffee and anti-inflammatories," he said wryly. "Did you sleep?"

"I did," she said. "You shouldn't have given up your bed for me."

"It was worth it," he said, "to see you looking so rested. You found a friend."

"She found me," Luella said, petting Sphinx on the head. "How did she get here?"

"Naleen Altaha," he said, braving a scratch under Sphinx's chin. "She and Terrence stopped by Ollero Creek to check on you early this morning. When they didn't find you, she called after me to see if I knew where you were."

"Why would she call you?" Luella asked.

"Because her sister, the deputy, told her if anybody knows where you are, it's me."

Luella frowned. "Oh."

"She brought the other one, too," he muttered, "in a cat carrier with some choice words. He seemed more interested in the stables so I let him go out there. That's okay?"

Luella nodded. "He's a free spirit."

"He's somethin'," Ellis opined. "Caesar's out there, too."

She gaped. "She brought my rooster?"

"And your purse and phone," he said. "And some extra clothes and toiletries, if you need them."

"Does she think I'm moving in?"

"Until we find out more about whoever's trying to attack your animals, I have a mind to keep you."

Keep you. The words echoed from far off. When she'd recovered from a beating from her father after recouping above the stables at the Edge, Ellis had wanted her to stay—permanently. *I could keep you,* he'd said, his brow touching hers. *My father kept Wolfe, for a time. He can keep you.*

Wolfe didn't have a home, she'd reminded him. *I do.*

You're not safe there. If you stay, nothing will ever hurt you again. I promise.

She shook her head to stop herself from going through the rest. She hadn't stayed. She hadn't been safe. And all that was good about her life—Ellis, college, everything— had fallen away from there.

"She won't feed us until you both sit."

Luella glanced back at Everett's complaint and saw, alarmed, that everyone at the table was watching. She stepped away from Ellis. "I'd like my things," she told him.

He nodded to the counter. "That's your bag there."

It was. And Naleen was blessedly thorough. Luella found clean jeans, shirts, underwear and socks. There was her own toothbrush, toothpaste, deodorant...

She was going to have to send Naleen something in return, though she had no idea what.

"Do you have everything you need?" Eveline asked.

Luella stuffed her things back into the bag. "It seems so."

"If you need anything else," Eveline told her, "let me know."

Everett groaned then threw his head back and shouted, *"Breakfast!"*

Paloma swatted him on the shoulder. "Manners!"

"We're coming," Ellis said. He pushed something at Luella.

It was a mug. "Oh," she said, looking down into the murky contents. "Thank you."

He winked. "Milk and honey."

She placed both hands around the cup of coffee. Milk and honey was how she used to take it. She lifted it to her nose. The aroma curled up her nostrils.

Paloma piled her plate high with *huevos rancheros*, salsa fresca, fried potatoes, avocado, and refried beans. Wolfe looked amused when she glanced up at him with wide eyes. "Wow," she mouthed.

He unrolled his fork and knife from his napkin and placed them on either side of his plate. He put the napkin in his lap and, with his hands, signed, *Eat up, little sister.*

Luella followed his example, unrolling her utensils and placing her napkin on her lap before digging in. She caught Ellis observing her from the corner of his eye. He only started eating after she did.

It was delicious. She noticed none of the others talked. Was it because the food was that good or because she was there?

She'd never had breakfast with the Eatons—not in all the months she'd been with Ellis in high school. He'd snuck her out the front door a few times while Everett and Eveline sat down to the early-morning meal with their father. Other than some snatched leftovers from Paloma's table, Luella had never been privy to a place at it.

"*Hola*, Eatons!" someone called from the front of the house.

Ellis dropped his fork, lifted his napkin to wipe his mouth and started to rise. "That's the deputy."

"Deputy Sweetheart?" Everett asked.

"Deputy Altaha," Paloma corrected him. "You'll be good."

Luella frowned at the food left on her plate. Taking one last sip of coffee, she started to rise, too.

"Ellis," Paloma said, "carry Luella's plate to the office. If the deputy's going to question the both of you, you might as well do it on a full stomach."

Luella began to shake her head. "That's not necessary…"

On her left, Everett made a noise. "Rule number one—don't argue with Paloma. She'll make your life a living hell."

"Language," Paloma barked.

"Number two," Everett continued, "swear all you like at the dinner table so someone can be further up her hit list than me."

Luella didn't know how to take this. She narrowed her eyes.

Eveline helped her out. "Rule number three—never listen to Everett. His interests are completely self-serving."

Altaha frowned behind the office desk. "I'm still confused as to why *you're* here."

Everett reached up to take the toothpick from the corner of his mouth. "I'm his representative."

Ellis exchanged a glance with Altaha and looked studiously back down at his written statement from yesterday's shootout. "I'll plead my own case, if it's all the same to you, brother."

"Nobody here's a suspect, cattle baron," Altaha explained to Everett. "I'm just taking statements. And some details of the case are being kept under wraps for investigative purposes."

"What's Jones's take on all this?" Everett asked curiously.

Altaha eyed him over the length of the room. It was similar to the long, cool look she'd extended him over cards. "Ellis, is your representative suggesting he wants a second opinion on this case?"

"Not my representative," Ellis repeated. "*So* not my representative."

"If you have a complaint about my performance," Altaha went on, "please do feel free to kiss my ass."

The corner of Everett's mouth quirked. Maybe to hide a grin, he stuck the toothpick between his teeth again. "Damned if I don't like you, Deputy Sweetheart."

"Are they…?" Luella began under her breath.

"I think he's trying?" Ellis muttered back.

The door opened at Everett's back, knocking him off balance. He scowled when Eveline poked her head in. "What are you doing?" she asked him.

"Leanin', if it's all the same to you," he grumbled.

She rolled her eyes then sought the others in the room. "Luella, this is for you."

Luella reached out for the phone. Everett gave in, taking it from his sister and walking it across the room.

"It's been ringing," Eveline revealed.

"Thanks," Luella said. She unlocked the phone and checked her call list. She frowned. "Oh."

"What is it?" Ellis asked.

"Nothing," Luella said. "It's just…my mother. She never calls me."

"Riane?" Ellis watched her stand and pace to the far corner of the room. As long as he could remember, Riane Decker, or Howard or whatever the woman went by now, had given Luella the cold shoulder. Where Whip's wrath had been all fire and brimstone, Riane's answer to that had been torrents of shooting ice.

"Paloma needs you," Eveline chided Everett.

"Now?" he asked.

"Now!" Eveline said.

Everett groaned and followed her out.

"You'll need to sign that," Altaha said, bringing Ellis's attention back to his statement.

He scratched his signature across the bottom and handed it over the desk. "We never got a good look at the guy."

Altaha tapped the edge of the documents on the desktop to straighten them. "We know the assailant carried a small caliber weapon."

"But other than that, no leads."

"Apart from the fact that he's escalated from breaking necks to using a handgun," Altaha commented, looking over their statements carefully. "It's a man. We know that now from both your and Luella's descriptions. He also likes to strike when Luella is home at Ollero Creek."

Ellis nodded. "That's what concerns me."

"It's ballsy, too," Altaha said. "Ballsy criminals are my favorite."

"Why's that?" Ellis asked, bewildered.

"Because they normally have an abundance of overconfidence. That leads quickly to recklessness and that leads inevitably to mistakes. If the storm didn't knock them out, Luella had her game cameras turned back on for this one."

Ellis thought about it. "Damn. You're right."

"We might have an APB out on this sucker by the afternoon. The sooner we get an arrest, the sooner Luella can go home again. I hope Liberty's not stopping by before then."

"Not until next weekend when she's supposed to drop off the girls," Ellis answered. Though who knew if she'd be doing that, after the threats she'd been making about his parental rights?

"Hmm," Altaha said. "Have you spoken with Rosalie, the former Mrs. Sullivan?"

"I've been busy," Ellis said.

"I see that," Altaha said pointedly.

He tried to think of a retort but heard a curse from Luella's direction. "What's the matter?"

Luella stared at her phone. "It's my aunt Mabel. She's just…passed away."

Altaha folded her hands as compassion took over her face. "I'm sorry to hear that."

Ellis rose but stayed back when Luella lifted a hand. "No," she anticipated him. "I… I need a minute."

"When is the service?" he wanted to know.

"Tomorrow," Luella said. She lifted the phone then lowered it. "She's been gone for a couple of days. My mother's just gotten around to telling me."

Frickin' Riane. "I'm sorry, Lu. I know how much you loved Mabel. Do you need a ride?"

He noticed she didn't meet his eye. "This is something I need to do alone. I need to check on Sheridan before I go…"

Altaha placed their statements together in a folder. "I can drive you there and back to your house."

Ellis shook his head. "I don't like the idea of you being there on your own."

"She won't be alone," Altaha informed him. "I'll be there."

"What about Sphinx, Nyx and Caesar?" Luella asked. "They should come home, too."

"No," Ellis said. "They stay here. I told you. Until this guy is caught, you all need to stay here."

Luella sighed. "I don't think it's up to you to decide what it is I need."

Chapter 10

Luella spent most of her time at the funeral looking at Mabel's self-portrait, a colorful abstract painting. It didn't have one straight edge or line. Mabel had had an abhorrence for straight edges and lines—neutral palettes. Realism.

It was a wonder she and Luella's mother, Riane, the bitter pragmatist, had lived together for two decades. Part of that was Mabel's disabilities, Luella knew. Mabel had had Treacher Collins syndrome, a rare disease she had suffered from even through childhood that had caused facial deformities. Because of negative reactions from people in the community of both Fuego where she grew up and San Gabriel where she moved to be closer to doctors, she had developed a strong aversion to leaving the house.

Luella remembered holding Mabel's hand as they

walked down the sidewalk. Her fingers had been so tense. Normally bubbly and loquacious, Mabel had been reticent, as if fear had given her lockjaw. Even as a teenage girl, Luella had known her hand was a lifeline and had refused to let go, especially when people pointed.

People who knew the real Mabel couldn't help but fall in love with her. She was a kind soul who liked to paint people against her signature abstract backgrounds. She'd especially loved working with the physically and mentally disabled and in later years had taught art classes to them in her backyard. She'd liked to laugh until she cried, always smoothing over Riane's harsher points with cheer and encouragement. Riane complained constantly about how Mabel saw the world through rose-colored glasses.

"Why didn't you tell me she was sick?" Luella muttered at her mother in the front pew of the church.

"Shh!" Riane replied. "We're in the middle of the service!"

"I had a right to know," Luella said, unhindered.

Riane glanced over each shoulder. The organist drowned out Luella's voice. No one was listening. "You've been busy, haven't you—in jail?"

She breathed the last two words in a scandalized undertone. Luella frowned at her. "I was allowed mail and phone calls. And I've been back now for two weeks. I'm sure it was in the newspaper."

"She didn't ask for you."

Riane knew that would be the deepest cut of all. Luella looked down at the program for the service. There were no pictures of Mabel's face. Shouldn't there be pictures? "I think you're a liar. She sent letters to my house—"

"Letters." Riane turned her head to look at Luella fully for the first time. "What letters?"

"Postcards," Luella said. "Photographs."

Riane visually flinched. "What did the postcards say?"

"Wouldn't you like to know?" Luella challenged.

Riane's lips firmed and she looked away.

"How did she post the letters if you didn't know about them?" Luella asked, confused. "I thought she was bed-ridden."

Riane stared rigidly at the altar. She spoke out of the side of her mouth, her voice vibrating with fury. "That nurse. The one from the hospice service. She must've snuck them out under my nose."

Luella scowled. "You denied a dying woman's wish to talk to her niece," Luella said. "I'd pray harder if I were you."

"If we're praying for our sins," Riane said through hardened teeth, "then you'll have to rush to get ahead of yours."

Devil's spawn. Harlot. Whore. Luella felt the sting of the words as if they were more than memories—as if Riane had spoken them here in the church. The satisfied smile that settled over Riane's mouth made Luella's posture cave and her will to stand up for herself wilt altogether.

While a good many people had turned up at the church service and subsequent burial, particularly Mabel's old students, Luella found herself alarmingly alone with her mother and stepfather at the old house on Tesuque Lane.

For a time, Luella stood outside the two-story abode. It was much like all the other houses on the street. Luella remembered how Mabel had made it different—a brighter coat of paint, untrimmed garden flowering most of the year in plumes and spikes with wacky wind-spinners galore. It had looked like an artist's haven.

Her mother had taken out much of the plants, leaving only square hedges along the house front. The house had been repainted a neutral tone, and the wind-spinners—where were they? Had Riane thrown them out, and if so, when—before or after Mabel's passing?

Was it even the same house? When Luella entered, would she be able to feel Mabel's spirit at all?

It was painful crossing the threshold, far worse than entering Eaton House. Not just because Mabel was gone, either. She didn't want to remember being eighteen in this house and all the disappointment and anguish she'd brought with her. No bags but far too much baggage. If not for Mabel…would she have survived any of it?

The mismatched, shabby-chic decor had indeed been replaced by a carefully culled assortment of antiques. There was no artwork anymore. Mabel's abstract world had been erased.

Biting her tongue, Luella veered into the kitchen, where she found Riane and Solomon. The former was making coffee while the latter read the newspaper. "Luella," Solomon said. He looked cautiously at Riane. "This is a surprise."

Luella reminded herself she had nothing against the man her mother had married—only how Riane had used him and his fine community standing as a means of covering up every aspect of her previous life in Fuego with Whip Decker. "Nice to see you, too, Sol." She placed her purse on the counter and noted that her mother's back was still to her. "I ran into the hospice aid you mentioned. Betty. She said something about a box for me?"

When Riane didn't answer, Solomon hefted himself to his feet. At three hundred pounds, he couldn't do this so easily. "I believe it's upstairs. You girls catch up. I'll go hunt it down."

"Thanks, Sol," Luella said. "You weren't going to tell me about the box," she surmised when she and Riane were alone. "Just like you didn't tell me Mabel wanted to see me—so much so she had to sneak messages out of the house."

"Don't be dramatic," Riane muttered, taking down two mugs. She poured coffee into the first, then the second. She sugared them both, poured in cream. Setting the second mug next to Solomon's newspaper, she faced Luella over the length of the kitchen table. Eyeing her in the detached way she'd grown so accustomed to, she lifted her mug to her lips and drank.

Run. The message always came —a scream of adrenaline after any small amount of time spent in her mother's company. Luella felt the stir of minute hairs on the back of her neck and the sharp twist behind her navel that made her feet itch for the exit. It wasn't just the biting words and dirty looks that made Luella want to head for the hills. Something in Riane's manner never failed to make Luella feel not just like the unwanted daughter but prey.

Riane sighed. "That man's slower than Christmas," she muttered. "It's a box full of junk. Nothing of value. You could leave without it."

"Mabel wanted me to have it," Luella said. "That means something."

"Don't expect anything from the will. She left the house to me and Solomon."

"What about the art?" Luella asked.

"What about it?"

"It's missing," Luella said. "What have you done with that? What were her wishes for it?"

Riane's mouth folded into a thin line. "It's being stored in her studio outside. Once we convert it into a garage, however—"

"Let me guess. You'll put it on the street."

"I'm sure her students will collect some of it."

Luella shook her head. "You're unbelievable."

"What would you have me do?" Riane challenged. "It's not worth anything. She wasn't a celebrated artist."

"She was known well enough regionally," Luella said. "You could open a gallery. Do showings. Sol's got some savings, hasn't he? Or have you blown it all on renovations and antiques?"

"Solomon's money is none of your concern," Riane said tightly. "None whatsoever."

"I don't want his money," Luella said. "I don't want Mabel's house. I want what she left me. And then I want never to speak with you again because the only reason you and I have interacted over the last ten years was because of her. Now she's gone and, I'm sure you'll be happy to know, so am I."

Riane searched her. "Where will you go?"

"I don't know," Luella said. "Somewhere where I'll never have to think about you or my father again, preferably."

"A sinner can't run from her sins," Riane opined.

Luella narrowed her eyes. "It's a sin to be born, Mother—or a sin to be your daughter?"

"It's a sin to carry a man's child out of wedlock," Riane retorted plainly enough.

Luella seamed her mouth shut to keep in the cry that wanted to pierce the jagged silence. She said nothing as twin wails of grief and anger keened inside her.

Riane was moved to smile by Luella's inner turmoil.

"You forget… I know all your nasty secrets. It was me who brought you to Mabel's so that you could be saved."

"Is that what happened?" Luella whispered, her voice lost.

"What happened was willed," Riane said pointedly, "by God, and no less than you deserved, whore that you are."

Luella blinked several times. She looked around the kitchen—at the oversized wooden knife, fork and spoon on the wall, at the large unadorned cross over the kitchen table. "Somebody should go check on Sol," she muttered. Before her mother could, she backed away. "I'll go. It'll give me a chance to say a proper goodbye to Mabel. Is her room still the one on the end with the windows?"

"Mind you don't slip anything in that bag of yours on the way there and back," Riane warned, taking several steps after her. "I'm not afraid to call the authorities."

Luella didn't dignify that with a response. She practically fled up the stairs to Mabel's room and almost bowled over Solomon on the landing.

"Careful there, darlin'," he said with a chuckle. "Don't want you taking a tumble down those stairs."

The comment was completely innocent. He couldn't have known. There was no way her mother would've told him anything. But nothing could be more devastating for Luella to hear. She accepted the box, cradling it to her. "Excuse me," she said and veered around him.

She shut herself inside Mabel's room. The medical bed was still in place but it had been stripped. Bouquets of flowers were packed across the raised surface of both the armoire and dresser, some on the floor. They were in various states of decay. The smell was heady, almost overwhelming. Luella set the box on the bed, along with her bag, and absorbed the silence.

Bracing her hands on her hips, she tried to find some semblance of Mabel.

Not even here, she thought. Her mother worked fast. Not one paintbrush lay scattered across the floor. The grains of the wood panels had been scrubbed of their paint flecks. There were no knickknacks—nothing.

She took the lid off the box. Pulling out the contents, she spread them across the blank canvas of the mattress.

They weren't Mabel's things, but her own—things she'd left when she departed the house after her convalescence. Books, she found. Comfort reads she'd found little comfort in at the time. Notebooks. She opened them not to find writings but pressed wildflowers from desert walks. She pulled out a sketchpad and flipped it open without thinking.

Charcoal sketches leaped out at her. They had been done at Mabel's tutelage. She let the pad fall away from her hands to the mattress, unable to touch the profile of Ellis's face, or any of the others she knew followed.

She'd sketched other things—thickets of rough Indian paintbrush, the gnarled twists of an old Colorado pinyon, constellations, mountains and clouds… But she'd always come back to Ellis's face like the glutton for punishment she was. She'd never drawn him from photographs. She hadn't had any. She'd sketched him from heady, passionate memory.

Mabel had begged her to go to art school. Luella hadn't been able to drum up the energy for more dreams. She'd seen too many tattered. So she'd rushed headlong into nursing school, determined to drown her grief with the busywork that came with being a trauma nurse.

The baby's layette made her hands fumble, too. Mabel had chosen things in fragile yellow, white and mint... The blanket they'd spent many a night cursing viciously over hooks and slip stitches had somehow managed to turn into something soft and delicate, if not perfect.

Luella raised it from its folds and pressed it to her cheek.

There's no end to a good mother's love, Mabel had told her soothingly when she'd returned home to Tesuque Lane, arms and womb empty. *You're a good mother, 'ella. You cry. I'll sit here with you as long as you do.*

She carefully placed everything back into the box. She did so neatly, in the same order as she'd found it.

When she put the lid on, Luella reached into her purse and took out the postcards. *Baby. Mother. Father.* Those were the first three messages. Luella set them aside, trying not to think of the broken triangle that pointed from her to Ellis and the life she'd hidden from him and lost.

W.J.

Luella bit her lip. Were these initials? She racked her brain and couldn't see how they connected to her, Ellis or the baby.

S.G.W.C.

The abbreviation was too long to be initials. Maybe it were an acronym—for an organization or a place...

S.G. could stand for San Gabriel. And *W.C....* Luella thought hard.

Baby. Mother. San Gabriel.

Luella stared at the letters as something dawned. Her lips parted. "San Gabriel Women's Center," she whispered to the walls.

She'd been taken to San Gabriel Women's Center

by her mother the day she fell down the stairs here on Tesuque Lane.

As she looked at the next postcard and the letter and numbers scrawled across them, she lost her breath. *S.9.06.*

September 9, 2006. The date it had happened.

How had she not seen it before? *Baby. Mother. Father. San Gabriel Women's Center. September 9, 2006.*

Mabel had needed to speak to her about her baby… or the day her baby had been brought into the world via Cesarean section without a heartbeat.

But why?

And how did that tie into the remaining messages— *W.J.* and *Nightstand*?

She eyed the nightstand close at her hip. Reaching out, she gripped the little round knob and pried it open.

Empty.

Damn it. Her head was starting to hurt but she went back to poring over the messages, willing them to make sense.

Nightstand.

Her gaze fell on the door. She'd been undisturbed by her mother or stepfather. She listened, trying to hear them in the hall and only found silence.

Her pulse quickened as she stood. She stuffed the cards back into her purse and lifted the box from the bed. She took one last look at the room that was no longer Mabel's then opened the door.

Studying the length of the hallway, she couldn't glean any signs of inhabitants. From downstairs, she heard the everyday echoes of kitchen dishes clanking together, water running, a man's voice then a woman's answering.

Luella edged down the wall to the master bedroom, feeling like a thief. The door was open. She peered inside.

It was clear whose side of the bed was whose. The nightstand on the right held a pair of thick reading glasses, a bestselling hardback crime drama and a framed photo of an unsmiling Riane. The nightstand on the right held a Bible, a bottle of hand lotion and a sleep mask.

Luella made sure again that Solomon and Riane were downstairs before she set the box down and moved past the door.

Was she really doing this? She had no doubt her mother had been telling the truth when she'd said she'd call the police. She'd likely find no greater satisfaction than watching officers take Luella away, maybe following it up with a restraining order. The more distance Riane could put between herself and her past with Whip Decker, the better.

However, if there *had* been something in Mabel's nightstand for Luella…where was the most likely place Riane would have stored it?

It was a long shot. Still, Luella's breathing was all too audible, practically thunderous, as she went down on her knees before the nightstand. Her hands were shaking as she lifted them to the drawer pull. Forcing it open, she was relieved to hear it whisper and not squeak along the tracks.

She peered into the dark contents. Here she found trinkets where she'd found so few in the rest of the house. A watch that looked expensive, a pretty paperweight prism that would shoot rainbows if it ever saw the light of day again, a thin book of psalms and blessings, a cross on a silver chain…

Luella didn't recognize anything. Nothing set off warning bells. She nearly shut the drawer again, defeated.

Then she saw the ring box. It was blank—no brand—

black and velvet. Still, something niggled Luella to reach in and pick it up.

She checked the door. It was still open—still empty. Sitting back on the floor, she opened the box with a soft creak…

…and nearly keeled straight over.

The diamond glittered in the lamplight. It was etched in a star shape. Four points—north, south, east, west.

Polaris, Ellis had told her when he'd given it to her for the first time. *True north, holding steady all through the year while the sky moves around it. That's us.*

The sob was tumultuous. It broke like a wave and the diamonds blurred.

She'd thought she had lost it. She hadn't been able to face him—not after losing his ring…and his baby.

"What is going on in here?" Riane came into the room. She saw Luella on the floor next to the bed she shared with her husband and fury hit her face. "How dare you?"

"How could you?" Luella said simultaneously. She held up the ring box for Riane to see. "You stole this! You *stole* it from me! Why?"

Riane stared at the ring, then Luella's red, hot face and narrowed her eyes. "It never should have been yours."

Luella laughed bitterly through the tears. "Here we go."

"You weren't meant for anything that fine," Riane told her. "It shouldn't have been given to you to begin with. It wouldn't have been if you'd given that boy time to think—if you'd shown him who you really are."

Luella's stomach cramped as her breath hitched, but she got to her feet and straightened to her full height. "You had no right. No right. This is mine. It was meant for me. There's nothing you can say anymore that can convince me otherwise."

"But I did convince you otherwise," Riane said. "You didn't tell him about the baby. You ran away, tried wearing his ring and hiding yourself and your bastard away because you were ashamed. You were ashamed you led that fine boy astray with your wiles."

"The only reason I left Fuego and Ellis behind was because Whip found out I was pregnant and threatened to kill him if I didn't take care of it. But what you did— it was worse! You spent the next six months convincing a vulnerable eighteen-year-old girl that she never deserved any of it— Ellis, his ring, the life we would've had together or the child that we made. You stole it all from me, starting with this!"

Riane made a grab for the ring box.

"Don't!" Luella was beyond sense or any vestige of calm. Where was the numbness now? She was somewhere beyond it. "If you try to take it from me again, I will give you a reason to call the cops on me."

Riane's eyes lit with malice. "Look at you! Every bit Jace Decker's daughter. It disgusts me, how you ever could have thought you could have it all."

"I could have," Luella realized. "You may have convinced me I couldn't have him…but I could have had a piece of him. You didn't take that from me. Fate did."

"It was God!" Riane argued. "He took what you should never have tried taking for yourself!"

"Shut up!" Luella yelled, covering her ears. "Shut up, shut up, shut up!"

The screams echoed off everything and nothing.

Solomon entered, brows high on his otherwise hairless head. "What is all the fuss about?"

Luella gathered the box from the floor. "Hey, Sol, did you know Riane here tried to give away her own grand-child? She didn't ask me to kill him like my father did. But she did try to sell him to some rich couple in Sante Fe. They offered a sight more than the couple in Lub-bock."

"We don't have to listen to this, Solomon," Riane said, placing her hand on his shoulder. "In fact, I don't feel safe with her in our house. Please do call the police for me."

"Please do know when to get the hell out," Luella advised the man on her way to the stairs. She couldn't leave fast enough. "The devil's a lot closer than you think. She wears stringed pearls and a twinset and likes to blame little girls for her mistakes."

Riane called over the rail of the landing, "Don't trip and fall on your way out like last time!"

Luella fled into the foyer, rounding the corner with speed enough to foot-race an elk…

…and ran headlong into Ellis.

Chapter 11

"Wh-what are you doing here?" Luella asked, stricken.

Ellis stared up the long stairwell. He felt like his heart was outside his body. What the hell had he just heard?

She put her hands on her head. Her fingers sank into his hair. She tugged on it as her eyes wheeled. "Ellis, *what are you doing here*?"

Ellis opened his mouth, closed it then remembered how he'd wound up on her mother's doorstep. "Everett. He had an appointment with his shrink in San Gabriel. It was my turn to drive him and I thought I'd check on you—make sure you're okay... What you said up there... about a child..."

"Nope," she said and darted around him before he could catch her. She opened the door and fled.

Ellis cursed and went after her.

"I have to get out of here," she said numbly as she

made for her truck. It was parked in front of his in the driveway. "I have to…"

Ellis grabbed her by the arm. "Lu, I need you to look at me."

"No, I need to go, Ellis," she said, snatching out of his grasp. "I have to go, now!"

"We need to talk about this," he said, chasing her around the driver's side. He beat her to the door and planted his hand on it. "Just look at me, all right? Tell me what I just heard."

She yanked on the handle of the door to no avail. "You heard *nothing*. Let me go!"

He'd had enough. He took the box from her, set it on the hood of the truck then grabbed her by the arms and held. *"Look at me!"*

She shook her head, closed her eyes but he glimpsed the wet over them anyway. "I can't," she chanted. "I can't. I can't…"

"Calm down," he said. It was as much for him as for her. "Just…calm down and let's talk about this rationally, okay? You said Riane had a grandchild." He ignored her when she shook her head again, frantic. "I heard it plain. You said she tried to give it away, sell it? You're going to have to clarify. I won't let you loose until you do."

"He was going to kill you." It bubbled up from somewhere inside her, the words tumbling over each other. "He said he would gut you like a fish, pull out your insides and tie them together. He said he'd make me watch!"

"What?" Ellis said, shocked. "Who?"

"My father." Her eyes were glassy. "Whip Decker. He was going to kill you if I didn't kill our baby. And he wasn't lying. I know he wasn't lying, Ellis. Look what he's done—to your mother, your sisters. He was sick and sadistic but he didn't lie."

"Okay," he said, trying to soothe when he felt like the world was tumbling, over and over in a sickening lurch. "Okay," he said again, running his hands over her arms. "When…when was this? When…did you find out?"

She went slack, leaning against the truck for support. "I can't. It's too much."

"I need to know, Lu," he insisted. "Please. I need to know."

Her face screwed up and she took a tremulous breath. "May. Just after graduation. He found my test in the trash. I was already far enough along I felt sick and heavy… I waited so long to take it I was in denial—and not thinking straight otherwise I never would've left it in the trash like that. I never should've taken it at home—"

"Slow down," he said, catching her face in his hands. "Slow down, honey." He touched his brow to hers, trying to breathe calm into both of them. "It's okay," he murmured, trying to believe it. "It's okay."

"I'm sorry," she said. He felt her hands balled in the front of his shirt. "I'm so sorry. I lost him. I lost our baby—"

"Shh," he soothed when the brittle, broken words trailed away like smoke. "You didn't… You didn't mean to. I know you didn't."

"I felt him kick," she said, "and I knew I couldn't let her give him away. She tried—tried talking me into it. She tried forcing me to sign the papers. But I couldn't… I couldn't give him away. He was yours."

"Mine." Ellis absorbed it, like a highway armadillo absorbs the impact of a four-by. "He?"

She nodded slightly. "Yes," she whispered. "I wasn't

supposed to know. Mother didn't want me to find out. She said I would get too attached to it. But Mabel took me to my appointment. I heard his heartbeat. They told me it was a boy. I saw the shape of him. His feet. His hands. His toes. And I knew he could never be anyone's but my own."

"What happened?" he asked, lifting his head from hers. When she balked, he rushed to soothe. "This is hard for you, sweetheart. I know. But I need to know."

"I was leaving," she mumbled. "I wanted to leave. Not to go back to Fuego. I wanted to go to Taos to find you. I thought we could go somewhere far enough away that neither my mother nor father would find us. I had a bag packed. I tripped at the top of the stairs and..."

He let loose a breath to relieve some of the screaming pressure inside him. It didn't work. Not in the least. "How...how far along were you?"

"Seven months," she said. "By that point, it was September. I'd had enough of her talk. She chased me to the stairs and I fell...all the way down. I started to bleed."

"God Jesus, Lu." The words had gone thick.

"Mother took me to the local women's center," she said. "The doctor there... He said I was in labor. It was too early. There were complications. The baby's pulse wasn't right. I wasn't in my right mind—scared and confused. I think I might have been in shock or...maybe I lost my mind. I don't know. They had to sedate me. I woke up and...he was gone. Just gone."

He took several careful breaths. The coping mechanism he always fell back on...it wasn't working. Why wasn't it working? There was too much inside him— too much building. It was going to come out—in all its messy, dark glory. "You should have told me," he said, sounding small even to his ears. "I could've been there. I could've helped you."

"He was going to kill you," she replied. "Gut you like a fish…"

"Your old man was a killer," he acknowledged. "You were right to believe he would've done it. But you forget. I had my brother, my father and half a dozen good ranch hands at my back. We would've taken care of him. I would've happily taken care of him, Lu, so that you and I could raise our child together and live the life we wanted in peace. The one I promised you. Remember?"

She was too lost to speak. He'd lost her, somewhere in the realms of past traumas. He pressed her face into his shoulder so he could wrap her up and hold her like he'd never had to stop. Giving in, he buried his face in her hair and tried to cull something of himself out of the scent of her.

Luella had been pregnant when he'd left for Taos. She hadn't fallen out of love with him. She hadn't wanted to break things off. She'd left to protect him from her father's cruelty, which she'd known all too well by that point. And Riane…

Riane had done the rest.

"I never should've let you go back to them," he said. "I never should've let you go home after that last time he beat you. None of this… You would've been okay…" He raised his face and lifted hers so he could see. "You watched me have children with another woman."

Her eyes remained closed. "You have two beautiful children, Ellis. The sweetest."

"I know I do," he said and nodded. "I love them. God, but I love my girls, Lu."

"How could you not?"

"And you and I—we had a son?"

"Yes, Ellis. You and I had a son."

He let out of laugh that wasn't a laugh. It was breathy and compromised. He was compromised—completely and utterly compromised. "I wish I could have held him."

"Me, too," she said and he saw the tears leak through, the wet getting caught in her lashes. "They never let me… I don't even know where he's buried. I don't…"

Something burned his throat. It was tight and things were trapped there, broken and ragged.

"The hell is going on?"

Luella turned her face away at the sound of Everett's caustic voice.

Ellis couldn't bring himself to look at him either. "You okay to drive?"

Everett paused. "Sure."

"Take the keys," Ellis said, digging into his pocket and tossing them Everett's way. "We'll follow you."

"Are *you* all right?" Everett asked. "You don't look so good."

"We'll follow you," Ellis repeated, leading Luella away from the driver's door. She didn't stop him from steering her around the front of the truck to the passenger side where he boosted her in and closed the door.

"Ellis?" Everett said. "Am I hearin' things right?"

"We'll talk about it later," Ellis said. "I need to get her home."

Everett waited a beat. "Watch the road." Without further argument, he stalked to the other truck.

Luella woke long after the witching hour. The room was dark, but the light beaming from the adjoining bathroom told her it was Ellis's and the silence said that the house was dead around it.

As she lifted her head, Sphinx stirred on the pillow next to hers. Luella reached out to drag her fingers through her fur. She felt drained. Her face felt tight, as if she'd fallen asleep with tears on it and they'd long since dried.

She stilled when she found Ellis's silhouette sitting on the bed's edge, his back to her. He was still fully dressed. Her box from Mabel lay open at his feet. The little ring box was clutched in his hand.

Luella turned on her side. As she stirred, his head swiveled in her direction. "Did I wake you?"

She shook her head. Fitting her hand under her cheek, she tried to gauge him.

He'd been quiet, too, when they'd come back to Eaton Edge. Over dinner, neither of them had eaten or said anything despite Paloma's and Eveline's attempts to pull them into conversation. Everett, at least, had known not to engage them. He'd eaten and kept his mouth shut, for once.

No one had said anything when Luella chose to turn in early. She'd made some excuse about needing to visit Sheridan early—and that was true. She did want to visit him at Dr. Wilstead's. Though mostly she'd just needed to be away from everyone.

It seemed grief would never be done with her. Watching Ellis grieve, too, for what was—for all that might have been—made it worse.

Shouldn't it have felt better—to have someone to grieve beside?

Luella swallowed. Her throat still felt raw. She knew she'd be hoarse when she spoke but she had to know.

"That day in the box canyon this summer…was it you who killed my father?"

Ellis looked at her long before answering. "Yes."

She ran her eyes over his profile, so like the charcoal sketches of the boy he'd been in the sketch pad at his feet. "How did it feel?" she asked.

His brow knit a second before he looked away. His shoulders lifted and fell on a long inhale and exhale. "It should've been Wolfe," he replied. "He wanted it. He had a vendetta. When he missed his chance and I had Whip in my sights, I didn't hesitate. Now I wish I could go back and squeeze the trigger again and again, like I should've done when you came to me beaten. I wanted to kill him then and I should've."

"You're not a killer, Ellis."

"Then why did it feel so good," he asked, "ending him?"

"Because he was a monster," she said. "A real, living, breathing monster."

"There've been too many of those between us," he observed.

"I wish it'd been me," she told him. "I had plenty of opportunity. Plenty of reason. Especially when he showed up at Ollero Creek expecting me to keep him alive. He told me he'd take me out of this world. I should have at least tried to do the same to him. A lot more people might've been saved."

"Maybe we both are better off not thinking about what should have been," he said, the words dredged from deep in his chest. "Though that's a lot harder now…knowing. I gave up finding you too easily when you disappeared."

"You did try to find me." She wanted it to be a question because she'd never been sure, entirely, how hard he'd looked for her once she escaped to San Gabriel.

"I went to the police. I went to your father's house."

She closed her eyes. "No. Ellis."

"He was too drunk to do anything more than laugh in my face," Ellis said. "I never knew what he was laughing about—until now. The sick son of a bitch. It was the police who told me. They knew where you were and they weren't saying, for your protection. They gave me Riane's number and when I got her on the phone, she made me feel so stupid. She said you didn't run away from him, like everybody thought. You ran away from me."

"She's an excellent liar," Luella told him. "She always has been."

She saw the weariness in his shoulders, the way they hung, in the way he scrubbed the lines in his brow with the back of his hand. She reached out for him, touching the place between his shoulder blades where she knew strength lived. "You're tired," she whispered.

He said nothing. Instead, he turned to look at her again. The light from the bathroom bathed her face. She knew he could see everything. He searched it for some time. She could feel his eyes roving in gentle glides and didn't want to hide.

She moved her touch down his arm, tugging. "You don't have to watch over me anymore."

"I want to."

"Ellis," she said softly. "Come to bed."

He wavered, watching. Then he reached down and pried his boots loose, one at a time. He set them next to the box of her things. Then he stood and unlatched his belt. He removed it, rolled it up and set it on the nightstand. Then he walked into the bathroom and she heard water running and him brushing his teeth.

He turned out the bathroom light. She heard him come

to the bed. She lifted the covers so he could slip underneath. She moved Sphinx closer to her.

The bed shifted and she felt his toes touch hers. He turned to face her. She felt his breath on her face, then his fingers in the thick coils of her hair. "Tell me what happened to you," he told her. "There were a good few years there you spent in San Gabriel...after what happened."

She licked her lips. "I wasn't well. Mabel tried to bring me out of it, but I spent a year in this...numbness. Sometimes, it was so much I couldn't breathe through it. It felt like this weight on my chest. I was either overwhelmed with grief or completely turned off from everything. I didn't have the energy to feel. And since that felt safer than grieving, I kind of stayed there and got to know it."

"You were depressed," he surmised.

She nodded. "I know its name now. Though it took me years to understand...and by then, it was like my shadow. Where I went, it came."

"How long did you stay in that house with your mother?"

"Too long," she admitted. "It did get to the point where I couldn't stand it. I got a job, worked days to rent a place above a pizza parlor. I went to night school. Nursing school. I worked in the emergency room of the hospital there for a time. And then, I got the call from the nursing director at Fuego County Hospital with a job offer. They needed a trauma nurse."

"You came back," he remembered.

"I thought my father was dead," she told him. "And I thought you were living in Taos."

"That was around the time Dad's health started going," Ellis remembered. "Everett asked me to come back. And I did, Liberty and the girls in tow."

"By that point, I'd already bought Ollero Creek and

started working. It was too late to run again. Even after Whip started showing up at my door, demanding a hand-out."

She felt him tracing the lines of her throat in feathery strokes. "Do you still get depressed?"

Unsure of how to answer, she opened her hand and closed it. She wanted to touch him. "Something's wrong with me. It's off. There are times I feel dead."

"You're not dead," he murmured.

"Maybe it's regret," she said, under her breath. "It's like Jacob Marley. He had to carry those chains through eternity."

"You're not dead," he said again. "And I don't regret anything…unless you count every man who's touched you since the last time you slept in this bed with me."

"I haven't…" she started to tell him. She pressed her lips together. Could she let go of this—her last remaining secret? "You're the only one who's touched me," she told him, so quietly she almost didn't hear her own admission.

His breath shuddered across her face. "Lu." His hand cupped the back of her neck and she knew what that meant before his mouth closed over hers, hot and wet and sweet.

His arms wound around her. His lips nipped ever-so-gently to part hers. After a moment's resistance, hers opened on a whimper.

"You're not dead," he breathed. "Say it."

She sighed, reaching for him. "I'm not dead."

"Good girl." He kissed her slow, dipping deep when her head dropped back into his open palm. Submission took hold. "Now say my name, here in the dark."

Her breath grew ragged. She spanned her hand across

the length of his throat, trailing her nails up to the hair-line at the nape of his neck.

He shivered, involuntarily, creating little fires in her blood. "Say it," he whispered again, his hand flattening against the heavy bottom curve of her breast.

She closed her eyes, feeling all those little fires take hold. "Ellis."

He groaned, taking his time unbuttoning her plaid button-down. He parted it, pushing it back from her shoulders. Underneath, she wore little and felt exposed. She was rounder than she had been before in this bed. It had been so long since she'd felt the glide of a man's gaze—Ellis's gaze.

She could see enough of his dark eyes in the dim light from the window. His touch followed the path of his eyes and undid her. She tugged the shirt over his head and pulled him back to her. She felt heady, alive, urgent for his mouth on her. Her body rose under the firm line of his.

"Mmm-hmm," he said in approval. His hands spread through her hair, smoothing it over the pillow until it crowned her head. He pressed a kiss to the center of her brow then between her eyes, down to the bridge of her nose. He touched his lips to the point of her cheekbone, then the other. He turned a kiss underneath the line of her jaw.

Her head dropped back, urging him to wind his way around. He followed suit, teasing her with kisses up the length of her throat to the lobe of her ear. The sensitive nerves there made her body bow in a fluid, involuntary motion as the furnace lit around her center.

She let him keep spreading kisses, weaving them in star maps over every hard point of her collarbone, down.

She arched as his kisses trailed between her breasts and his hands followed, over peaks and into valleys. They were barely there and everywhere. His lips followed the center line of her abdomen, her navel.

Luella panted, crazy with kisses. He tugged her panties and she shrugged them down her legs, kicking them away.

The heels of his hands nudged her knees outward and his head lowered between her legs. His mouth covered her.

She reached up to grip the iron post of his headboard. He didn't stop and her cries grew loud in the quiet dark. Her palm was damp around the metal as he indulged her in hypnotic pulls in tune with the beat of lust alive now inside her.

She began to make little keening cries and covered her own mouth to stop from waking the house. "Stop," she moaned. "Stop, please. I'm dying…"

He made a noise, somewhere between longing and protest and pulled himself away.

"Oh, my God," she sighed.

"Look at you shinin', honey."

His voice was rough and sexy. He unsnapped his jeans. She let out a shuddering breath at the promise of more.

He was hard and she was hungry for that weight. The space between her legs ached, pulsing like he was inside her already.

He came down to meet her, laughing silently, breathlessly, as he kicked to free his legs from his jeans. The smile felt foreign on her face, but it wasn't a lie. She hadn't had to work for it. The giddiness of being here in the dark with him—it was memory bubbling to the surface, bursting to meet and match the reality of tonight.

I'm not dead.

He scooped his hands beneath her and hitched her into his lap. His hands ranged over her back from waist to shoulders and back in a possessive wave. His gaze had a gleam to it that was hard and soft. It echoed need and promised things deeper—things she couldn't contemplate. He was smiling. He knew he had her—all of her.

So not dead.

A sigh of relief and pleasure fell as he slid inside her. His, hers? She wasn't entirely sure. Her arms hemmed around his shoulders even as his bracketed her waist. She blazed, hot for him.

He lit a goddamn fire—another fire she'd never be able to put out.

He began to churn, fine strokes that drove her up in increments and took her apart. When the cries hit her throat again, she turned her mouth to his. She was definitely going to wake the house.

The heat built to a flash point, the finest point imaginable. *Polaris.* He made it worse when he said her name. He said it like a prayer and she was done. She let her nails dig into the skin of his shoulders until he grunted and she skittered over the brink.

Ellis stilled. She could feel his heart slamming against hers. For a second, she worried neither of them was breathing anymore.

His lungs released in an immense wave, rocking them both. He came, too, just as hard.

"Look," he said. When she didn't lift her head from his shoulder, he steadied his voice and tugged lightly on her hair. "Look, Lu."

She managed to lift her head and look at him.

His hand stroked her cheek. His eyes were hooded. She expected him to kiss her, but he held back—looking.

The intimacy came to a staggering point and she understood. She was his woman. She'd long been his woman. In that moment, it didn't matter— all the years in between.

He'd devastated her. He always did—so much so she was afraid of how little she'd find of herself in the morning.

Chapter 12

"We can't keep meeting like this, Deputy Sweetheart."

Ellis rolled his eyes at his brother as Deputy Altaha propped one hand on her uniformed hip in the kitchen the next morning. Everett leaned against the counter, a cup of coffee in his hand and a large grin spreading across his face.

Altaha sized him up, slowly. "You know…when most people find an officer of the law on their doorstep before breakfast, they tend to react differently."

Everett thought about it. "I like a challenge."

She lowered her chin. "You *are* the challenge."

"That is a compliment, Deputy," he drawled, "of the highest caliber. I thank you."

Altaha exchanged a look with Ellis, who shrugged helplessly. Paloma saved them all by shoving a *sopaipilla* in Everett's mouth on her way to the table with a platter. "Chew, *niño*," she advised. "*Buenos días*, Deputy."

Altaha took off her hat. *"Buenos días, Señora."* She looked to Ellis. *"Cómo estás?"*

"Bien," he replied. "Join us for breakfast?"

Altaha eyed the setup on the table with intrigue. "I'm supposed to drop in for a quick word and return to the station, but I see Paloma's made her sopaipillas."

"Later," Everett announced. He grabbed Ellis by the elbow and tipped his head toward the door for Altaha to follow. "I've got some business to discuss with the both of you."

"Business?" Ellis mumbled. It was unlike Everett to want to discuss any sort of business before breakfast. And since when did their business involve the deputy?

"Okay," Altaha said slowly as Everett quickly ushered them down the hall and all but pushed them through the door to the office. As he shut the door, she rounded on him. "What's going on, cattle baron? I thought it was Ellis who needed to speak with me. Not you."

"Hmm," Everett said, feigning ignorance as he walked around the brawny desk. "That's odd, as it was me who called."

Altaha narrowed her eyes. "Pretending to be your brother?"

"We do sound a lot alike on the phone," Everett considered, distracted now as he riffled through desk drawers, brows drawn together.

"We sound nothing alike," Ellis argued. "On the phone, or otherwise."

Altaha stopped talking to study Everett more closely as he located a flash drive. He drew up the chair behind the desk and sat. In his big, working hand, the drive looked tiny. It looked downright foreign there as he turned his head sideways to try fitting it into one of the ports on the desktop PC.

"Oh, for heaven's sake," she muttered. She took the flash drive and easily found the correct port to plug it into. "You're liable to break it at this rate."

He sat back, wiggling the mouse insistently. "What's happening here?"

"Your monitor's off." She reached across him to turn it on then halted, bringing her eyes around to his.

Everett stared, somewhat innocently—as innocent as Everett could manage, in any case.

She pursed her lips, easing back into a professional stance. "Real smooth, cowboy."

Everett didn't have the decency to keep up the charade. "Got to give a man points for trying."

"Or," she considered, "I could arrest you."

He hissed through his teeth when her hand went to the small of her back to palm the set of handcuffs. "I almost wish you would."

Ellis had had enough. "Look, as much fun as this is, I'm going back to my breakfast." He wanted to see if Luella had come down yet. He'd left her wrapped in his bed, her red hair a fan around her face.

He'd wanted to wake her and had only just checked the urge to trace the parting of her lush red lips with his fingertips. There was more inside him. He had more to show her, more to give.

But she'd needed rest. And he'd wanted a bit of time to process what was and what had been.

How could so much change in one day, past and present?

Everett, sobering, turned to the computer screen. "The trip to San Gabriel joggled some memories."

"What kind of memories?" Ellis asked, coming around the desk to see the monitor. His brother was viewing the files from the drive. There were hundreds. "What could you possibly find in this mess?"

"Dad might not have taken care of himself," Everett ventured, "but he was an excellent businessman and an even better record-keeper. He kept everything he wrote down."

"I know this," Ellis said, remembering the nightmare that had been his father's file boxes. They'd all been meticulously organized, but there had been *so many.*

"When I heard the word *baby* yesterday from Luella," Everett elaborated, turning to stare at his brother pointedly, "I remembered a meeting Dad had around the time of her disappearance—the summer after you graduated high school."

"Whoa," Altaha said, holding up her hands. "Time-out. What about a baby?"

Ellis frowned at Everett. "It's not public knowledge."

"What exactly?" the deputy asked. Her eyes widened slightly when Ellis could say no more out loud without Luella's say-so. "Oh."

"Good." Everett nodded, satisfied. "We're all on the same page now."

"Against our will," Ellis noted.

Everett leaned toward the screen, slowing his scroll. He chewed his lower lip as he got closer to what he was looking for. The file names were dates, Ellis saw. These went back over a decade. "You remember a meeting Dad had with someone seventeen years ago?" he asked in disbelief.

"It stuck out," Everett weighed. "We don't get many people doctors at the Edge."

"The meeting was with a doctor," Altaha said, trying to string together the details.

Everett growled low in his throat as he highlighted a file name with the mouse and double-clicked it. "Right around this time… We were sending off a truckful of heifers. I was about to see it off when this guy arrived, white coat and everything—said he was from San Gabriel."

The file opened and filled the screen with an overhead shot of a desktop planner.

"Hell," Ellis groaned. "I forgot he used to keep notes by hand."

"Little ones," Everett acknowledged, "that spilled into the margins when he was feeling wordy. Like this one…" He double-clicked again and the screen zoomed in on the bottom right corner of the calendar.

Everyone leaned in, trying to read Hammond's tiny, precise lettering.

Altaha read out loud, "'Transport at 10:00 a.m. Fence check. Payroll. Dr. Bridestone, no appointment, 9:20 a.m.'"

"I'll be damned," Ellis said with a shake of his head. "Seventeen years ago."

"When did Luella say the baby was born?" Everett asked him.

"She didn't," Ellis said. "She lost the baby."

"When?" Everett persisted.

The urgency in him spooked Ellis. "September. What does this have to do with Dr. Bridestone?"

"The good doctor wanted to know if Dad was interested in adopting an orphaned kid from San Gabriel."

Altaha stared openly at Everett. "I'd say that's something to remember."

"He…wanted to give Dad a baby?" Ellis said. He shook his head. "Why, exactly? What were his reasons?"

"He said it was well known that Dad liked to take in the odd kid or two," Everett revealed.

"Was it?" Altaha asked.

Ellis thought it over. "He tried to adopt Wolfe but backed off when Santiago claimed him. I thought about asking him to take in Luella…after Whip nearly killed her. I think he would have said yes. But I don't know anyone who would've known that other than her."

"What else did this doctor say?" Altaha inquired.

"He said Dad could have the kid by Christmas," Everett explained.

"Did Dad seem interested?" Ellis asked.

"He didn't turn the man out," Everett said. "Dad didn't have a habit of turning anyone out."

"Especially not a kid in need," Ellis considered.

Everett nodded. "Yeah."

"How could any of this have been legal?" Altaha asked.

"Well, that's the part of the conversation that struck me as off," Everett said. "Dad wanted records, paperwork, permissions from the parents or system so that if— and, frankly, when—he chose to accept the child into his home, there would be no pushback. No chance a young mother might come looking for him."

"A boy," Ellis repeated and his heart dropped out from under him.

"Sit down," Everett said immediately.

"I'm fine," Ellis replied with a shake of his head.

"Sit down," Everett said through his teeth. "You look like you did when she dropped the bomb on you yesterday—like you've been torpedoed."

"I can stand," Ellis informed him, shifting his feet just to prove he could.

"Was there anything else?" Altaha asked. "Any other details that could be important?"

"Only that there was a price," Everett explained. "The baby came in exchange for a five-figure lump sum, paid up front in cash."

"Jesus," Ellis uttered.

Altaha shook her head. "The cost of adoption is up there, even by traditional means. This whole thing stinks, however. Who was Dr. Bridestone? And what business did he have leading the adoption process like this? And why Hammond? Why Fuego and Eaton Edge? There's far too many red flags."

"I'll leave that with you," Everett said, selecting the print function so that the machine in the corner began to whir to life. "Though I have some theories of my own."

Ellis thought about it, then automatically rejected the idea. "No."

"It's no less than finding out I'd have a seventeen-year-old nephew if Luella hadn't miscarried," Everett pointed out.

Ellis turned away. His was sweating at the implications. "You changed your tune toward Luella last night," he remembered. "You stopped barking at her and me. Is this why?"

"No," Everett noted. "Blood's thicker than water. If she's the mother to one of ours, whether or not the kid lived, that means something."

"It means everything," Ellis murmured.

"Ellis," Altaha said slowly, "I'll look into this, starting with Dr. Bridestone in San Gabriel. We'll see where that leads."

He nodded.

"Will you tell Luella?"

He rejected the idea. "Not until we know more. All this.. it could lead to nothing. You said you were looking at Luella's game cams from the night Sheridan was kidnapped."

Altaha frowned at the pivot. "Snowfall made the picture unclear."

He cursed, louder than he wanted to. "Did you canvass? Were there witnesses?"

"There was a blizzard," Altaha reminded him. "How far out in front of you could you see? Farther than Luella's neighbors, I'll wager."

Ellis ground his teeth. The frustration gnawed at his cool.

Everett watched him with more understanding than Ellis liked.

Altaha patted Everett on the shoulder. "It's good to see you behind the desk again, cattle baron."

Everett looked down at his hands, which were both clamped around the arms of the chair. "Feels good, I guess. What do you say, Deputy Sweetheart? Fancy joining me for breakfast?"

A distant smile flirted with the corners of her mouth, but before she could answer, the phone on the desk rang.

"It's probably the buyer from Bozeman," Ellis said. He reached for the receiver.

Everett beat him to it and answered in a bark. "Yeah?"

Ellis's hand fumbled to his face where he scrubbed. Before surgery, his brother's business demeanor had always been more Billy Goat Gruff than Ellis thought necessary. It appeared postsurgery wasn't going to be much different.

Everett frowned as he pulled the receiver away from

his mouth. "For you," he said, pushing the phone at his brother.

Was that resentment in the lightning-blue flash of Everett's eyes—or was he just being his normal, recalcitrant self? When Ellis did hand the reins of Eaton Edge back to Everett, he hoped it would be a smooth transition with no hard feelings on the part of his big brother and rightful boss. Ellis and Paloma had prevented him from ignoring his therapist's warning of not returning to work too soon during his journey toward physical and mental recovery.

Ellis made a mental note to assure Everett that when the time was right for him to return to his position of chief of operations that Ellis would happily return to the support position their father had wanted for him. He cupped the phone to his ear. "This is Ellis."

"Ellis," a brisk, feminine voice greeted. "I'm so glad I reached you. This is Rosalie. Rosalie Quetzal—from town council?"

Ellis lifted his chin. Rosalie Quetzal…formerly Sullivan, he realized. He turned his gaze to Altaha with a lift of his brows. "Of course. How are you, Ms. Quetzal?"

"Fine." Her tone was strained around the edges. "Listen, I know this may seem out of left field, but I was wondering if you'd like to get together sometime and talk."

Talk, Ellis mused. The only thing he and Rosalie had to talk about that he knew of was their respective spouses' apparent habit of jumping into bed together. "Yes. I've been meaning to call, too. Things have been crazy."

"I could come to Eaton Edge," she offered. "Would that be better for you?"

He thought about it. "Why not Hickley's BBQ?" He

shifted so he could read the desk calendar where he'd taken to scrawling notes, just like their father had. The calf didn't fall far from the dam. "Is eight o'clock this evening too late for you?"

"That sounds just fine," Rosalie noted. "But, just for kicks, let's make it Mimi's—same time, my treat."

"I'll see you there," Ellis agreed though he had other thoughts about letting a lady pay for a meal.

"Bye now," she said and hung up quickly.

Ellis let the phone dangle from his hand for several seconds before he replaced it in the cradle. "You put her up to this."

"I did nothing of the sort," Altaha claimed. "But I may have put a bug in my sister's ear."

"What kind of bug, exactly?"

"The kind that goes, 'Buzz-buzz, his ex-wife's a con artist,'" Altaha drawled.

"It's been on my mind," he told her, "contacting Rosalie."

"I'm sure it has," she granted. "You've had a lot going on."

"Speaking of ex-wives," Everett said, leaning back in his chair, "is she bringing the girls this weekend? It's your turn."

"Last time I spoke to her on the phone, she made it sound like my visitation rights are over unless I sign my shares over to her," Ellis explained.

Everett muttered something uncomplimentary. Then his gaze flicked to Altaha. "Pardon."

She pulled a face. "Hey, I'm with you."

His eyes narrowed and his mouth softened toward her. "You want to help us out with this little problem?"

It took her a moment to soften toward him in return.

"I like how you think sometimes, I've got to admit." Looking to Ellis, she said, "I think I'll give the former Mrs. Eaton a call."

"You're not going to threaten her," Ellis said. "You could lose your job."

"Did I say I was going to threaten her?" Altaha asked. "She just needs to be reminded that she's in violation of your rights and that won't reflect well on her when her case goes in front of a judge."

"It won't make her happy," he warned.

"You want to see your girls," Everett guessed. "You need to see your girls. Hell, we all do. The place isn't right without them. Do it," he told Altaha. "I'll owe you one."

"I like that, too, I think," Altaha weighed. If Ellis wasn't mistaken, she sent him an infinitesimal wink on the way out.

Everett looked far too smug for Ellis's peace of mind. "Careful there," he cautioned.

Everett laced his hands behind his head and grinned. "Don't piss on my parade, *mano.*"

No, Ellis thought, seeing his brother more relaxed than he had in a long time. *I couldn't.* "We need to check fences in the southwest quarter. Ride with me?"

Everett shifted to his feet. "Only if you're on gate duty."

"That means you're driving," Ellis said, pulling a face. Everett was notorious for being a terror behind the wheel.

"You're damn right I am. While we're out, you can tell me what the nature of your business with sexy town-council lady is."

Ellis heaved a sigh. "You're incorrigible."

Luella didn't know what to think, much less feel, when she came out of Dr. Wilstead's office and saw Ellis holding the door open across the street to Mimi's Steakhouse for Rosalie Quetzal.

Rosalie was a single woman again after her divorce. She'd quickly gone back to her maiden name and was a lot like Eveline in the looks department. Tall, blonde, regal, she was a woman who carried herself well and enjoyed her high standing in the Fuego community.

She was on the city council, as her father had been before her, and could be mayor if True Claymore would loosen his hold on the position. For a rodeo cowboy's wife, she'd gone far beyond any buckle bunny Luella had ever heard of.

As they disappeared into the restaurant—Fuego's finest—Luella stood on the stoop, all the warm, fuzzy feelings she'd felt after her last few hours helping Wilstead care for Sheridan wafting away like smoke. An involuntary exhale left her on a rush. The emptiness that followed was insurmountable.

Last night. Last night, he'd touched her and tasted her, claimed her. It had only been last night that she'd realized she was his woman. She was Ellis's woman, unequivocally.

Had she forgotten what she'd had to go through years before and the harsh understanding that had come with it?

She might be Ellis Eaton's woman. But he would never be her man. She had worn his ring. She'd planned for a future with him. She may be his lover again, the mother of his child, the woman he'd thought about even when he was with his wife...

But she couldn't think of him as her own any more than she could think of the moon and stars as her own.

She started to cross the street to the windows of Mimi's,

but then thought of the pathetic picture it would make with her face pressed to her glass—the cold without and the warm within with Ellis and Rosalie wrapped up in it over wine and appetizers.

Stumbling back a step, she nearly tripped over the curb.

"Luella?"

She looked around and was distressed to find witnesses. "Eveline," she said, sounding dull even to her own ears. "Paloma."

"Oh, *niña*," Paloma murmured, reaching up with a gloved hand. She cradled Luella's cheek. "You've forgotten your hat."

"Come with us," Eveline invited, closing in on her other side. Luella didn't know what to think when her arm linked through hers. "We were going to see what the new axe-throwing place is like."

"I don't think so," Luella said, digging in her heels before they could think about urging her in the direction of people and lights. "I'm not sure I'm in the mindset for axe-throwing."

Eveline studied her. A knowing light hit her eyes. "Oh, I think you might be. And it's not every day I convince Paloma to leave the sanctity of her kitchen. Come on. Let's try it."

"Okay," Luella said unwillingly as she was coaxed along. They tuned off Main Street together and onto 2nd Avenue and approached the adobe-style building that had once been a run-down furniture store. A neon sign read Hatchet House. It buzzed busily over the double-door entrance. Luella frowned when she saw the mash of people inside.

"I reserved a time," Eveline said as they took off their

coats and gloves. "I'll talk to the owner, see if we can't cut the line."

Luella and Paloma were left to stare at their surroundings. The place had been refurbished to look like a saloon with snack booths in deep red leather and the same rough wood furnish on everything from the floors to the ceilings, tables and chairs. "Well, they certainly did improve on the place," Paloma opined.

"I don't think I can do this," Luella said, her feet itching for the doors.

Eveline swooped back in. "We've got the target on the end. It just opened up. This way."

Luella once again found herself practically frogmarched, this time through a tight clutch of people, most of whom openly stared at the unlikely trio—the model, the housekeeper, the home-wrecking felon who had no business here or anywhere else in Fuego, if you asked them.

"Drinks, ladies?" the waitress asked as they hung their coats on handy hooks nearby.

Eveline was already rolling up her sleeves. "Three beers?"

Paloma chuckled in her throat. "It's my night off. Margaritas, all around. I'm buying."

Eveline whooped happily. She grabbed an axe from the sideboard then stepped up to the mark. "Now, how do you do this, exactly?"

Paloma pursed her lips, eyeing the target. "I think we can all assume you just chuck the blessed thing."

Eveline turned toward the far wall, lifted the axe and heaved it. It didn't hit the mark. It buried itself beneath the outermost circle. "Oh," she said with a grin. "That was satisfying. Give me another."

Paloma made a disagreeable noise. "Let Luella have a turn."

"Oh, yes," Eveline said, stepping back to let Luella have a throw. She handed her the next axe. "You have to try it. It's fantastic."

"Erm, okay," Luella said, unsure. The axe didn't feel foreign in her hand. She'd chopped her fair share of wood at Ollero Creek and had the arms to prove it. Or she had, before her incarceration. Feeling silly nonetheless, she tried to ignore the people around her as she faced up to the target and eyed the center. She planted her feet, lifted the axe in both hands and released, throwing her weight into it.

Eveline cheered and Paloma applauded soundly when the blade found the middle ring. "Look at you, Luella Belle," the latter said with a shake of her head. "You're a natural."

"She's a Viking," Eveline said admirably. She hugged Luella around the shoulders. "I knew you'd love it."

"I…" Luella stopped, wondering what the odd sensation was around the lower half of her face. Jesus, was that a smile? The adrenaline she recognized and there was plenty of it. It *was* satisfying, she found, surveying her axe on the board with something akin to pride.

"Margaritas," the waitress said, returning with a tray full.

"Wow…" Luella couldn't believe her eyes. "Are those glasses or fishbowls?"

Eveline cackled, raising one. She clinked it first to Paloma's then handed Luella hers and clinked it, too. "To girls' night out."

"Girls' night out," Paloma repeated.

Luella stared, wide-eyed, at them both as they drank.

She blinked several times, smelling all the sweet and salty goodness in her bowl. Then she lifted a shoulder. *What the hell?* she thought and drank, too.

Luella closed one eye, trying to sight that center circle like she had before. It wavered and she frowned. "You know… I don't drink a lot. Alcoholics are a pox on my family tree, my father being the biggest and loudest and ugliest…"

Eveline snorted a laugh. She was leaning against the nearby wall, nursing the remains of her fishbowl and looked a little worse for wear despite the happy flush on her cheeks.

"I'd forgotten how great margaritas are," Luella went on. She was rambling. She knew she was rambling. And slurring, slightly—only slightly. "It's no fun to drink them alone. Drinking in company…*so* much better…"

"Damn right," Paloma said, raising her glass.

"Paloma!" Eveline said, overloud. "You swore!"

"It's you children," Paloma opined. Her words leaned heavy on her Latin accent. "Bad influences. Your brother, especially."

"Which brother?" Eveline wanted to know.

"The one who didn't spend last night cozy in Luella Belle's arms," Paloma noted.

Luella threw and missed. "Beg pardon?"

"Oh, *please!*" Eveline said, grabbing the next axe for herself. She didn't relinquish her drink as she stepped up to the line again. "Ellis came down all dope-faced this morning. Like he had sunshine beaming out from between his ass cheeks."

The *s*'s ran together, making Luella grin loudly. The mental picture of Ellis's cheeks helped. She picked up her drink but hiccupped before she could get it to her mouth. She placed it carefully back on the table with both hands. "That's enough, I think."

"Oh, no," Eveline said after another ill-timed throw. Sober or drunk, she had no talent for axe-throwing. "Another, *please*. I never do this. And I love you guys." She hugged them both around the neck and pulled them in for a squeeze.

Luella found herself laughing even as she choked on Eveline's designer perfume. "I can't do another. I'm sorry."

"Don't be sorry," Paloma said, patting her on the hand and leaning toward her in an empathetic way. "You sweet girl. You've come a long way tonight."

"I have," she said in wonder. "God. I never did this with I was younger. I never had girlfriends."

"Not one?" Eveline asked, stunned.

"Not one," Luella said with a shake of her head. "When I was little, I knew making friends meant play-dates and sleepovers, right? All the normal things. But what mama or daddy would let their little girl spend the night in Whip Decker's double-wide? Plus, playdates would only ever bring questions about the bruises I carried like a patchwork quilt. The kind little girls with normal fathers don't have…"

Eveline and Paloma fell silent. Luella was distressed to see Eveline's eyes swell with tears. "Oh, no. I didn't mean… I told you I'm no good at this. Damn, I'm *such* a downer."

"No," Eveline said even as a wet, round drop escaped down her cheek. "No, Luella. Don't you dare apologize. You're doing so great."

"So great," Paloma echoed. "I wish you'd run away to

the Edge, like Wolfe did. I would've taken care of you. Like my own."

Luella felt tears of her own stinging her eyes. "You would have?"

"Without question," Paloma said. "Aw, *niña*. Come here to Paloma."

She found herself enveloped in a warm hug. The circle of Paloma's arms felt safe. She pressed her face into her wide shoulder. Her eyes closed. There was warmth inside her instead of the devastating emptiness that had been there on the street.

"You shouldn't leave," Eveline said, patting Luella on the back as she pulled away to wipe her face on a napkin. Paloma used hers to blow her nose. "Whip Decker is finally gone. You're free now to do whatever the hell it is you want. What have you always wanted to do, Luella? Why did you come back to Fuego after being away so long?"

Luella sighed. "Oh, I don't know. At first, I told myself it was because I got a job at the hospital and it was just convenient. But after being back at the Edge... I'm starting to think it's because I wanted to be close to it again. I fell in love with it, every bit as much as I fell in love with...you know who. Some part of me never forgot that feeling of being there or...belonging to it. I just wanted to belong to something, in the permanent sense."

Paloma nodded. "I know exactly what you mean, *niña*. When I came to the Edge, I was a young woman. I've never left—and not just because I have people there who need me. The land...the sky...the way they reach for each other...the way the river comes down out of the mountains and never ceases, no matter how hot or dry the desert country is… It's miraculous. It's vital. It grabs you by the soul, and it doesn't let you go."

"No," Luella agreed. The land—that sky—those stars…so many stars…she'd fallen in love under those stars in more ways than one, she realized.

"It brings people together," Eveline mused, cupping her chin in her hands, axes and margarita forgotten. "Normally, land drives people apart. It is the most coveted resource on earth. But the Edge is different. That's why I wanted my wedding there. If not for the Edge, I'm not sure Wolfe and I would've ever been together."

Paloma nodded. "The land draws the right ones in and it holds them. They may go away, like the both of you did, but it never stops calling them back."

Luella ran a hand under her nose. "I want to belong there. But I don't."

"Bite your tongue, girl," Paloma snapped, stern for the first time that night.

"It's true," Luella said. "Ellis and I… Things didn't work out. Now everything's so complicated. There's too much there—too much hurt and too much grief. It's like a friggin' mountain I can't use my hands to move, just my heart and my mind and I'm not sure either of those are strong. And even if I could use my hands, they're not strong enough either. It's a no-win scenario."

Eveline put her cheek on Luella's shoulder. "I told you, didn't I, that Ellis is in love with you?"

"Oh yeah?" Luella asked. "Then why did I just see him going into Mimi's with Rosalie Quetzal?"

She saw Eveline and Paloma exchange a significant look. Her heart turned over. "What?" she asked. Could she handle the portents behind that look? She was already on the edge. The bubble of warmth and friendship they'd created was a fragile thing with the emptiness just below—an ill-fated net waiting to catch her when she tripped and fell on her face once again…

Paloma made a face. "Rosalie was married to Walker Sullivan. The rodeo king."

"I know," Luella said. "What does that have to do with—"

Eveline cleared her throat, lowering her voice. "He was sleeping with her."

"Rosalie?" Luella said. She shook her head, trying to clear it. "Wait. I've had too much to drink…"

"Not with Rosalie," Paloma said, patiently.

"Well, not exclusively," Eveline clarified. When Luella still couldn't grasp the meaning behind any of it, Eveline threw her a bone. "With Liberty."

It was spoken under Eveline's breath but it rang through Luella head like a gong. She sat up straight. *"What?"*

Paloma nodded. "Unbelievable. We know."

"Sh-she… Hold on." Luella raised her hands and stared hard at the tabletop, making the wavy age lines in the wood fix themselves in place. She needed absolute clarity here. "That…that…"

"Minx," Paloma supplied.

"Hussy," Eveline offered.

"That *bitch*—"

"Oh, that's good," Eveline agreed. "I like that better."

"— she waltzes 'round town telling everything that breathes that Ellis is a no-account cheater who's been sleeping with me, his ex-girlfriend, for all these years and watching everyone tear the two of us down piece by every little piece and all that time…the whole *damn* time, she's the one who was having the affair? With a *married man*?"

"Mmm-hmm," Eveline agreed, widening her eyes for effect. "She's a real class act, right?"

"She's a phony," Paloma added. "She's a…oh, what's it?"

"Use your words," Eveline encouraged, nodding fervently.

"She's a…" Paloma snapped her fingers. "A *hypocrite*!"

"Yes!" Eveline said, raising both hands. "Preach!"

"For Christ's sake," Luella said, grabbing her head in both hands. It was starting to hurt—really hurt. The anger…the shock…it pulsed and writhed. "I… I need to get out of here."

"Ohmagod," Eveline cried, grabbing her by the shoulders. "Are you going to yak? Here, I'll take you to the restroom. I'm actually feeling a little queasy myself… Too much Cuervo."

"No," Luella said, rising quickly. "I need to… Too many people… Too many axes… Too *mad*. Do you *know* what I'm saying?"

Paloma hefted herself to her feet. "I know *exactly* what you're saying, *niña*." She slapped money on the table. "We're leaving." She picked up her glass, downed the remains of her margarita in one go then let it clack back to the table. "Eatons out!"

"Yeah, we are," Eveline said as she hooked her purse over her shoulder. She gathered their coats off the hooks and followed close on their heels.

The crowd between them and the door parted, miraculously. They cut a fine swath through the Hatchet

House patrons. Luella was proud of the fact that she didn't stumble or appear too tipsy.

They were just about to reach the exit when something blocked their path. Or, someone.

Eveline groaned. "Not now, Conway."

Rowdy leered at them all from his medium height. He had a medium build to match his coveralls. Luella's nose curled. He smelled like it'd been several days since he'd changed out of them. "Barf," she moaned.

He drew his head back on his neck. "That's not very nice, is it?" His eyes did a dive over her knit sweater. "You look plenty nice. You smell plenty nice. But you ain't nice. Are you, devil's daughter?"

Paloma stuck her finger in his face and shook it. "You will watch your mouth, Theodore Conway, or I'll knock the Rowdy right out of you the way your mother should have the day she decided to call you that instead."

"Let's go," Luella begged, trying to vie for the exit. "I want to go."

"We're going," Eveline agreed, sneering at Rowdy as they went.

Luella touched the handle. Behind her, Eveline shrieked. Turning back, Luella saw Rowdy's hand cupping the back of Eveline's jeans in a firm hold.

Eveline whirled on Rowdy, who was grinning like a fiend, dislodging his grip. "Ah," he said, pressing a hand to his heart. "It feels just as round and sweet as it looks in the pictures." And he laughed.

Eveline balled her hand into a fist and brought it up, humming with fury. Luella stopped her, grabbing a bottle off the nearest table. She brought it down with a great deal of force on Rowdy's head.

There were screams. The music stopped. All eyes

were on Rowdy as he slumped stupidly to the ground, then Luella, who held the neck of the broken bottle in her hand.

"You did that so well," Paloma murmured as Luella tossed the offending bottle away.

"I wish I could've done something like that," Eveline said. "Heaven knows he deserves it."

"Next time," Luella promised.

"Hey!" The owner, a large mountain of a man named Homer, barreled down on them. "You're not going anywhere!"

"We are, too," Paloma said.

"You can't knock out my patrons and leave," he argued, pointing to the coveralls that were Rowdy slumped across the floor like a lumpy potato sack.

"We *are* your patrons," Paloma informed him. "Good paying ones, too, who were enjoying themselves just fine until Theodore here copped a feel on Ms. Eveline."

"I'm going to have to ask Luella here to wait for the sheriff," he told them, banding his arms over his chest. "The rest of you can go."

"You can't arrest her," Eveline said. "She was defending me."

"I can't," he granted. "But the sheriff can."

"We're not leaving without Luella," Eveline said, getting right up in his face. Or as close to it as she could. He was a really large man.

"Fine," he said, dipping his red face down into hers to drive the word home. "I'll tell them you tried inciting a riot in my place of business. *All* of you."

"Fine," Paloma volleyed back, nonplussed. She drew Luella and Eveline back toward the bench by the door. "We'll wait right here. Won't we, girls?"

As Eveline and Paloma both settled in with determined faces, Luella wondered, dazed, why she'd waited
until she was leaving Fuego to make friends there.

Chapter 13

Being taken down to the station again in handcuffs was another low point, Luella would admit. But sharing a cell with Paloma Coldero and Eveline Eaton was a high one. When Ellis, Everett and Wolfe appeared on the other side of the bars, they found the three women in fits of laughter as they recounted how Rowdy had looked as he sidled to the wooden planks at Luella's feet.

Everett raised his hand to the bars over his head. "Well," he drawled, pushing his hat up from his brow. "This is a turn of events."

That only made Paloma and Eveline laugh harder. Luella's laughter fizzled at the sight of Ellis's quiet stare. She cleared her throat, remembering how quiet the room had gone when she'd smashed the bottle over Rowdy's head. She also remembered how for about an hour—a entirely miserable hour—she'd thought he'd been going into Mimi's with Rosalie for a date.

How could she doubt him when she was the one locked up in a jail cell again? And she'd gotten his sister and houseekeeper thrown in here with her...

She licked her lips. "It's my fault they're here. They didn't do anything. Homer's a liar. Nobody incited a riot. Rowdy copped a feel on Eveline—"

"Wait, *what*?" Everett barked.

"There he goes," Paloma said, amused.

"Zero to rage in three milliseconds," Eveline measured. "That can't be good for his health."

"What are we going to do about him?" Paloma said, eyeing Everett with pity.

"Get him a woman?" Eveline suggested.

"You'd wish that on a woman?"

Eveline narrowed her eyes. "She'd have to be as strong as you."

"Stronger, *niña*."

"Y'all 'bout done?" Ellis asked, sounding maybe a little amused, too.

"Oh, I don't think so," Paloma said. "This is the most fun old Paloma's had in a long time."

"Aw," Eveline cooed, tipping her head to Paloma's shoulder.

Wolfe blew a low whistle.

"What are the charges?" Luella asked. "Jones wouldn't tell us." What she didn't ask—what made her heart pound in dread—was whether her night in jail was going to be a violation of her parole.

"He wouldn't tell us either," Everett said. "He may hate you more than he hates me. And here I was thinking that wasn't possible."

"Jealous?" Eveline teased.

"He's threatened to charge the three of you with drunk and disorderly," Ellis revealed.

"Ooh, nice," Eveline said.

Luella frowned because she sensed there was more.

"And disturbing the peace," he finished.

"It's an axe-throwing place," Eveline said, humor vanishing in another upsurge of indignation. "It's not exactly a peaceful establishment."

"It was Theodore who disturbed the peace," Paloma added. "We were trying to make an exit."

"When he groped you," Everett said, dropping the words like grenades.

"Yes," Eveline said, thrusting her chin in the air. "And I would've given him the what-for if Luella hadn't stopped me by dropping a bottle over his head."

Ellis raised his brows. His gaze passed over her face first in a considering sweep before feathering over the points of her torso.

Her navel gathered the heat of that. It helped tamp down on the shame, somewhat. She wanted his warmth. She hated what she'd done. But she hadn't wanted Eveline to get in trouble and Rowdy had needed the comeuppance.

"The lawyer will take care of all of it," Everett said with a shrug. "From the sound of things, Jones will have to drop the charges."

"Even against Luella?" Paloma asked.

Everett exchanged a glance with Luella. He must've seen the way she was gnawing her lower lip. "Yes," he said without question, surprising her.

She opened her mouth to say "thank you," but stopped at the sound of footsteps.Altaha nudged the men out of the way. "Make a space, people. Geez." She fit the keys in the lock. "Ladies, your bail's been paid. You may go now."

"Thank you, Deputy," Paloma said, coming to her feet as the others did. "My purse?"

"See Officer Jenkins," Altaha suggested. She looked tired. Then again, it was near midnight. "He'll get your things back to you."

"Might I suggest some cushions for those benches?" Paloma advised her.

Altaha tucked a smile behind the pursing of her lips. "I'll look into it, ma'am." She let Eveline out but stopped Luella from passing. "A word?"

"Okay," Luella said, apprehensive.

Eveline grabbed Wolfe by the face and mashed a kiss to his lips before he escorted her out, every bit the doe-eyed intended. Everett groaned but followed. Ellis hung back with Luella and Altaha. "What's the trouble, Kaya?" he asked.

"You should know, too, I guess," Altaha informed him. "Jones has taken me off the Ollero Creek case."

"What?" Luella and Ellis said as one. "How could he?" Luella asked. "You've been working on it for weeks…"

"He doesn't feel I'm making enough headway in the investigation," Altaha revealed, grim. "He also feels that I'm too close to the family."

"What family?" Luella asked.

"Our family," Ellis murmured.

She glanced up and caught his gaze. It was round and dark and bursting with meaning. Her stomach flipped and she looked away quickly.

"I'm sorry," Altaha said in an undertone. "But you'll have to deal with him now on this."

"Isn't there anything you can do?" Luella asked.

Altaha eyed her with sympathy. "Look, Luella, I'm surprised the sheriff let me take this case to begin with. He's been trying to push me out for a while now."

"Why would he do that?" Ellis asked. "What's he got against you?"

"I don't know," Altaha said slowly. "Could be that I have breasts, a badge *and* a brain. Could be I'm Jicarilla. All I know is I've had to work four times as hard as everybody else in this station house to make any kind of ground and I get no reward for it where others who do half the work do."

"That's bullshit," Ellis muttered.

"He's the sheriff," Altaha reminded him. "And until that changes, I don't see things being any different."

"You're a good cop," Ellis pointed out. "A damn good cop. The best we have in this county."

"Thanks," she said with a little smile. Turning her attention to Luella, she said, "You need anything, don't hesitate to call. He can take me off your case but he can't stop me from answering a distress call."

Luella thought about it. "There may be something I could use your help with. Something I can't and won't discuss with your boss."

"Sure thing," Altaha said. "I'd say step into my office but he's got eyes all over this place. We can meet tomorrow, lunchtime, if I don't get any calls away from the station."

"How about at Ollero Creek?" Luella asked.

"Lu," Ellis said in warning. "It's still not safe."

"She's the deputy," Luella reminded him.

"I am the deputy," Altaha said with a nod. "Oh, by the way, I called your ex in Taos."

Ellis's eyes opened up with possibility and, in equal amounts, dread. "Yeah?"

"Expect to see your girls the day after next. She'll be bringing them for the weekend."

He released a heavy breath. "I'd hug you, Deputy, but your boss may frown upon that."

"Oh, he'd definitely frown," Altaha stated. She patted him on the arm. "Enjoy them, will you, and see if you can't end this thing with the missus?"

"Already on it," he said, taking Luella by the wrist. He tugged her toward the exit.

Ellis escorted her out of the station. They rounded the corner where they found his truck waiting. The others had gone, probably in another Eaton Edge truck. Before she could reach for her door handle, he used the circle of his hand around her wrist to tug her around.

She gasped, her front buffered suddenly by his.

His arm hooked around her waist and he brought her to her toes for a firm kiss.

She fumbled for his shoulders. "Wh-what…"

"Did you really break a bottle over Rowdy Conway's head?" he asked.

His eyes were glittering in the dark. She licked her lips, trying to tamp down on the mystifying urge to grin. "Yes."

He made a noise in his throat then brought his mouth back to hers for a kiss as thorough as it was disarming. She felt the door of his truck at her back and embraced the feeling of being trapped between it and his body. She moaned when his hips churned against hers. Gasping, she turned her face away from his but kept her hand firmly thatched in the hair on the back of his head. "We're in the middle of town."

"I don't give a hot damn where we are or who sees," he whispered. The words breezed across her cheek. He touched his temple to her cheekbone. "I could get lost in you. Right here."

She'd lost herself to him a long time ago. She closed her eyes. "Say my name."

"What?" he asked, touching her chin. "What'd you say, honey?"

She gathered her voice above a whisper. "Say my name, Ellis." *Like you said it with her. Show me how you said my name.* "I need to hear you say my name."

It was ridiculous but she could almost hear him smiling. She could feel it. "Luella," he said.

She sighed, turning into him again. "Again."

"Luella," he said. He tugged her into another kiss, this one soft as rain.

"Again, damn it," she said, bringing herself up to her toes to reach the lines of his face… "Say it again."

"God Jesus, I like you strict," he breathed across her mouth. He groaned when she fished his bottom lip between her own, his hands flat against the windows of the truck. "Luella, honey. My always."

"Oh," she sighed again, this time giving in—just throwing in the whole damn towel. Who was she if she didn't need him?

A car passed on the street and she broke away. She was hidden from view by Ellis's breadth and found distraction in the fragrant hollow of his throat. "Let's…let's think for a second."

"Why?" he whined.

A smile dangled from her lips. "Because your girls are coming home."

He lowered his head. There was light in his eyes. "Thank God."

"I shouldn't be there when they do."

"You can't go back to Ollero Creek," he told her.

"I'll find somewhere to go," she told him. "Someplace safe."

"Where's safe when I can't be there to protect you?"

"I'll be okay, Ellis," she told him. "I want you to focus on the girls this weekend. Enjoy them." She pressed her lips together for a second and inhaled, unsteady. "And…if it comes down to it, I need you to promise me something."

"What?"

"If Liberty tries to take them from you again," she said slowly, "and you come to a point where you have to let me go to keep them, I don't want you to hesitate. I want… I need you to keep your girls."

"Lu—"

"Don't," she said. "I didn't get to spend one single moment with my baby…our baby. You can't miss a single moment with your girls. You know that."

"I know that," he told her. "I'd do whatever I could to get those moments with our son back for you. You know that?"

"I do," she whispered. "You didn't promise me."

"I promise," he said with a nod. His hands cupped her hips, tugging her against him once more. They slid around to the small of her back and crossed and he leaned the side of his head against hers. "I'm working my hardest to take it all back."

"What?"

"My life," he said. "My parenthood. My standing. Yours, too. Redemption. The girls need the Edge, their lives there, just as much as I need them."

He was a wonderful father, she saw—such a good daddy. She hated Liberty all the more for trying to erase him from his daughters' lives.

"What do you need to talk to Altaha about tomorrow?"

"Oh." She eased back, spanning her palms across her chest. "Just some decoding. My aunt left me postcards and a photograph of my mother. I've been able to figure out some of the messages. But I was hoping she could help me with some of the others. They helped me find my ring. Did I tell you that?"

"Good old Mabel," he said running his hands over her back.

"Dear old Mabel," she murmured.

"Come home to my bed?" he asked. "Once more at least. Please." When she thought about it, he added, "Don't make me beg." It wavered out of him on a nervous chuckle. "I'll do it on my knees—right here on the pavement."

It might have been the dregs of tequila that made her say it. She'd definitely blame it on tequila in the morning. But she smiled, sly, and said, "I can think of better things for you to do on your knees, Ellis Eaton."

A satisfactory rumble sounded in his chest. "Keep talking like that, sweetheart, and I may not make it back."

"Ellis, where are you?"

Ellis exchanged a wary look with Eveline over the long line of Shy's back in the stable two days later. The horse jerked at the shout from somewhere near the stable entrance. He set aside his hoof pick and brushed his hands off as he peered into the aisle.

Liberty was looking for him.

Unlatching the gate, he left his sister to see to Shy's

care. "I didn't think you'd show," he revealed. "Did you bring the girls with you?"

"I have a bone to pick with you!" she shouted. Five stalls down, the young ranch hand, Lucas, poked his head out, brows raised to the ceiling. "Why are you in cahoots with Rosalie Sullivan?"

Ellis took off his hat in a weary motion. He frowned. "I take that as a no. And I see you're still in touch with the town gossips."

"You met her at Mimi's Steakhouse," Liberty accused. "What did you discuss?"

"That's not really any of your business, is it?" he contemplated. "You wouldn't be so worried about it, either, if you hadn't slept with her husband."

She balked. Turning red as a poppy, she went up to her full height. "How dare you—"

"Let's talk truth for once, shall we?" he intervened neatly. He was stunned he could sound so level when everything inside him came up to a wicked point. "I have something you never did."

"What is that?" she wanted to know.

"Clear and present evidence of my spouse's infidelity," he stated. "You waited for the right moment to pin this whole mess on me. When I said Luella's name, that was your opportunity, to get out of the marriage and take something for yourself. You never thought it'd come back on you like this—not after getting the entire town to side with you and spread your rumors to the far corners of the county and back. You'd have gotten away with it, too, if it hadn't been for Rosalie."

"What're you, sleeping with *her* now, too?" she accused.

Ellis nearly smiled. It was a petty response. "Say

goodbye to my shares and that seat on the board and have my girls here tomorrow morning, eight o'clock sharp. Then you're going to call Greasy and tell him the new terms of our divorce."

"Fine," she grumbled. "What do *you* want?"

"Split custody," he said. "I'm not going to take them away from you completely, even though you threatened to do that to me. They need you every bit as much as they need me. I'll even cut you a check, and a generous one to pay for their tuition should you decide they need to stay in private school. But they will have a life here at the Edge. They can have the best of both worlds and when it comes time, they can choose for themselves where they want their lives to unfold. That's the arrangement we should've had from the beginning. They need to come first, Lib. It always should've been them first."

Her eyes moved from his left to his right and back and forth in quick succession. When she looked away, around at the hands that had gathered to watch the spectacle, she released a breath. "I did bring the girls. They're in the house with Paloma."

"Good."

"Your deputy didn't leave me much choice," she said. "I'll be back to pick them up Sunday morning."

"Sunday afternoon," he countered. "You forget Paloma likes to take us to church."

"Fine, if you tell me how long you've been seeing Luella Decker again," she snapped back. "You were spotted outside the police station the other night—"

"That's a real nice surveillance team you've got on my tail," he remarked.

"—and some say she sleeps here most nights now. Is that true?"

He rocked back to his heels and crossed his arms. "As our marriage has been over for some time now, I'd say that's none of your business, either."

"It won't help you," she warned. "You have to know that."

"I know I'm done playing your games," he replied. "I'll see you Sunday afternoon."

"I don't want her around the girls," Liberty warned. "I won't have it."

He tilted his head. "Sure. If you can look me in the eye and tell me neither of the girls ever saw you flirt with the rodeo king."

She knew he had her. It was why she set her teeth behind her lips. She turned away quickly.

When she reached the open barn doors, Luella's cat Nyx snuck like a black wraith out of the shadows and attacked her ankles. Liberty cursed and shrieked and shook him off. The cat went flying with a yowl and she pushed her hands through her hair, her steps quickening with every stride.

It was only after Luella told Ellis that she was staying with Altaha that he let her go. The deputy lived not far from downtown Fuego in a one-bedroom house with a chain link fence around the front yard and a screen door with decorative iron over the front. "It's cozy," Altaha said as she led Luella inside. "A little too cozy at times but, hey, I'm single. What do I need the room for?"

Luella assured her it was fine. She slept on the couch the first night, Sphinx curled against her belly.

She turned twice in the night toward phantom warmth that wasn't there. Already she'd grown used to having Ellis beside her.

Over breakfast the following morning in the little windowed space off the kitchen that the deputy called her conservatory, Luella tried to figure out if that was going to be a problem.

She still expected more chaos. If she'd been able to count on anything in life, it was that.

Altaha joined her with a plate of toast. Her reams of glossy black hair were piled messily on top of her head and her gel sleep mask was still wrapped across her forehead. A buttered knife rasped across the surface of her bread. It clattered to the tabletop and she reached for her coffee with a deep frown. "Look, I got something to say and it isn't good so I'm going to have to ask you to brace yourself."

Luella, her feet in her seat and knees between her torso and the table, set her mug aside. "Is this about the postcards I gave you?"

"No," Altaha said with a shake of her head. "Though that photograph does bug me something fierce."

"What about it?"

"I don't know," Altaha said, contemplative. "The man. He rattles something." She gestured to her head. "I can't put my finger on what."

"Okay," Luella said cautiously. "Is what you wanted to tell me something about Ollero Creek?"

"No. Jones has really shut me out of that one. The man's a steel trap when he wants to be."

"What then?" Luella asked. "It's not Ellis…is it?"

"Your boyfriend's fine," Altaha said. "I got a phone call saying Liberty showed up with the girls as instructed so that's something. No, it's…more to do with you and what happened to you in San Gabriel seventeen years ago."

"What?" Luella asked. She lifted her napkin and

wiped her mouth, setting her feet down on the floor where they belonged. "Why would it be about that?"

Altaha looked uncomfortable. She turned her gaze to the ice-entrusted backyard that was about the size of a postage stamp and seemed to gather herself. "Everett asked me to look into something that happened back then. A visit his father had on July 20—from a doctor named Dr. Bridestone. Does that name ring a bell?"

Luella thought about it. It did sound familiar in some vague, distant way. "I… I don't know. It might."

"We'll cover that in a minute," Altaha said. "The first thing you need to know is that Hammond Eaton was offered a large sum of money for a newborn baby that would have been delivered to him in December of that year if he met the demands of the closed adoption."

Luella's eyes had gone wide. "A newborn."

"Yes," Altaha said. "So I looked into it. I dug back through your records from the time of your hospitalization without asking. As a friend who isn't on this case in any official capacity, I have to say I'm sorry."

Friend? Luella nodded, distracted.

"Do you remember the name of the obstetrician who happened to be on call that night?" Altaha asked.

Luella squinted down the long lens of her memory. "Dr. Gladbreed? No, that's not right. Dr. Stonewell." A frustrated noise escaped her. "Damn it. It was something along those lines. Some combination of the two."

Altaha waited for Luella to piece it together, watchful.

Luella rubbed her lips together, thinking fast. She snapped her finger. "Dr. Bredston. That was it. Sorry. It was so long ago…" She fumbled to a stop when she saw Altaha's brows drawn together, concerned. It didn't strike her like lightning, as some ideas did. It unveiled itself in slow, utter horror. Luella shoved her chair back from the table and stood. "Oh, my God. Dr. *Bridestone*."

Altaha took a careful breath. "I'm afraid so. You see, I tracked down his wife. His records stated he died eight years ago. Heart attack. She didn't give me much, but it was enough for me to piece some of the puzzle together, for the most part. She admitted that in September of 2006, he came into some hefty cash. She asked him where it came from. He wouldn't tell her, initially. But she managed to needle it out of him. He admitted to his part in exchanging a baby he'd delivered via C-section at the women's center to Fuego County Hospital into the waiting arms of his adoptive parents for the money."

Luella had to open a window. She tried releasing the nearest one from the jamb. It wouldn't budge.

"It's stuck shut." Altaha rose and went to the little patio door. "Here." She pushed it open and let the cold in, propping it open with a potted snake plant. "Just breathe for a second."

Luella made a noise. *Just breathe?* Her baby had been born—alive. Her son had been stolen from her by a corrupt obstetrician and given to complete strangers for a heap of cash.

Heap of cash. Heaps of cash…

She lifted her head slowly. She turned to meet Altaha's gaze and saw something hidden there. Missing information that Luella knew… "Did my mother, Riane Howard, have anything to do with this?"

Altaha licked her lips in a furtive motion. "Luella, your mother arranged the entire thing from start to finish."

A sob bubbled forth. "Oh, God," she cried. There were

bitter, bitter waves of grief and horror building inside of her. She turned away quickly and raced from the room.

Down the little hallway, she found the door to the powder room. She closed the door then went down on her knees and rocked herself through waves of sickness.

It reduced her to dry heaves—uncontrolled, gut-wrenching dry heaving that left her weak as a kitten. At that point, she lay on the floor and pressed her brow to the cold tile, trembling and wet with sweat. Her stomach cramped and her mind took her back not to the emptiness it was familiar with when trauma came for a visit... but to those long, long months in her mother and Mabel's house seventeen years ago when she'd felt trapped and panicked and helpless.

She thought of her mother then shut her eyes to hide.

She *was* the devil's daughter, in more than one regard.

Chapter 14

Ellis, Isla and Ingrid spent the weekend riding together, going for long walks and stargazing. He took them up to the roof where he'd set up the old telescope and talked about the stars until they fell asleep on either side of him, their little heads slumped to each of his shoulders. He took them into town for lunch at Hickley's. He took them into the hills to find the little bits of crunchy snow left over for a snowman and then the inevitable iceball fight.

They returned to Eaton House hungry as trolls. Everett, also hungry, colored in coloring books with vigor alongside them while they waited at the table for Paloma to finish dinner. Eveline brought them new boots to try on as they were rapidly growing out of their current ones. They modeled them up and down the entryway, mimicking their aunt's supermodel pout and gliding walk. Wolfe taught them how to build fires in the fire pit on the bricked patio and watched over them as they roasted marshmallows, making sure they didn't burn their hands or any other part of their bodies.

There were reams of laughter around the dinner table again. Paloma told stories from Ellis, Everett and Eveline's youth that Ingrid in particular couldn't seem to get enough of—perhaps because she shared whatever chromosome that had led them on their misadventures.

At night, he missed Luella but soon found himself crowded into the center of his bed when Isla and then Ingrid snuck in from their bunkroom down the hallway and joined him. He listened to their breathing slow and then deepen into repose, almost in sync, and tried not to count the days he had been away from them—and how many more they were going to spend apart before this was all over.

No one came to wake him the following morning —not Paloma, not Everett, not even the restless dogs he kept at his heels. They slept in then tromped downstairs, Ingrid still sleepily invested on his shoulder, to scrounge up a late breakfast.

Sunday afternoon caught up with him all-too-quickly. After church, they had time enough for one more ride across the Edge. He helped them strap on their helmets and mount their ponies and he and Shy led them out into open country air.

"Yechaw!" Ingrid whooped to his right.

He snuck a glance at Isla. Her form was still superb. Better still was the broad grin on her face. "Faster?" he asked.

"Faster!" Ingrid chirped. "I want to fly!"

"Faster," Isla agreed with a certain nod.

"Yah!" He gave Shy a tap with his heel and the horse

broke into a near gallop. The girls' mounts followed suit until they were all in flight.

"That was fun," Ingrid said with a sleepy, smug expression as they walked the horses back to the stable half an hour later.

"I wish we could ride all day," Isla said with a touch of melancholy.

"Me, too," Ellis agreed. "When it gets warm, I want to take you camping on the back of Ol' Whalebones."

"Ol' what?" Ingrid asked.

"The mountain you see to the north," he said.

"It's where the Edge ends," Isla said sagely. "Everybody calls it Ol' Whalebones because it looks like the backbone of a whale."

"The Apaches have another name for it," Ellis told her. "Do you remember it?"

Before Isla could answer, Ingrid stood up in the stirrups. "What's that?" she asked, pointing over her pony Dander's ears.

Ellis looked ahead and saw the black spot in what was left of the ice. He drew back on the reins. "Whoa."

The girls followed suit as he sat and looked at the smudge against the white landscape. He shifted back in the saddle, flicking the reins over Shy's head. "Stay here. Understand?"

"Yes, Daddy," Isla said obediently.

"Yes, Daddy," Ingrid echoed.

Ellis dismounted. He grabbed the reins and led Shy behind him as he approached the figure.

Shy's feet began to dance backward. He whinnied, his nose turning up once, then again.

Ellis stopped long enough to pat him on the neck. He could get closer, but he didn't have to.

Inside, he cursed. It was a black cat.

It was Luella's. The one that had attacked him and then her at Ollero Creek and Liberty just the other day. The cat had been skulking around the stables, chasing mice and boots to his heart's content.

He watched the cat's belly, willing the bastard to breathe.

Instead, it was eerily still against the ice-and-dirt-strewn grass.

Ellis looked around. He scanned the fence to the east and the shadow of the river to the west. His eyes fell on the buildings in the near distance.

The cat was alone out here. More, it had died inside the bounds of the Edge   meaning that whoever had brought harm to Ollero Creek had penetrated the safe harbor that was his home.

He cursed a stream, unable to help himself.

"What is it, Daddy?" Ingrid called. "Is it hurt?"

He glanced back at his girls. He scanned the shape of their pale faces, the little tufts of air that escaped their mouths.

He was going to send them away this time. They wouldn't be able to return until he hunted down the killer and finished this.

Ellis knocked on Altaha's door that evening, hat in hand. He studied the worn texture of her welcome mat, hating the news he carried.

The door behind the screen opened. Altaha appeared in plainclothes, her hair braided black over her shoulder. "What are you doing here?" she asked.

"I need Luella," he said without preamble.

She pushed the screen open. "Now's not a good time."

"Why not?" he asked. "Has she been talking to someone at the Edge?"

She tilted her chin. "No. Why?"

"Something's happened," he told her. "Another animal attack."

Altaha lifted a brow. "How do you know it's related to the others?"

"It was Luella's cat," he said.

"Just hers?"

"Yes." He took a step forward but she didn't budge. "Damn it, Kaya, let me in."

"It's not a good time," she repeated.

"What's going on?"

"She's had a hard few days," Altaha revealed. "She's had some news... It's been difficult. She's processing."

"What news?" he demanded.

"You can't come in," she told him, "until she says you can. Do you understand?"

He met her stare and knew he wasn't getting past her. "I just want to talk to her. She needs to know about her cat."

"Jones," Altaha said in realization. She nodded. "He's the lead on this now. He'll want to talk to her, too."

"I need to warn her," he told her.

"Leave it with me."

"Kaya," he said before she could close the door. "I can't walk away not knowing what's hurt her."

She frowned. "Look, lover boy—"

"Let him in," Luella said from behind her.

"Lu," he started then stopped. She looked like actual hell. Her hair was a mess around her face and her cheeks were splotched with red and white in patches. The red had washed down her neck to the open collar of her chambray shirt. Worst of all, her eyes—they were rimmed with dark circles and they didn't so much look at him as through him.

"I'll make coffee," she said before shuffling into the depths of the house.

Wide-eyed, Ellis looked to Altaha for answers.

She heaved a sigh and held the door open. "You heard the woman."

Carrying his hat, he stepped over the threshold, knowing on some level the news that waited for him was twice as bad as the news he'd come to deliver.

"I could get fired for this," Altaha said as Ellis sped past the sign for San Gabriel.

They'd been driving for some time with Luella riding quiet in the backseat. He glanced in the rearview mirror at her remote face. She'd remained motionless for much of the drive, staring out the window.

That empty stare was scaring the hell out of him.

As the speed limit signs narrowed to the town limit, he didn't lift his foot from the gas. "Nobody asked you to come," he told the deputy.

"Damn it, Eaton. I'm a cop. Slow the eff down!"

He did—but only by a fraction. "Tell it to me again."

"We've been over it three times," Altaha told him wearily. They blew past the police station and she gave a little wave.

"Once more," he insisted.

She sighed. "I know *some* of the timeline."

"Starting with?"

"Luella had an accident at the home she was sharing with her mother and aunt," Altaha recounted, turning to look into the backseat for confirmation that didn't come.

"She fell down the stairs," he remembered, filling the silence delicately. God, if she'd just say *something*—let him know she was going to be okay. The news that their baby had been stolen was enough. But the silence was crushing him.

"Riane took her to San Gabriel Women's Center where she was admitted around five o'clock in the afternoon," Altaha continued. "The doctor on call at that time was Dr. Bredston. He arrived shortly after, clocking in around half an hour later, which is pretty impressive considering it was a Sunday and he lived some forty-five minutes outside of town. The RN who first attended Luella that evening was one Scott, Lacey. She was the only nurse in the room."

"The whole time?"

"From what the file said, yes. Luella corroborated that."

Ellis thought about it. "There were at least three in the room when each of the girls were born—plus the obstetrician. Not to mention the anesthesiologist and interns. Weren't there any other nurses on staff that night?"

"There had to have been," Altaha reasoned. "It's the largest women's center in the county. Even on a Sunday, you'd think they'd need at least two or three."

"Go through the rest of it," Ellis said, turning down the road toward the residential side of town.

"According to Luella, she was sedated an hour or so after she was admitted," Altaha went on. "The reason being that she was hysterical. When she woke up, the doctor had gone home. The only people with her were RN Scott and her mother, Riane, who told her her baby had been stillborn."

"But the files tell another story?" Ellis prompted.

"Yes. They took her into the OR not long after she

was sedated where Bredston performed an emergency C-section. The baby's time of birth was reported as seven twenty-two that night."

"From there?" Ellis asked, his pulse swimming in his ears.

"A bus was called from the nearest hospital—that's Fuego County Hospital—and arrived around eight thirty. The baby was taken directly to the NICU."

"What was the reason?" Ellis wondered, the words punchy. His hands hardened on the wheel.

"Premature birth," she said. "Other than that, no medical reason was noted in the file. From there, the baby's whereabouts taper off. I'll have to quibble with the hospital for those. Luella, however, was discharged from the women's center three days later. Bredston discharged her with a script for a high dose of ibuprofen and an antidepressant. She followed up with her post-op appointments."

He ground his back teeth together as he pulled onto Tesuque Lane. "I don't buy that the nurse, Scott, wasn't in on it, too."

Altaha grabbed the panic bar over her head when he swerved into Riane's driveway. "Christ," she muttered.

He'd unclipped his seat belt and opened the driver's door before he'd shut off the engine. He eyed the front line of the tidy two-story, scowling at the curtains over the windows. He reached for Luella's door but she'd already opened it and was climbing to the ground. Grabbing her arm, he muttered, "Easy there, honey."

"I'm not made of glass, Ellis," she informed him.

The blotchiness he'd seen on her complexion yesterday had been replaced by an almost translucent pallor.

She *looked* like glass. "You don't have to come in. You can wait out here, if you need to."

"I want to see her," Luella said. "Hear what she has to say for herself."

"It's not going to be easy."

"What part of this is?" she asked. "What part of our lives has *ever* been easy?"

He could hardly breathe. Everything he had to say seemed too paltry an offering in the face of her disillusionment.

Altaha led them up the front steps to the front door. She pounded on it several times with a closed fist. As they waited, she asked him, "So, you wanna be good cop or bad cop?"

Ellis eyed her blandly before the door opened and a large man in a polo shirt and khakis barely hanging on by a belt answered the door. He looked from Ellis to Altaha, who was in her official uniform and hat, and frowned. "Can I help you, Officer?"

"Deputy Altaha," she greeted, extending a hand for him to shake. When he did, hesitantly, she asked, "Are you Solomon Howard?"

"I am," he said, reaching up for his browline. He stopped to scratch it. "Is there some kind of trouble?"

"We just have a few questions," Altaha explained. "Is your wife, Riane, home?"

"She is," Solomon said, glancing over his shoulder. He tapped his fingers on the edge of the door.

"Let us in, Sol," Luella said at Ellis's back.

"Luella? What are you doing here? Your mother's not going to be happy to see you. I can tell you that."

"She can deal with it," Ellis told him.

"Ellis," Altaha said, setting her teeth. "I do have to insist," she told Solomon. "It's official business."

"I guess." He narrowed his eyes on Ellis. "Can I ask what this is about?"

"We're following up on a case," Altaha noted as they followed him through the foyer into the kitchen breaking off to the left, "to which she was a witness some years ago. We have a couple of follow-up questions then we'll be out of your hair."

"Riane? There's some people here to see you."

Riane was sitting at the table with a pair of scissors and what looked like coupons spread across the table. When she looked up from her business, she stiffened first at the sight of Altaha then stilled completely when her gaze locked on Ellis and Luella standing shoulder to shoulder. She got to her feet, the chair moving back with a screech across the floor. "What are you doing with him?"

"Long time, Moms," Ellis greeted cheerlessly. There was a muscle ticing in his jaw incessantly. "How's it hangin'?"

She scowled at him then Luella, the scissors clamped in her fist. "What's she told you?" she asked, staring hard at Altaha's nameplate on her shirtfront. "My daughter's a pathological liar. Always has been. You know that, Ellis."

"Shut up and sit down," Ellis said, pulling out a chair for himself.

"Now," Solomon said, inching forward, "you can't speak to my wife like that."

Altaha raised her hand to him. "Sir, I'm going to have to ask you to wait outside."

"You said you were just going to question her," Solomon said, eyes peeled.

"Be quiet, Solomon, and go call the lawyer," Riane snapped. "Make yourself useful, for God's sake."

"What do you need a lawyer for, Riane?" he asked, bewildered.

"Go on!" Riane yelled.

Ellis ran a hand down his shirtfront, contemplative. He waited until Solomon left the room, chastised, before he pulled a chair out for Luella and gestured for her to sit beside him. When she did so, facing her mother again with silent reluctance, he decided to take the lead. "You were ready with that lawyer bit, weren't you?" he asked Riane.

"I don't have to speak to you," she said.

"You are wrong about that."

Altaha had been poised between the only exit and Riane. She moved the only remaining chair, motioning for Riane to sit back down. "It's like we told your husband, Mrs. Howard. We'd like you to answer a few questions about the night your daughter went into labor. That's all."

"Luella never went into labor," Riane sneered. "She miscarried. They had to go in and get the baby out. It was stillborn."

"Nope," Ellis put in. Luella flinched and he laid his arm across the line of her shoulders, steadying.

Altaha spared him a glance. "Please, sit down, Mrs. Howard."

"What if I don't submit to these questions of yours?" she asked.

"Then we can take this down to the station," Altaha told her, evenly. There was a finality behind it, though, that made Riane's head snap back. "It's up to you."

Riane's eyes followed Altaha's hand as it reached around on her belt. She shoveled out a breath then pursed her lips in an unhappy pout and dropped unceremoniously to her chair.

"The real story this time," Ellis said with a hurry-up motion. "Come on. Take us through it, step-by-step."

"I don't know what you want from me," Riane claimed.

"You could start with whatever relationship or arrangement you had with Dr. Graham Bredston," Altaha suggested.

She made a disgusted noise. "We didn't have a relationship. He was the doctor in the delivery room that night."

"Dr. Bredston, did you say?" Solomon asked, coming into the room. His phone was in his hand. He shuffled to the table, his temples lined. "Isn't that the obstetrician from church who died a few years ago?"

"Be quiet, Solomon."

"He was a big donor for those fundraisers you do every year. The ones for the foster children."

"I said quiet, Sol!" Riane screeched.

He stopped and looked from his wife's stern expression to Ellis and Luella. His mouth formed an *O*. "Sorry. I called the lawyer."

"Is he coming?" Riane asked.

"Ah, yes," Solomon said. "But he's an hour away. There was some court case in Santa Fe he had to attend this morning. I could sit with you until he gets here…" He trailed off when she quailed him with another one of her looks. He jerked a thumb behind him. "All righty then. I'll be out back…"

They waited for him the shamble out again. "Idiot," Riane muttered.

"So your relationship with Dr. Bredston," Altaha picked up. "It was monetary, in some fashion."

"He donated money to a good cause," Riane supplied.

"How long have you been attending the same church as him?" Altaha asked.

"I never attended church here in San Gabriel," Altaha claimed. "Not before I met Solomon."

"That's a lie," Luella said, under her breath.

"Shut up, girl."

Ellis went cold. "I've never hit a woman in my life, but you say that to her again and I might."

"You've got your own family now, don't you?" Riane asked him. "Why're you getting so worked up over my daughter? She left you, remember? Ran away, hid her baby so you wouldn't have to worry yourself over it."

Altaha cleared her throat. "Everybody remembers you in Fuego for your perfect attendance at church every Sunday. First to get there. Last to leave. You organized fundraisers there, too—as well as luncheons, bazaars… You practically ran the nursery. Reverend Claymore describes you to this day as the incredible one-woman show."

"Did you try to sell those babies, too?" Ellis wondered out loud.

"Ellis," Altaha said. It was a low warning.

He didn't want to back down. He didn't want to settle back and watch. She'd sold his and Luella's baby. He was sure of it. He eased off only because he knew if anybody could get a confession out of her, it was Altaha. And they needed it.

"Mrs. Howard," Altaha said, carefully, "I've already warned you. You can cooperate or you can answer these questions at the station. We have evidence that Luella's newborn was born via C-section at San Gabriel Women's Center before being rushed to the NICU at Fuego County Hospital. We also are certain that Dr. Bredston and the nurse on staff that night, Lacey Scott, lied to Luella about the baby's whereabouts."

"Sounds like they're the ones you need to question," Riane said. "Not me."

"So when we question Lacey Scott," Altaha continued, "she won't confess to having colluded with you to make this happen?"

Riane was silent on that point. She turned her face to the window. The sun fell harshly against the creases of her face.

"How did you convince them to do it?" Ellis pushed. "Were you paid that much for the baby that you were able to cut them both in on it?"

Her nose twitched. She stared at nothing, motionless.

Ellis sat back against the ladderback chair. He wanted to flip the table over. He wanted to break something. He wanted to scare the truth out of her.

He needed to know where his son was.

Reaching for Luella's hand, he used it to bring himself back. Her fingers were so chilled, he curled his around them and tucked them against his navel. Looking around, he noted the glass-front cabinets, the fine china, silver and crystal on display at every corner. "It was enough, wasn't it—to fix you up for life? How else could you afford this? Mabel taught art classes. You work at the church, like you always have. Solomon doesn't fetch much at the grocery store he manages."

When Riane again said nothing, he shook his head. "Hell, at least tell me why you did it—how you could sell your own grandson like that. You owe us that much, at least."

At first, he thought she wouldn't respond. He thought they'd sit the whole hour in silence waiting for her damn lawyer. Then, quietly, as if from far away, he heard her say, "I didn't want my daughter to raise a bastard, like I had to."

Ellis stared, wondering if Riane had said it or he'd imagined it. Luella whimpered.

Altaha leaned forward. "Can you repeat that, Mrs. Howard?"

"You've got ears, Deputy," she hissed. "I'll say nothing more until the lawyer comes." Her arms knit across her chest and she closed her eyes, as if exhausted.

Bastard. Ellis heard the word over and over.

He didn't realize he was grinding his teeth until Luella's hand turned into his, reaching. She met his gaze. Shock penetrated the blank wall of her composure. Her eyes were big and blue and desperate. Tears filled them and he nearly broke.

"You two should go outside," Altaha told them. "Walk it off."

He never should have brought Luella back here. He never should've made her sit through this. Keeping ahold of her hand, he brought himself then her to their feet. His hand on the small of her back, he ushered her toward the door.

Before he left Riane's kitchen, he turned to face her. "If there is a hell, you're going there. And when you get there, I hope you meet your ex-husband. It's nothing less than you deserve after what you've put her through."

"Ellis," Luella said at his back.

He followed her urging, opening the door for her. They escaped the house together.

He watched her sit on the front steps and, after a moment, drop her face into her hands.

Heavily, he sat next to her. He sat with her as the

weight of everything came to the surface. He put his arm around her, soothing as best as he could as he heard her cry. She'd suffered so much here without him.

Not anymore, he thought. She wasn't going to be without him anymore.

Fighting his own emotions, he rocked against her. "Hey," he said, sounding gruff.

She lifted her face and wiped away the wet. She'd cried silent tears, the only sound her breath hitching every few seconds. He wished she'd wail until there was nothing left of it—until she was free of it, the whole terrible weight of it.

He waited until her eyes came back to his. "I love you," he said.

Her lips trembled. She shook her head.

"No," he said. "You'll hear it here, where you ran from Whip and your mother hurt you. You'll hear it because it's still true. I love you, Luella. I'll say it however many times I need to. I will work until I make a believer out of you, like I did before. I love you. I will never stop loving you. No matter what comes."

She stared, her eyes softening as they circled his face. It was her only response, beyond the biting of her lip.

He touched his lips to the center of her brow. "I'm sorry," he said, reaching up to wipe away her tears. "I can't change the fact that you were born to her. But I can tell you every day that you're worth ten of her. More. You're worth more." He traced the curve of her ear. "Remember? 'All the stars and the ones we can't see...' That's you."

She closed her eyes. He'd said it before when he'd proposed. Her hand slid up his arm, clutched his wrist then touched him palm-to-palm. Fingers lacing through his, she brought his hand to her cheek and pillowed her head there. "I always knew I was yours," she said after some time. "I never thought...you could be mine, too."

"I never wanted to be anything else."

"Stop," she said automatically.

He turned his hand to her cheek, bringing her focus back to him. He made sure he had it, before he challenged her. "Why?"

Her lips parted. She eyed his mouth. She exhaled quickly. "I'm not sure anymore," she murmured.

"Me either," he said. "I will make this right. If our son's out there, I will find him. And I will bring him back to you. I swear."

Chapter 15

Luella walked Sheridan around the paddock on a lunge line in a wide circle, wary of the crazy look in his eyes. "Walk," she instructed. He'd been cooped up in a stall too long, waiting for his wound to heal enough for sport. Until he could be ridden again, the lunge line was his best means of exercise. And until she was sure he was limbered up, he would have to walk. "I know, baby," she cooed. "You're doing great. Just...walk."

It did her good to see him walking. It must be nice, getting outdoors again. As soon as she'd led him out of the stall and into the paddock, he'd bobbed his head as if to say, *Yes! Yes!* She found a smile on her lips as she gave him subtle urgings through the rein. "Turn. Good boy. Let's walk the other way."

He snorted, tugging lightly on the line.

"It's boring," she granted. "I get it. But you're a good boy and you're doing great."

She'd debated whether to bring him back to Eaton Edge or not. Since she and Ellis had buried Nyx, it had become clear to her that whoever had been able to hurt her animals at Ollero Creek could hurt them here, too. She couldn't help but question whether Sheridan would be safe.

Extra security measures had been stepped up. Hands were posted outside the barn at all times. She didn't envy those on the graveyard shift, and she knew them all. Wolfe and Eveline took it in turns as well as Everett, their head wrangler, Javier, and Griff MacKay, the stable manager.

Luella knew each of them personally. It helped that they were the ones who Sheridan seemed least likely to take a bite out of.

"He's almost ready for tack."

Luella found Ellis standing at the gate. His gloved hands were wrapped around the top rung, but he kept himself on the other side. Sheridan had come a long way since leaving the clinic, but he still wouldn't let Ellis near him without nipping. Luella had started to wonder if it was because he sensed how much Luella liked him.

Loved him.

Her stomach fluttered. The sun was bright in the midday sky, casting shadows under the brim of his white hat. But she saw the intensity beyond the smile—the deep portals of his eyes. It transported her to someplace diverting. There was safety there and heat—so much heat, it made her knees weak.

She was back in his bed. Their nights had been filled with everything his eyes promised—intensity, sweetness, need and safety.

My always.

It was a wonder she managed to get any sleep at all. If not for exhaustion, she'd lie awake thinking how she was going to handle loving him and leaving again.

She went back to watching the placement of Sheridan's hooves. Ms. Breslin had stopped by yesterday. The inspection at Ollero Creek had gone well. She'd worked up a list price and had wanted Luella to approve it and the listing so it could finally go on the market.

Luella had panicked. She'd waited until Ms. Breslin left before escaping outdoors into the fresh air, wondering why her flight reflex had kicked in.

Isn't this what she'd wanted? She'd *wanted* to sell, leave Fuego, start over. And someone wanted her gone, enough that he'd killed just to get that message across.

Luella pivoted toward the gate as Sheridan completed his next circle. Ellis knew her moods. He fell into companionable silence.

Perfect, she thought. He was so damn perfect…for her.

It was a strange thought. She'd never thought of him that way. Perfect, yes. But not perfect *for her*.

The idea was like candy. Hell, it was a drug.

Should she really think of Ellis in those terms?

Perfect. For me.

Whether she should or not, she couldn't seem to stop. "Ellis!"

The stare broke, leaving Luella with a pleasant shiver as she shortened the lunge line, bringing Sheridan to a slow stop. "Whoa," she murmured, shortening the rein until he was within reach. As the young hand, Lucas, came to the gate to meet Ellis, Luella stroked Sheridan's winter coat, checking his wound to make sure it hadn't torn with any of the new activity. She couldn't help but eavesdrop, especially when the words *the sheriff* fell from the boy's mouth.

"Thanks," Ellis told him. "You're on gate duty today?"

"Yeah," Lucas said. "With Everett."

Ellis made a face. "Good luck with that."

"Any idea when I'll be able to call him chief again?" Lucas asked.

"Not sure why you stopped," Ellis replied. They heard ringing in the distance. "That's the lunch bell. Head in for a bite. We'll be there shortly."

As Lucas trudged back in the direction of the house, Luella walked Sheridan to the gate. "What about the sheriff?"

"He's here," Ellis said. "In the house."

He gauged her reaction. She set her jaw. "Maybe there's news."

He nodded though she could read his doubt for what it was. "Do you want me to stable him?"

He reached for Sheridan's halter. The horse pulled away.

Ellis sighed but offered something of a smile. "I'm not going anywhere, partner. You're going to have to learn to put up with me."

Luella made soft noises until Sheridan relaxed. She pressed her cheek against his face.

Ellis watched, looking hard and soft and all manner of wonderful, forbidden things. When his glove closed over the top of her hand on the gate, she stilled.

He smiled, using the hold to bring her close.

She followed his bidding, coming up to her toes. The gate was between them but it didn't matter. Despite Sheridan pushing his nose at her hip for attention, she accepted the bidding of Ellis's mouth.

It was so tender, she felt her legs buckle. They'd made his iron bed frame rock the night before. How could something this demure be just as effective?

"Mmm," he murmured, thick tawny lashes coming down to reveal the freckle on his eyelid. His sigh blew across her mouth. She shivered again and he grinned. "Who needs lunch? I've got you, honey."

She sank her teeth into her lip to stop herself from moaning. "If you're still planning on taking that ride into the southwest quadrant, kissing won't sustain you."

"I don't know 'bout that," he said, sly. "It sure keeps me toasty thinking about this mouth." Her lips parted under the urging of his thumb. She checked the urge to insert it into her mouth. "Other things about you, too. All the other things."

She closed her eyes, turning her cheek to his palm. "You're making me blush."

"That helps, too," he said, "as I know all the little places that blush leads me when I'm taking off your clothes, one layer at a time."

He was touching her now through the gate, hands soft on her curves. She stopped thinking—just stopped. How was she supposed to concentrate or, hell, function on any level when she knew he thought about her like this? She had hay stuck to her sweater, rips in her jeans and mud on her boots. This morning, she'd tied her hair back in a tangled mess at the base of her neck. She smelled like horse—horse hair, horse sweat, horse slobber. Still, this was how he thought about her. "You can't take off my clothes here."

"We could go skinny-dipping," he suggested, framing her hips as his mouth turned its attention to the column of her throat. "Like we used to. You remember."

She did, vividly. "It'd be more of a polar plunge at this point. I'm not sure you could perform after a shock like that."

"Ain't no harm in trying, sweetheart."

It brought a laugh out of her, as he'd intended. She pushed him away. "Recall that the sheriff's here."

"I'm going to have to have a word with him," he said, hanging his head as she opened the gate and guided Sheridan through.

"About?"

"Wiping away that smile," he said. "I'm helpless when you smile. You know that, don't you?"

"You need to stop talking."

He'd fallen into step as she made her way to the stable yard. The easy way his hand found hers, linked and held, didn't go unnoticed. It was natural to walk hand in hand with him. "To you? Never."

"Sheridan's going to take a bite out of you," she warned.

"Tell me it's not worth it."

She started to laugh again. It died in her throat when Sheriff Jones came around the side of the building. "Uh-oh."

Ellis growled. "I'll take care of him."

"No," she said. "I'll see what he wants."

"What he wants is to rattle your cage." His hand tightened on hers. "Let him try it. I might be in the mood for a misdemeanor."

"Ellis," she said. As they drew closer, the sunlight glinted off the sheriff's sunglasses. Something stirred in her blood. She frowned when she recognized it as a frisson of fear.

"Can I help you, Sheriff?" Ellis asked.

"Eaton," he greeted. "I'd like a word with Ms. Decker, if you don't mind."

"Oh, but I do," Ellis said in a tumbled rush that spoke of his irritation.

Luella frowned at them. "What can I do for you, Sheriff?"

"You can give me your whereabouts from last Sunday," he said, drawing his writing pad from his back pocket. He flipped through. "The eighteenth, around noon."

"What is this about?" she asked as Ellis shifted his feet, impatient.

"I'd like your whereabouts," he stated again, stubbornly.

"I was at Kaya Altaha's house most of the weekend," she answered.

"My deputy's?"

"She let me stay a couple of nights there," Luella explained.

"And you'd say that's your alibi for the time in question?"

"Alibi?" Ellis snapped. "You mind telling us what your meaning is exactly?"

The frisson of fear had started to drench her in a cold sweat.

"Rowdy Conway," Jones said.

"What about him?" Luella wondered.

"Somebody tried to run him off the road between the southeast pasture here at Eaton Edge and town," Jones said. He planted his hands on his belt. "It was a truck driven by someone that matched your description."

"He saw *me*?" she said doubtfully.

"He said he thought it was you," Jones explained. "And since it was you who assaulted him at Hatchet House days before—"

"Oh, for God's sake—" she began.

"—I'd say he's got his reasons for assuming so."

She shook her head. "It wasn't me, Sheriff."

"You're certain?"

"Pretty darn," she drawled.

"I'll be checking with Deputy Altaha to ascertain your whereabouts," he said, stuffing the notebook back in his pocket. "Until then…don't leave town."

"Jesus Christ," Ellis muttered.

Luella narrowed her eyes on Jones's back as he strolled in the direction of Eaton House. "What was Rowdy Conway doing near the Edge's southeast gate the same afternoon Ellis found my cat dead out there?" she called after him. When he stopped and rotated half-way around to study her again, she shrugged. "Did you think to ask him that question when he came to you with these claims?"

Jones considered her. Then he lifted a hand to pinch the brim of his hat in parting and kept going.

"Son of a bitch," Ellis groaned. "Surprised he didn't arrest you, just for the fun of it. Give it time. He'll be back."

"Yes," she said wearily.

"We'll be ready."

She glowered at the determined glint in his eyes. "Don't do anything stupid."

"I'm an Eaton, honey," he argued. "We don't call it stupidity. We call it defense, and there's nothing we take more seriously than defending our own." His gaze was a hot, dark lance as he snuck a kiss over her stunned lips. "You're mine. My own. Nothing's going to stand in the way of that. Not even the goddamn sheriff of Fuego County. Let him come. I'm waitin'."

As he walked away, too, she released a heavy breath.

Why did he always say the words that were bound to disarm her most? She closed her eyes, briefly, before petting Sheridan on the neck and leading him into the safety of the stables.

She jumped when she nearly ran into Everett. "Make some noise, why don't you?" she suggested.

"He's right," he told her.

"Which part?" she asked. "There's a lot there to digest."

"All of it," Everett said. "We're Eatons. We defend ours—all of ours. Doesn't matter who from."

"*You'd* defend me?" she challenged. "From the sheriff?"

"In a heartbeat."

There was no hesitation. Luella was stunned beyond belief.

"I'd have done it," he claimed, "had you let him keep you seventeen years ago. We might've been better off if we'd finished off your father then."

"And I'm the one who has to live with that," she assured him.

"We all live with it," he told her. "Ellis has carried it for almost twenty years. You'll remember that before you think about leaving him again. When he says he's all in, he's all in, baby. There's nothing more certain in this world than my brother when it comes to his kids and his woman." She opened her mouth to reply, but he intervened. "*You're* his woman. It was never that other one. Let him give you the life he wants to—the life he's always wanted to give you. I'd say he's earned it."

Before she could offer any sort of reply, he stalked off in long strides. She heard him holler at Lucas.

It was hard enough trying to figure out her own heart and mind—never mind having to deal with two tall, dark and brooding Eaton men.

* * *

Luella and Altaha had taken to meeting at Ollero Creek a couple of mornings a week. It was the deputy's opportunity to update her on the San Gabriel case as well as try taking another crack at Mabel's messages. It was Luella's chance to sit with the rooms and try to figure out if she really wanted to sell them.

She didn't take her panic attack after speaking to Ms. Breslin lightly. Did she really want to leave Fuego—or was she just being chicken about the final plunge? Once the house was on the market, that was it. No turning back. No changing her mind. But she wasn't going to do it unless she was absolutely certain it was the right choice.

The trouble was, she had no idea what was right anymore.

She stood in front of the window overlooking the plain. The snow was all melted. In the distance, she could see clouds, but not the kind that brought snow from the mountains. It would bring cold rain and thunder. By nightfall, everybody in Fuego would be sheltering from the storm.

Deer were visible, she saw with a start. She stepped closer to the glass, squinting. Three does. Or perhaps a mother and two large fawns. She saw the smile in her reflection and blinked.

She'd caught herself doing that quite a bit over the last few days.

A few days of contentment—were they enough to make the decision that would determine where she should spend the rest of her life? A few days of happiness amid a lifetime of chaos.

She couldn't count on happiness. Or, at least she hadn't thought she could. After the lecture from Everett and

Ellis's intimate attentions of the last few days... Well, she was starting to believe. That was a hell of a lot scarier than a storm. Her whole belief system was in upheaval and it was all their fault.

It wasn't just the brothers. It was Eveline, who she'd been sharing stable duties with. They'd discussed her dream of opening a horse rescue either at the Edge or on the property she now shared with Wolfe just outside Fuego city limits. It sounded not just like a noble pursuit but an important one. Her excitement had been tangible.

Hell, it was contagious. Luella bit her lip. Wouldn't it be nice helping rehabilitate horses who'd had a rough start in life? Horses like Sheridan.

The kitchen door opened and Altaha breezed in with a burst of cold. "Wind's picking up," she noted, stomping her feet on the rug. "It's going to get wicked."

"Yes," Luella said, frowning at those storm clouds on the horizon. "Did you find anything out there?"

"Nothing," the deputy said, removing her hat. "Everything's clear."

Luella breathed a little easier as Altaha joined her near the window. On the long expanse of wall next to it, the deputy had already started an elaborate link chart. Mabel's postcard messages had been tacked amongst various names—Luella, Ellis, Hammond, Everett, Dr. Bredston (aka Bridestone), RN Lacey Scott, Mabel, Riane and Baby. Altaha had used Post-its to make notes under each name. The messages Luella had already figured out also had Post-its with the meaning written on each.

In the center hung the photograph Mabel had sent her of her mother and the mystery man.

Altaha bounced on the balls of her feet. "I feel closer."

Luella narrowed her eyes on the board. "Nothing's changed here. How could you feel closer?"

"I feel it," Altaha repeated with a bob of her head. "Starting here." She tapped the face of the mystery man in the photograph. "Why would your aunt send you this particular photograph?"

Luella lifted her shoulders. "I don't know."

Altaha pursed her lips. "You remember what Riane said during our sit-down at her house."

"She said a lot of things," Luella remembered. "None of them good."

"She said she did what she did with your baby so that you didn't have to raise a bastard…"

Luella's stomach clutched. "Like she did," she finished dimly. She had mulled over the words. Had Riane meant that? Was Luella a product of a relationship other than the disastrous one Riane had had with Whip Decker… or had Riane said it simply to hurt her?

It was a toss-up, really.

Nonetheless, Luella found her focus returning to the mystery man. "You believed her. And you think this man may be my father."

"It's a theory I've been working," Altaha admitted. "You have to see it makes sense." She pointed to Mabel's postcards, one by one. "'Mother.' 'Father…'"

Luella stared at the third. "'Baby.'"

"Maybe Mabel was wiser than any of us thought," Altaha suggested. "Maybe everything about this comes full circle."

"Maybe…" Luella let the possibilities hang in the air. "She hasn't led us wrong with any of the others. 'Night-stand.'"

"The date," Altaha added, nodding to the card with *S.9.06.*

"And the abbreviation," Luella said, frowning at *S.G.W.C.*

"We'll need the testimony of Lacey Scott to charge Riane as most of Bredston's wife's statement is supposition and probably won't hold up once Riane's lawyers sink their teeth into it…"

"Have you had any luck finding the baby?" Luella asked. In her mind, her son was still a baby. It'd taken a while to bring herself around to fully accept the miracle that he was alive, much less a teenage boy fast approaching adulthood.

"No," Altaha said. "Adoptions have a lot of red tape around them, particularly closed adoptions. It may take weeks. Maybe months before we get through it."

Luella nodded. "We'll keep trying."

"Of course, we will," Altaha assured her. "Until then, we should figure out what the last message means."

"'W.J.' It's got to be initials," Luella stated.

"I ran a search through county residents to see how many people with the initials W.J. there are around here."

"What'd you come up with?"

Altaha made a face. "Roughly a hundred."

"Wow," Luella said. She shook her head. "That's discouraging."

"I printed lists from both San Gabriel and Fuego in 1987, 2006 and now, but I've only just started combing for names that are familiar. I want you to take a look at them, too. Something, or someone, might pop out at you. We just need to narrow it down. Once we get fifteen or so, I can start knocking on doors, asking questions…"

Luella nodded. "I can do that." She stared at the *Baby*

card again. "I wish we knew his name. If I just knew his name…all this would be better."

"We'll find it," Altaha told her. "I won't stop looking for your child. Not until he's found."

"Thank you," Luella said, "Kaya."

Altaha's mouth formed into a warm smile. "You're welcome, Luella. Hey, I forgot to mention. I checked your game camera footage again this morning."

As the deputy pulled out her phone and logged into Luella's security server, Luella leaned over her shoulder. Altaha backtracked through the footage from the night before. "At approximately two twenty-two…"

Luella made herself take a steadying breath as she watched a large figure lumber across her empty yard. "His back's to the cameras."

"Look at the way he's walking."

Luella hated how ghostly the image of the man looked in night vision. Everything was pixelated in shades of gray while the killer's form floated like an apparition.

No, *floated* was the wrong word, Luella realized, looking again. "He's limping."

"Mmm-hmm," Altaha said, her smile fixed. "The injury's to his right leg or hip."

Luella's eyes grew round. "You could check the hospital—see if there's been someone admitted for an injury."

"I did, before I knew where Ellis's bullet hit the guy," Altaha informed her. "There were no gunshot wounds reported within seventy-two hours at Fuego County Hospital or the urgent cares around here."

"Oh," Luella said, deflating.

"But knowing it's his right side… If he knows how to work the system then he may have convinced a doctor to supply him with pain meds, anti-inflammatories, antibiotics."

"What was he doing, do you think—at the house?"

"I think he was checking to see whether or not you were home."

"If I had been?" Luella wondered, quietly.

"Best you not dwell on that one," Altaha said. "You're not leaving Eaton Edge anytime soon, are you?"

"I don't know what I'm doing." The words spilled faster than Luella could catch them. When Altaha only stared, Luella licked her lips. "Well. It's true. I don't know what I'm doing...or what to do."

"About your living situation...," Altaha asked, "or the other thing?"

The other thing was Ellis, of course, and his feelings for her. Her feelings for him. Their feelings for each other. "It's hard to think about leaving," Luella admitted in a low voice, "when I don't know where our son is. How would you contact me if you did find him?"

"*When* we find him," Altaha amended. "Is that the only thing keeping you here?"

"I don't know," Luella lied, pacing to the other end of the kitchen. "It would be easier to sell everything...start over somewhere new. Somewhere no one knows who I am...who my family is..."

Altaha gave a nod. "That would be easier. I know I haven't had it as hard as you. But if you'd told me a year ago that Wolfe Coldero—that kid who showed up on the Edge beaten and silent and nearly broken—could be living life as good as he is now, I wouldn't have believed it."

Luella thought about it. "Wolfe's lucky. And he deserves a good life."

"You deserve one, too," Altaha insisted. "And if anybody in this town disagrees with that, they can go straight to hell."

Luella laughed in a sudden burst. Miracles did happen, she was finding, one confidante at a time.

Before either of them could speak, Altaha's phone rang. She frowned at the caller ID. "Well, well. Lacey Scott found us." She glanced at Luella. "I need to take this."

"Go ahead," Luella said. "I'll be outside."

Chapter 16

The wind stung her eyes but she stared nonetheless at the land. Now that the ice was gone, the grass stirred. It whispered.

So much space, she thought. How many times had she thought about buying a telescope, building some sort of shed out in the open so that she could observe the heavens from its roof?

The thought had brought too many memories of her and Ellis at Eaton Edge. She'd always dismissed it.

Space, she considered. It wasn't the cosmos, she realized. It was right here, on Earth.

Why *had* she bought all this space? It was too much for one person. She'd wanted to make use of it, somehow. But the thought of her father lurking out there somewhere when she'd known he was alive had scared her enough to give up any ideas or possibilities...

Possibilities.

"Eveline," Luella said. "Eveline's horses."

Eveline had admitted that her and Wolfe's place was too shrubby. The desert terrain out near them was too unfriendly. It would require a lot of work to turn it into a horse haven. And the Edge was already a multitiered operation in and of itself. The Eatons and their cowboys had their hands full.

But here… Why not here, where the grasses ran wild… where there was plenty of room to build and for animals to roam?

It was be a risk. But Luella had known it would be worth it, from the moment Evenline had mentioned it.

Risk. Possibilities. Dreams.

Luella grinned until her cheeks ached. Her heart beat a little faster, a little lighter. *Finally*, something she wanted. Something she could do. Something she could be passionate about other than Ellis and the search for her baby… This might be the thing—like Sheridan, the thing that quieted all the noise in her head, that brought her back from the edge of numbness and disquiet…

And if she could reach for that…was it really that much more of a stretch—reaching for a future with the man she loved?

She'd done it once. She'd fallen on her face—but not because he hadn't loved her.

They would have built, too. She and Ellis…they wouldn't just have dreamed it. They'd have built it—the lives that they'd mapped out in words.

Castles in the sky were real, Luella knew now. With the right amount of intention and the love she knew she felt for him and he felt for her, those castles became homes. And they'd live in one together, with Isla and Ingrid and maybe—*oh, God*—one day, their son, too.

She heard Altaha coming down the porch steps. She turned, beaming. "I know what I want now. I know *everything* I want. I..." She stopped. "What? What is it?"

"Lacey Scott," Altaha said, lifting her phone in indication. "She says she had knowledge of the con your mother and Bredston ran. She lied to you in the delivery, but not because your mother got to her or the doctor. She refused them both when they approached her."

"Then why did she do it?"

"She was coerced," Altaha stated, "by a cop."

"A cop?" Since when was there *a cop* in this story? They should have been narrowing down the perpetrators, not chasing new leads. "A real cop?"

"A deputy, as a matter of fact," Altaha revealed. "A Fuego County deputy."

"Does she remember his name?" Luella asked.

"He didn't give one," Altaha said. "But she gave a description of him. Luella, I'm sorry. It's been right in front of me."

"What?" Luella asked. "*Who is it?*"

"It's Jones," Altaha said.

Luella faltered. "The...sheriff?"

"It fits," Altaha said, moving with her thoughts. Her feet took her around in circles as she laid it all out. "He wouldn't have been a sheriff in 2006. He was a deputy, like me. He's been around since then. Born in Taos, moved to Fuego with the wife in the mideighties. 'W.J.?' His name's Wendell, for God's sake. Damn it, I'm such an idiot. I mean, look. Look at this!"

She was holding Mabel's photograph. With new eyes, Luella stared at the mystery man next to her mother. Full head of hair, slim hips, mustache...but she saw it now, too. She saw Sheriff Jones all but screaming at her out of the man's face. "Oh, my God." She felt sick. All her good feelings from moments before were gone. "Wh-what do we do?"

"I'd like to visit his wife, Katie. She should see the photo. We can't confirm it's him in the photograph... not until she does."

"Okay," Luella said. She trailed Altaha to her police vehicle. "This is my fight. If Jones is involved in my baby's disappearance, I'd like to see you bring him in."

"I'll allow it," Altaha decided. "Your head's cooler than your boyfriend's. I don't think I have to worry about you running off doing vigilante nonsense."

Jones shared a pretty cabin with his wife, a dental hygienist. Altaha knocked on the front door. There was a wooden sign hanging underneath the peephole. It read *The Jones Family, Est. 1985*. Luella had gone to school with the sheriff's son, Mark. He'd been quarterback of the Fuego football team.

He'd called her *devil's daughter*, just as Rowdy Conway did.

Luella felt light-headed. She rocked herself from side to side.

"Do you need to wait in the truck?" Altaha asked without turning her head.

"I'm good. Just...weird feeling, is all."

"Hold it together for me," Altaha urged. She straightened when the door unlocked from the inside and Katie Jones peered out. "Mrs. Jones."

"Deputy Altaha," Katie said, pulling the door back from the jamb. Her smile started then stopped when she found Luella next to her. "Oh. What—"

"Is the sheriff at home?" Altaha kept her tone even.

"No," Katie said, "As far as I know, he's at the station house today."

Altaha relaxed. Luella felt it more than saw it.

"I'd invite you in," Katie said, glancing over her shoulder, "but we've got the kids home for the holidays."

"That's a fine thing," Altaha said. She was trying to set Katie at ease, Luella knew. "It's been a while since the both of them have come home at the same time, hasn't it?"

"Yes." Katie's dimples flashed in a brief smile. "Yes, Mark and his wife, Keegan, flew in last night. Sybil and the grands have been here for several days. Her husband, Jim, will join us over the weekend."

"A full house for Christmas, then?"

"Yes. Isn't it wonderful?"

"Absolutely. Listen, Mrs. Jones, I know you're busy and I don't want to take up too much of your time, but I was hoping you could help me with something."

"Okay," Katie said. She stepped out on the porch, closing the door behind her. Luella didn't miss how her eyes strayed to her and the smile dimmed.

Altaha took the photograph out of a manila folder. "I was wondering if you could identify this man here for me."

Katie took the picture in both hands. "Oh," she said, a quick grin flashing across her face. "Oh, Wendell. Look how handsome. It's been so long since…"

The grin tapered off little by little. Her eyes raced across other details in the snapshot. She shook her head. "Why…?" She stopped, cleared her throat and thrust the photograph back at Altaha. "When was this taken?"

"March 11, 1987," Altaha explained. "It was taken by

Luella's aunt, Mabel Brinkley. We're certain the woman in the photograph with him is—"

"Riane," Katie said. She rubbed her lips together, as if she'd blurted it out by accident. "Riane Decker." Her frown strengthened. "This one's mother."

"She was a Brinkley, too, at the time," Luella threw in. "She married my father in February of the following year."

"A shotgun wedding," Katie remembered.

Altaha studied her closely. "I'm sorry, Katie, but I have to ask. What was the nature of your husband's relationship with Riane at the time this picture was taken?"

"We were friends," Katie murmured, her mouth drawn. "We were good friends...for a time. Riane...she was good fun. Always at the rodeo. She liked the men. The cowboys. She fancied herself a buckle bunny."

"My mother?" Luella said, shocked by the idea.

"Oh, yes," Katie said, drawing her sweater around her. She didn't meet Luella's eye. "She... I... Well, we were all different back then."

"What do you mean by that?" Altaha asked.

Katie rolled her eyes. "Oh, come on, Kaya. You weren't born yesterday." When Altaha only continued to wait for an explanation, she blew out a breath. "We were swingers, all right? Wendell and I. Hell, all us newlyweds were."

"Was Riane involved in this lifestyle, too?" Altaha ventured.

"Very much so," Katie said with a nod.

"Were she and your husband involved sexually?" Altaha asked delicately.

Katie closed her eyes. She brought her forehead down to her hand and scrubbed her temple. "It was so long ago. So damn long ago. What does it *matter* anymore what they were?"

"It's important, I'm afraid."

Katie dropped her hand. She kept her eyes closed. "Yes. They were involved."

"How long, would you say?" Altaha asked.

"Long enough."

"Can you be a little more exact?"

Katie cursed impressively. For the first time, she raised her voice. "I don't know, Deputy. I don't know. For a while, it was just harmless fun. I slept around, too, but no one shows up on my doorstep asking about that."

"So you knew about the affair."

Katie's expression grew frosty. "Did I say it was an affair?"

"My mistake," Altaha said.

Katie's shoulders rose and fell quickly. Her breathing had quickened.

Altaha gave her a moment to gather herself. "You knew they were sleeping together."

"I did," Katie said. "It meant little."

"I'm trying to establish a timeline," Altaha said, carefully. "When would you say they stopped? They did stop. Didn't they?"

"He said they did. I found out I was pregnant with Mark. He was Wendell's child. I never had any doubt about that. But I wanted to stop. The parties…the drinking… I don't mind telling you, the drugs that came along with it…it wasn't healthy. I wanted us both to be healthy. Stable. So we stopped being swingers."

Altaha waited, as if she could smell more.

Luella tried to fade into the background. Was there more?

It came slowly, the distress. First, Katie's breathing increased once more. Then she blinked, and there it was in her eyes. She looked to Luella, accusation painted there.

Luella's lips parted. "It didn't stop," she realized in a whisper. "He went back to her."

"She chased after him," Katie returned. "Like a *bitch* in heat. She practically stalked him, for Christ's sake. I caught her in the house once. He said she'd been waiting when he came home…in our room. It's disgusting."

"Did he indicate that the encounter was nonconsensual?" Altaha asked.

"No," Katie said. "Not exactly. But…he told her he was done. And she couldn't accept it."

"Okay," Altaha said. "One more question and I'll let you go back to your family."

"That would be nice," Katie said irritably.

"How long was it between Riane's last encounter with your husband and her marriage to Jace Decker?" Altaha wanted to know.

Katie shook her head. "I can't answer that."

"Why not?" Luella found herself asking.

Katie scowled at her. "Because I don't know when the last time was! The doctor put me on bed rest and Wendell said he wasn't going to the rodeo anymore. But sometimes he'd come in late, drunk or high as a kite and smelling of her cheap perfume…like he was addicted to her. It was horrible—absolutely horrible. It only stopped after Jace entered the picture. He put a stop to it. Your father wasn't a good man, but at least he put a stop to Riane's exploits. Once he entered the picture, Wendell stopped going to the rodeo. Once she stopped chasing him, he had a chance to straighten out—to become the husband and father I knew he could be."

Luella didn't know where it came from, but the question leaped out of her mouth. "Has the sheriff been acting oddly over the last month?"

Katie shook her head. "In what way?"

"Coming in late at odd hours," Luella elaborated.

"He's a police officer," Katie said "Of course, he comes in at odd hours."

Altaha took up the line of questioning. "Yes, but has he seemed off to you?"

Katie scoffed. "No. I mean, he's been in some pain. But other than that—"

"Pain." Altaha latched onto the word, a dog with a bone. "What kind of pain?"

"You know he was hurt on the job," Katie said. When Altaha said nothing, she added quickly, "A few weeks ago. He said there was some scuffle out in the county. A domestic dispute that got out of hand. He took a bullet."

"Where?"

"What?"

"What part of his body, Katie?" Altaha insisted.

"His leg."

"The right or the left?"

"The right!" Katie shrieked. "Jesus, you *know* this!"

Altaha exchanged a look with Luella.

Luella felt her color draining. Little black spots floated around the edges of her vision.

The sheriff wasn't just the cop who had most likely coerced Lacey Scott to participate in her baby's kidnapping. He'd had a blistering affair with her mother. And he was the one who'd killed her chickens, her cat, and who had abducted and shot Sheridan and Ellis.

"You say he's been at the station," Altaha clarified with Katie.

"That's what he told me." As they both moved off the

porch in quick strides, Katie came after them. "Wait. What is this about? Why is Luella here? And why do you need to find him?"

Altaha spoke into the radio on the shoulder of her uniform. "Hey, Wyatt. Do you read?"

Some static screeched over the line then the voice of her fellow deputy. "Ten-four, Altaha."

"Switch to Channel Two, will you?" Altaha asked him, opening the door to her truck and piling in. She waited until Luella joined her before cranking the engine. Katie stood outside the truck, her face a map of questions. When Deputy Wyatt replied that he had changed channels, she asked, "Are you at the station?"

"Root and I just left."

"Was Jones there?"

"That's a negative."

Altaha cursed. "Has anybody had eyes on him today?"

"Ah… I haven't. Root says he hasn't. If you open the channel, I'm sure you could contact him directly."

Luella straightened in her seat. "She's making a call." She pointed at Katie outside of the truck. Her cell phone was in her hands and she was dialing.

"We're out of time," Altaha agreed. She turned her mouth to the speaker again. "This is an APB. I need a location on the sheriff, boys."

"An APB? On *Jones*?"

"I believe he is armed and dangerous," Altaha reported, putting the truck in reverse.

Luella grabbed the handle over her head as the tires skidded across the driveway and Altaha backed out to the highway, jerking the wheel. Luella glanced back in the direction of the home. "Three miles," she muttered. "His house is three miles from Ollero Creek."

"If that."

"But…why did he kill my animals? I don't understand *anything*."

"We'll find out," Altaha asserted, "if we catch him before he flees town. Hang on." She toggled the siren and mashed on the gas.

Chapter 17

The clouds fretted and flickered. They swept in sideways across the Edge, bringing a downpour. It was too hard a rain to spit sleet, and the sky was far too hot-tempered for snow.

This storm had been building. It'd worked itself into a fine fury, one that made the horses out in pasture spook and the cattle low fitfully.

"Get 'em all in," Ellis instructed. "Make sure the gates are locked. I don't want to be chasing them in this mess. Lucas, watch that bull. He'll take the hide off of you. Javier, make sure Eveline and Griff have a handle on the horses."

Everett sprinted up. "A moment?"

"We don't really have one," Ellis said. "You see what's coming."

"It's Jones," Everett said.

That got Ellis's attention. "What about him?"

"He's back, looking for Luella."

"Is he?" Ellis considered. "Did he give a reason?"

"No. He's not leaving without her."

Ellis exchanged a meaningful look with his brother. "It might be time he stepped into my office, for a change," he said, nodding toward the barn.

Everett's grin was sharp. He rocked back on his heels, considering. "I like where your mind's at."

As Everett walked back toward the house, Ellis scanned the yard. The others had a handle on things. Even Lucas. The boy was coming along. When he saw Wolfe come out of the stables, he waved him over. At his approach, Ellis said, "Trouble's here. Stick around?"

Wolfe raised a brow but didn't question him. He nodded.

Ellis ushered him inside because he could see Jones, his head low to stop the wind from carrying off his hat, making his way around the first corral.

The sound and smell of cattle would've been oppressive had Ellis not grown up with it. He checked in with the other hands, made sure everyone had a handle on their business. He reached through the rungs of a fence to check the hay. It was dry.

Wolfe tapped Ellis on the back. He turned and saw the sheriff duck inside. "Be ready," he muttered before he stood up. "Sheriff."

"Eaton," Jones returned.

"You interested in joining the cattle business?" Ellis wondered. "You can't seem to stay away."

"I'm looking for Ms. Decker," Jones said briskly. "Your brother said you know her location."

"I do," Ellis said, reaching back to scratch his neck. "Unfortunately for you, I'm not willing to share it."

Jones's gaze had been roving over the restless heifers in the nearest pen. It seized on Ellis. "She's a suspect in my case."

"She's nothing of the sort," Ellis rebutted.

Jones shifted his weight.

Ellis stilled when the sheriff's hands went to his gun belt. Behind him, he could all but feel Wolfe's readiness.

"What're you a cop now, too?" Jones asked him.

"No," Ellis said. "But I know the truth and that's that you're making her life difficult. I think it's time you admit why."

A humorless smile touched Jones's mouth as he scanned Wolfe. "You Eatons. You're all the same. You think you're above the law, one step ahead of us... Before all this, I thought you may have been the sane one. But you live so long with crazy, you become it. You crossed the line, right around the time you started screwing Luella again."

"You don't get to say her name, Sheriff," Ellis warned. "Not in my house."

"I can call her what I damn well want. And I can make her life harder."

"Can you?"

"You have no idea what I am capable of, Mr. Eaton," Jones said. "No idea."

Before the two men could square off, the chirping of a ringtone reached Ellis's ears. Jones stopped. His teeth showed as he took a step back, dug into the pocket of his slacks and pulled out his cell phone. He scanned the screen. "We're not done here," he said before turning halfway away to answer.

"I sure hope not," Ellis returned.

As Jones took the call, Ellis risked a look back at Wolfe. Wolfe may have looked unflappable to anyone else.

But Ellis recognized the ticcing muscle in his jaw, the flexed tendons of his neck. The tension was enormous.

His friend sensed exactly what he did. Something about Jones was off and for once it had little to do with Wolfe's or Ellis's personal aversion of the man.

"What?" Jones snapped. His face hardened. Ellis saw the sheen of sweat on it for the first time as he cast a furtive look in their direction. "When? When did they…" He listened. His free hand fisted, the knuckles white. "Listen carefully," he said, lowering his voice. He turned on his heel and retreated toward the door.

Ellis let him go. Then he saw the hitch in Jones's gait.

With every step, Jones favored his right leg.

Ellis's mind flew back to the snowstorm—the shadow in his scope—how it had bowled over after Ellis squeezed the trigger before it disappeared into the whiteout…

His heart racked his ribs as he told himself to stay calm. Following Jones, he thought quickly.

The sheriff lived on the same side of town as Ollero Creek.

He'd been dogging Luella since her return.

You have no idea what I'm capable of.

I'll be goddammed, Ellis thought. He caught sight of Javier near the door. He gave him a tip of the chin.

Javier did the same in response then shut the barn door soundly, blocking the sheriff's exit.

Jones's feet faltered. He stopped muttering instructions into the phone, bringing his hand up to block sound from entering the receiver. "Open that door," he demanded of Javier.

"I don't think so, Sheriff," Ellis answered for him, putting himself, too, between Jones and the exit.

Jones looked around, found Wolfe ready at his back.

He pulled his hand away from the phone. "I'll call you back," he said before he shoved the phone in his pocket. "Open the door and this will end peacefully."

"Fine," Ellis said. "Tell me why you did it."

"Did what?" Jones snapped.

"Tell me why you slaughtered Luella's flock," Ellis told him. "Tell me why you shot her horse and killed her cat."

Jones's expression went carefully blank. "Stand down," Jones said and he reached for the Glock strapped to his hip.

Ellis reached around, too, to palm the pistol he kept nestled in the waistband of his jeans. "You first."

Jones didn't move but for the beads of perspiration creeping down his cheeks. Then his grip on the gun tightened.

Ellis swung his around and up as Jones raised his. Shots rang out. The herd moaned and milled, straining against the fences, as the hands ducked down with shouts of "Get down!"

Altaha and Luella tracked Jones to the Edge, thanks to a 911 call. The words *shots fired* rang in Luella's head as Altaha drove her truck right up to the front porch of Eaton House, killing the siren.

The deputy unbuckled, her weapon ready in her hand. "Stay here."

"Like hell," Luella said, grabbing her shotgun and scrambling out the passenger door. She saw Paloma. "Are you okay?"

"They're in the barn," Paloma said. "Is it true the sheriff—"

"Stay here," Altaha instructed. "If any other deputies arrive, tell them what you told me. Luella, you stay, damn it!"

"I'm coming," Luella said and cocked the shotgun for good measure. As they rounded the house, she choked back a scream when Everett nearly ran into them.

"Deputy," he said, breathing hard. He, too, was carrying a weapon. "Sweetheart. You seen Paloma?"

"She's that way," Altaha said, pointing. "Give me a rundown."

Everett opened his mouth but the sound of gunfire made them brace themselves against the wall of the house. "Get down," he said, pressing a hand into Altaha's shoulder.

She shrugged it off. "*I'm* the police officer. *You* get down."

"Ellis has got him pinned in the barn," Everett stated.

"Ellis?" Luella asked, distressed. "He's in there?"

"Him, Wolfe, Javier, Lucas and one or two more of our men," he explained.

"How did it start?" Altaha asked.

"The sheriff came looking for you," Everett said of Luella.

"How long has the standoff been in progress?"

"Fifteen minutes."

"Is anyone down?"

"I'd be surprised if everyone's still standing after all the shots we've heard."

Altaha placed a hand on his arm. His attention came back to her. Luella noticed for the first time the line of sweat along his upper lip and his unnatural pallor.

"Are you okay?" Altaha asked, quietly.

"I need my brother and my men out of there," Everett said in no uncertain terms.

"How many access points does that barn have?" she asked.

"One on the east side. There's a weak spot on the north side. We did a quick patch on it a few weeks ago with plywood. With the right tools, we can breach it in seconds."

"That sounds like the best bet. Wait here for backup. Send them my way."

"You're not going alone," Everett asserted, jumping to his feet as she did. "Those are my men in there."

Luella stood, too. "I'm coming with you, too."

"Don't either of you understand?" Altaha asked. "Jones is armed and dangerous and we now know he's capable of murder."

"Come again?" Everett asked. More gunfire made Altaha take off running. Everett and Luella didn't stay behind. He took the safety off his pistol and frowned at Luella as she kept pace with him. "Nice weapon you got there. You know how to shoot it?"

Luella groaned at him. "Just stay out of my way."

"Likewise."

Ellis stayed low behind a large rolled-up section of barbed wire. As cover, it wasn't ideal but it was working for the moment. He tried to listen over the frantic sounds of the cows for Jones's movements. As far as he knew, they still had him pinned behind a stack of lumber.

At least their position was between Jones and the door. Ellis glanced over at the sound of a pained moan.

Wolfe was tending to Javier. He'd been hit in the first exchange of gunfire. The bullet from Jones's gun had been meant for Ellis but had bounced off the wall and hit Javier instead. "How much time do we have?" he asked, concerned by the amount of blood on the shoulder of Javier's shirt.

Wolfe's hands were strained with it. They moved quickly. *Need a doctor. Now.*

Ellis tried peeking out from behind his position. Another shot volleyed from Jones's position. It hit somewhere over Ellis's head. He ducked back down. "I don't have enough ammo left for the cover fire you need to get him to the door." He narrowed his eyes in the direction he knew Lucas and the other young ranch hand Mateo were hiding out some twenty feet away. He hoped to God they stayed there. "We need a distraction."

As if on cue, the wall near to Jones's position splintered. More, the plywood over a weak section of wood caved in. An unmanned Polaris buzzed into the arena, sending heifers scattering, their eyes whiting. "What the hell?" Ellis said a split second before Altaha rushed in with Everett on her heels.

Wolfe made a noise. Ellis waved him on as Altaha and Everett drew Jones's fire. "Go," he said. "Go!"

Wolfe hauled Javier onto his shoulder and, in a crouch, headed for the door. Ellis's heart was in his ears as he counted the seconds it took for the two of them to get through. When the door closed behind them, he breathed a sigh of relief.

They weren't out of the woods yet. He looked around the wiring, trying to get a sense of what was happening.

Jones was shooting in the direction Everett and Altaha had taken toward an alcove where they could hunker down.

Altaha didn't make it. Ellis saw her go down, heard her cry over the din. Everett didn't miss a beat. He scooped her up and got her behind the wall before Jones squeezed off another round.

Ellis heard the sound he'd been anticipating for the last few minutes.

The empty click from Jones's weapon's chamber. There was a curse that followed. The sheriff was out of ammo.

Ellis thought about advancing then hesitated. Did Jones carry an extra clip on him?

Ellis wet his throat and called, "I know you're out! Stand up and let me see your hands!"

There wasn't an answer. Nor did Ellis see those hands.

Gritting his teeth, Ellis thought quickly. "We'll lay down our weapons, all of us, if you come out nice and slow." A shadow crept through the opening in the wall near Jones's position. Ellis squinted. His eyes went wide when he saw Luella's silhouette.

Jones's attention was on his belt. His Glock was on the floor between his knees, empty. His baton was in one hand and he was searching for something else.

Keeping to the shadows of the wall, Luella kept her shotgun out in front of her, her finger on the trigger. Putting one foot in front of the other, she crept like she'd seen a mountain lion creep through the tall grass at Ollero Creek. It'd been stalking a family of pronghorns.

Ellis raised his voice. "I'm going to give you to the count of three, Sheriff! One…two…"

The barrel of her gun came up against the side of Jones's head just as he pulled a Taser out of his belt. "Drop it," she told him.

Every muscle in Jones's body froze.

"I said drop it!" she hollered. "Now!"

His fingers loosened around the Taser. It bounced to the barn floor.

"Hands," she said, kicking the Taser away. "In the air. Now."

His palms came up, reaching for the sky.

"Stand," she said, taking a few steps back, enough space so he couldn't snatch the shotgun barrel from her.

He stood, slow and obedient.

"Now turn," she instructed. As his feet shuffled around, she saw him favoring his right side. "Take off the belt and toss it this way. Then empty your pockets—all of them." As he started to, throwing everything out of reach, she shook her head. "It was you."

"It was me," he admitted.

"Why?" she demanded. "*Why* did you do it?"

"For your mother."

Luella's chin dropped. She planted her feet again, to keep herself fixed. "After all this time...she still has a hold on you?"

"Not the kind you're thinking," he argued.

Ellis appeared, his weapon in his hand. He kept it trained on the center of Jones's body. "You got him, honey."

"Are you okay?" she needed to know.

"I'm fine. Javier and Altaha need medical attention."

"I called it in," Everett said from somewhere beyond her. His voice didn't sound right. "Luella..."

"Go," Ellis said, bringing himself around to her position. "I've got this guy."

Luella lowered her weapon slowly, backing away. She found Everett near the alcove he and Altaha had discussed before breaching the wall and dropped to her knees beside him. His hands were pressed, one over the other, on Altaha's left thigh. "I can't stop the bleeding," he said.

"You're doing good," she told him. "Keep pressure on it. Use your knee, if you have to."

"She can't stay awake."

Luella heard the quaver underneath what he said. She leaned the shotgun against the wall after putting the safety back on. It was only as it slipped out of her hands that she realized how slick her palms were. She unclipped her belt and pulled it off quickly. Working in quick, steady movements, she fashioned a tourniquet around Altaha's leg and secured it. Then she checked Altaha's eyes, prying back each lid. "Kaya." She tapped her on the cheek.

Altaha's eyes rolled from the back of her head. "Hm?"

"Hey, friend," Luella greeted. "You've got the hard-ass cattle baron out of sorts over here."

"Mmm," Altaha mumbled. Pain worked over her face and she hissed.

"Sorry," Everett said quickly. "I'm sorry. My hands are only good for cattle branding."

Altaha tilted her head to look at him. "Geez, Eaton," she said, dull. "Go lie down somewhere."

"Once you stop bleeding, sweetheart, I'll do just that."

She closed her eyes, started shaking her head listlessly. "…love your hands…hate it when you call me that…"

Luella tapped her cheek again. "Stay with me. Help's on the way." She kept her voice even, but she breathed a tumultuous sigh when she heard the paramedics rushing in. "Gunshot wound to the left thigh." She rattled off Altaha's status and anything else that might help. Then she pulled Everett back so they could go to work on her.

He winced when the deputy cried out in pain. "It's the tourniquet," Luella explained. "It's supposed to hurt." She found herself rubbing his arm, up and down. "She's in capable hands."

When Everett remained silent, watching them place Altaha on the stretcher, Luella brought her attention back to him. "You're not hurt, are you?"

Everett shook his head.

Luella remembered suddenly what had happened in the box canyon the summer before—how he'd been dealing with PTSD episodes ever since. "You ran into the line of fire," she realized. "That must've been difficult."

"My people were in here. I couldn't sit back and let them…" He trailed off as the medics carted the stretcher out.

Luella gave him something of a smile. "You should be proud of yourself."

He cleared his throat. "I guess we've both made some strides today." At a grunt of protest behind them, they turned to see Jones up against the barn wall. Ellis was cuffing his hands behind his back. "That must do you some good."

Luella's lips thinned. "The police are coming. But I'd like to hear what you have to say, Sheriff—about my mother. You said you did what you did because of her. Explain that."

When Jones hesitated, Ellis pushed him harder against the wall. Jones cursed. "Riane wanted you to leave town," Jones said, his cheek mushed against the plywood. "When you returned from jail, she wanted you gone as fast as possible."

"Why?" Luella asked. "She left Fuego years ago. Is San Gabriel not far enough away?"

"That husband of hers had to leave a good-paying job when news of Whip Decker and his accomplice daughter hit the papers and Riane's connection to it came to light. That was when she contacted me and said if I didn't find some way to get you to leave Fuego after your sentence, she would tell Katie…"

Luella felt her heart in her throat, beating wildly. "Tell her what?"

"…that I'm your father," Jones said. "Your real father."

"How do you know she was telling the truth?" Luella wanted to know. "My mother lies. Don't you know that?"

"When Riane met Whip Decker, she was already pregnant," he revealed, "with my child."

"And you didn't tell your wife any of this," Luella said.

"She was pregnant with Mark," he said. "She was late-term, on bed rest. Her blood pressure was through the roof. How could I tell her I'd put another woman in that position?"

"The woman she didn't want you anywhere near," Luella added.

"Riane was like a fever I couldn't break. She wouldn't let up until you came into the equation."

No wonder Riane had resented her so much. She'd been the other woman and, suddenly, a mother with no means to raise a child. "So she never saw anything in Whip Decker…other than a means to an end."

"She got the short end of that stick," he said.

"You'd have me pity her?" she wondered. "After she made you kill my chickens, my cat and almost my horse?"

"I admit to killing the chickens," he said. "A chicken's nothing more than a meal, when it comes down to it. I couldn't kill the horse. She asked me to. She said that would be the jumping-off point for you. But a horse is another animal altogether. As for the cat, I had nothing to do with that."

"Then who did?" Ellis asked. They could hear people again rustling outside the barn.

"Rowdy Conway all but confessed to it the day he said Luella ran him off the road," Jones stated.

"But you didn't charge him."

"No."

"Why?"

"Because I needed you scared," he said. "I needed you gone. If you'd have just left, none of this mess would've happened."

"If you'd just have come clean with your wife, my chickens and my cat would still be alive," Luella argued. "Ellis wouldn't have been shot. Javier or Altaha, either. You've got a lot to answer for, Sheriff. I hope you're prepared to live with that."

The deputies, Root and Wyatt, filed in. They faltered when they saw the sheriff cornered and restrained. "What…what happened here?" Wyatt asked. "Sir?"

Jones waited several beats, long enough for Ellis to make a frustrated noise behind him. Then he closed his eyes. The muscles around his mouth trembled, making the bristled hairs of mustache vibrate. "Put me in the back of the wagon and take me to the station, boys. You can lower your weapons. I'll come quietly."

Luella watched them lead Jones away through a wide swath of Edge employees. It was raining buckets and running off the men's hats in streams. She stayed under cover of the barn, the smell of animal and hay and blood thick in her nose.

Warmth cloaked her shoulders as hands draped over them. They massaged. Ellis's words flowed over her ear.

"I just about lost my mind when I saw you sneaking up on him. He could've had an extra clip on him. He could've tased you, swung at you…"

"I was ready," she said. "It felt how I think you might have…in the box canyon this summer when you had Whip in your sights."

His arms slid around her. They knitted against her belly, gathering her hands in his as his cheek came to rest against hers. The line of his back was damp from rain or sweat or both. Nothing had ever felt that good. "Whip Decker wasn't your father."

She closed her eyes, turning her temple to his cheek, seeking comfort against the cold. "No."

"You never were the devil's daughter."

Riane's harsh features formed in her mind. She shivered. "That depends on your perspective."

"I'll need to get to the hospital soon to see how Javy's doing. Someone needs to let his wife, Grace, know what's happening, if she doesn't already know."

He'd see to all of that, she thought. He'd see to everything. That was Ellis's way. She gripped his arms tighter, bringing him in closer.

"Do you think Altaha's going to be all right?"

"I don't know," she said, truthfully. "It could just be tissue damage, but if the bullet punctured a bone or a major vessel…"

He nodded off the rest. "What do you want to do, honey? Do you want to go to the hospital or the station?"

She was so tired. She couldn't imagine doing anything but curling up in bed…with him. Tipping her head back to his shoulder, she swayed with him in their little space over the hay. "I want…" she began in a whisper.

"Yeah?"

She pressed her lips together as the certainty washed through her—a fresh, hot wave of excitement. "I want to get married."

He stilled. They stopped swaying. "Do what?"

"I want to get married, Ellis," she stated again, surer.

He turned her to face him, his grip on her upper arms as insistent as his gaze. "Are you serious?"

"We just came out of a gunfight," she said. "We're both covered in blood, sweat, gunpowder and God knows what else... How could I not be serious?"

"You want to marry me," he realized, surprise bleeding into naked joy.

"I want to marry you," she said—because it felt good, so good, to say it again.

He expelled an unsteady breath. His hands reached for her face. "Lu," he whispered.

"I know you aren't free," she said. "But once you are, I'd like to make you mine. I think we've both waited long enough to belong to each other."

"Yes. Yes, we have." He grinned widely. "You just proposed to me."

"I didn't get on one knee like you did," she said with a sentimental smile. "Should I have?"

"Nah. And I like that we've come full circle."

"I'm tired of circling—running, hurting... I want to take up my place here with you. You'll be my constant?"

"It'd be my honor," he said, kissing the point of her cheek, then the other, "and my pleasure to be your constant, Luella Decker."

"Not Decker. I don't have to be a Decker anymore." She smiled, her eyes wet with tears. "That's not my legacy anymore—and it won't have to be our son's either once we find him."

"You're damn right. But what do I call you?" he asked, weaving his hands through hers. "When we get up to the altar and I take you as my own, finally."

"I'll be your Luella Belle," she told him. "Always."

"Always," he said with a satisfactory nod. "Luella Belle Eaton."

She grabbed hold of him. "I like that very much."

Ellis waited outside the police station. He'd wanted to be there when she arrived. He'd needed to be there when it all came to a close.

When he saw the car coming down Main Street, he pushed off the building. Taking off his hat, he waited on the curb for her to bring the vehicle to a slow creep then a complete stop. He tapped the hat against his leg as she stretched her long body out of the driver's seat and looked at him across the hood.

"What's this about, Ellis?" Liberty asked.

"Did you drop the girls off?"

"With Paloma," she stated, shutting her door. She tucked her handbag against her hip.

"Everett delivered my message."

"With relish," she said, lips curling in distaste. "Looks like he's back at the helm."

Ellis nodded. "He's back in his rightful place."

She shook her head. "You could've been so much more."

"I am what I am," he told her. "I'm a brother. I'm a father. I'm my father's son. This is the life he wanted for me, and it's the life I love, the life that I fight for."

"Is it really safe to have the girls at the ranch?" she said, doubtfully. "Gunfights. Cat killings. I didn't feel comfortable leaving them there."

"It's funny you mention cat killings."

"Why's that?"

He tilted his head, wanting to watch the trapdoor shut. "Because a cat killing was never part of the official report," he explained. "It was never part of any news story. It was kept under wraps by Sheriff Jones. He was responsible for all the other killings. It unsettled him when he realized there was a copycat killer running around town, too."

Briefly, Liberty bit her lower lip. She stopped herself, glancing at some point over his shoulder. "You sound like you're accusing me of something."

"Of killing Luella's cat?" He shook his head. "No. You never did like to get your hands dirty. But you knew what was going on with Luella's animals. You knew she was staying at the Edge. And when you left the stable that day you dropped the girls off, the cat, Nyx, attacked you on your way out. You kicked him halfway across the yard."

"So?" she asked, jutting out her chin. "How am I the guilty one, all of a sudden?"

"Because Rowdy Conway isn't the steel trap you thought he was when you told him to do it," Ellis explained. "Deputy Wyatt never had to lean on him. He cracked, just as soon as they brought him into the station for questioning. He says you sought him out on your way out of town that day, having heard that Luella broke a bottle over his head. You targeted him because you knew he'd be feeling humiliated. You even threw in a few hundred dollars, just to make it worth his while."

"I didn't do anything wrong," Liberty claimed. "My hands are clean. I didn't kill the cat. He did."

The door to the station opened. Deputy Wyatt and another officer, Deputy Boot, stepped out into the white winter sunshine. "Ms. Eaton?" Wyatt said. "We'd like you to come with us."

She drew up straight as a pencil. Her jaw worked soundlessly. She took a step back. "What for?"

"We need to ask you a few questions about where you were Friday, December 16."

"This is not happening," she said, looking wildly around for Ellis as they escorted her into the building. "Ellis! Are you just going to stand there and let them do this?"

Ellis bent his head as he lifted his hat. He set it on his head and pulled it low over his brow. "Good luck, Lib," he said simply before the door closed behind them and he was left alone on the street. Sinking his hands into his pockets, he walked back to his truck so he could get back to building the future he wanted for his girls and Luella.

The storm wasn't gone. He wasn't sure it ever would be completely. But he'd found peace in it. He'd made his peace with it. As long as he had the three of them, he was content.

Epilogue

"**O**pen the door!" Eveline called to Wolfe as she held the gate to the open pasture.

Wolfe unlatched the door to the horse trailer and opened it wide.

Luella waited, holding on to Ingrid's shoulders so the little one wouldn't rush toward their new arrival. She felt the girl go up on her toes in anticipation. "Why doesn't she come out?" she asked.

"She's scared," Isla said. Her hand threaded through Luella's elbow, comfortably. "Isn't she, Lu?"

Luella couldn't stop the smile. It always came whenever the girls referred to her by the pet name. "Yes. She's been through a lot."

"Doesn't she know she's home now?" Ingrid asked, all but dancing on those toes. "She doesn't have to be cooped up ever again like she was in that stockyard. She can run and play and canter and race however much she wants and she never has to stop!"

"She'll learn all of that," Eveline told them. "She just has to give it a chance."

"Baby steps," Luella agreed. "She's going to take one day at a time, each moment in baby steps, until she learns to trust us. We just have to be patient and let her go at her pace."

Eveline called to the horse. Wolfe offered his soothing noises, the ones that normally worked.

Luella sighed. "I think it's time we brought him out."

Eveline nodded. "Call him. Let's see if we can't tempt her out."

Luella unclipped the radio from her belt and raised it to her mouth. "Ellis, do you read me?"

The radio crackled. Then Ellis's voice smoothed out. "Always, honey."

Another grin she couldn't fight, Luella thought as it spilled across her face. "Bring him around, please."

"Ten-four."

They waited. Ingrid started to squirm. Luella rubbed her shoulders. Patience was not one of Ingrid's virtues but Luella loved her spirit. Isla leaned her head against Luella's hip. "I can't wait to see her run," she breathed.

Luella put her arm around Isla and hugged her close. Over the last three months, things had moved much slower in her relationship with Ellis's oldest. Luella and Isla had bonded over quiet walks at the Edge and quiet talks.

Baby steps, Luella thought again.

They heard the far-off sound of a neigh. In the trailer, Luella heard the shuffling of curious hooves. She looked in the direction of the house with its retired waterwheel and dry creek-bed and saw the man and horse coming up the lane. She leaned down to the girls' ears. "It's your daddy," she whispered.

Ingrid cackled. "Sheridan's not trying to bite him in the butt today."

"It's early," Eveline drawled. "Give it time."

Luella watched her horse and shook her head when she saw how he'd come to accept Ellis's lead. While Sheridan still liked to take the occasional nip out of her man—and, really, how could she blame him—they'd come to understand one another, at least. It helped that, as the weather warmed toward spring, Ellis had been taking him on cattle runs, first on a lead rope next to Shy so he could get the lay of the land. Then, in the saddle, where Ellis had let him follow the herd and put his biting to use on the stragglers.

Luella had to admit it had worked to temper Sheridan's aggression, his restlessness, even bolster his confidence.

Ellis and Sheridan came to the gate, where Ellis paraded the roan in front of the trailer. Sheridan sniffed in the direction of the mare, gave an intrigued bugle and danced a little in place.

Isla gasped when, finally, the mare's nose poked out into the open air.

"Come on," Ingrid murmured. "Come on, girl."

Ellis looked to Luella and winked. "Should I let him be wild?"

She nodded. "Let's hope she follows."

"Easy," Ellis said to Sheridan when he came around to his front. He unlatched the bridle, loosening it enough to get it over his ears and off. "Show her how it's done," he said, patting his withers before he let out a rallying "Yah!"

Sheridan's front legs waved once in the air before he took off through the gate, the wind catching his mane and tail, just as it caught the prairie grass.

From the mare, there came a nicker. Sheridan, at a distance now, slowed and whinnied, arcing in a half circle.

"What's happening?" Ingrid asked.

"They're talking," Ellis said, coming to stand with them at the fence.

"What's he telling her?" Isla asked.

Ellis met Luella's gaze. "He's saying, 'Come on, girl. Live this life with me.'"

"What's *she* saying?" Ingrid asked, tugging on Luella's hand for an answer.

Luella couldn't look away from Ellis. "'Give me a second. I'm trying to catch my breath.'"

He laughed quietly, laying his arm across the top rung of the fence so that his hand could splay across the surface of her hair. She felt the sun warm on her face and had to catch her breath, as well, as she thought about how long it'd taken them to get here.

"Here she comes!" Ingrid said, giving in to a hop.

The mare came down the ramp in hesitant steps. She was a paint horse. Luella and Eveline had wanted to bring home all the horses in the stockyard. And that was the long-term goal. But the paint...after hearing her story, they'd wanted her to be the first.

She moved through the gate, skittish of the humans on the fringes. Then she took off into the pasture, moving like lightning.

Eveline closed the gate. Wolfe came to stand with her and they all watched as the paint let the wind take her.

As Sheridan turned and galloped toward the cliffs in the distance, on some unspoken plane where only the purest beings interacted with each other, the mare turned, too, in unison.

"She's free," Isla said as she and Ingrid climbed the fence to watch.

"She sure is," Ellis murmured. He turned his head and dipped a kiss to her head then Ingrid's. "Aren't they a picture?"

Luella made a noise. She feared if she spoke, it would come out all watery and she didn't want the girls to think she was upset.

She and Ellis had worked to shield the worst of what had happened over the last months from them. They knew that their time with their mother had been limited by the judge in the custody case.

In the future, they would have more time with Liberty. Ellis had never wanted them to be apart from her completely. Split custody was still what he had his sights on. But after being charged with the cat killing after her arrangement with Rowdy had come to the surface, the judge had thought it best for the girls to live at Eaton Edge for the time being.

More change was on the horizon. Ellis and Liberty would have to reach some co-parenting arrangement. And there would be a wedding.

Luella ran the tip of her thumb over the ring band on her left ring finger. She'd finally gotten used to wearing Ellis's engagement ring again, though it still made her blink in surprise when she saw the Polaris diamond winking light at her.

The Eatons had refused to accept Luella's suggestion of a city hall ceremony. There would be a wedding, they insisted, at the Edge or Ollero Creek—wherever she wished. It helped that the girls had taken the news of the engagement well. They wanted their father to be happy, and they had grown to accept Luella's place in his life. They'd accepted her in their lives, as well, which was the greatest gift of all, she thought, gathering Ingrid's golden strands of hair in her hands gingerly.

She'd wanted the two of them to feel as if Ollero Creek Horse Rescue was theirs, too. It would be their job to name the paint, and others who came to live here. Luella was determined that they would never miss a release.

Luella did what Isla had done for her. She rested her head on Ellis's frame as they watched the pair become specks against the backdrop of the plateau and sandstone cliffs. She had a family. She would have a wedding. She was going to live this life with Ellis and his girls and the horses she, Eveline and Wolfe were going to rescue together.

Second chances were the stuff of dreams and she was living them.

The sound of a truck rumbling toward them brought her head around. She laid her hand on Ellis's back when she saw the sheriff's vehicle.

He tensed, too, automatically. Then, he relaxed. "It's a friend."

It was easy to forget that the weight of the Fuego County police was no longer stacked against her. Wendell Jones was serving his time. His reputation had saved him from a long sentence. It had helped him that both Ellis, Javier and Altaha had survived their gunshot wounds. His reputation as a sheriff and his exemplary record as a police officer with over thirty years on the job had gone a long way, too.

Jones wouldn't be gone forever. But now wasn't the time to dwell on that.

Luella walked with Ellis to meet Altaha.

The sheriff's badge on her uniform gleamed as she removed her sunshades and smiled in greeting. "Howdy, Eatons," she called, hitching only slightly on her bad leg as she walked to them. "How was the first release?"

"Perfect," Luella admitted. "I'm sorry you missed it."

"Me, too," she said, squinting to find the paint and Sheridan in the distance. "I got held up at the station."

Ellis studied her. "What can we do you for, Sheriff? No more bad news, I hope."

"Nope," Altaha admitted. "Though there is news and I wanted you to know immediately."

Luella felt her heart pick up pace and didn't know what to feel, exactly.

Altaha took an envelope from her back pocket and held it out for Luella. "This came via fax this afternoon."

"From who?" Ellis asked as Luella lifted the flap of the envelope and took out the contents.

"Odessa," Altaha answered.

Luella was having trouble reading Altaha's expression. "Texas?"

"Read it," she urged.

Luella unfolded the fresh-printed papers. She read the first few lines. Her hand trembled as it came up to meet her mouth. "Oh, God, Ellis."

He took the papers and scanned the first few lines. His arm went around her shoulder immediately, drawing her close. "You…found him."

Altaha tilted her head. "Told you I would."

Luella couldn't speak past the knot in her throat. Instead, she stepped to Altaha and enveloped her in a hug.

Altaha patted her on the back. "I'm just sorry it took so long."

When Luella stepped back, wiping her eyes, Ellis took his turn, bringing Altaha in for a strong-armed embrace. "Thank you, Kaya."

"This is the best thing I've done on the job yet. Believe me when I say it's my pleasure. You'll have to be the ones who establish contact."

"His adoptive parents are open to that?" Ellis asked, stepping back to scan the paperwork.

"They are," Altaha said, "just as long as you contact them first."

"This is incredible," Luella breathed. "It's got his name."

"Look at that," Ellis said with a soft smile. "Our son's name is Kai."

She lifted her face to his. "We have a teenager."

"I'm old, Lu," he said. "You still want to marry me?"

"If you can handle these fine lines," she told him. "And ignore the wrinkles."

"Puppies have wrinkles, too," he said, touching his brow to hers. "Nobody can say no to them any more than I can say no to you."

"I've got to be getting back to the station," Altaha said, shifting toward her truck as the two kissed. She stopped, however, and turned back. "Oh. Could you do something for me?"

"Anything," Luella said.

Altaha pursed her lips. "Tell your brother I've thought about it. I've thought about it a lot. And my answer is yes. He'll know what it means."

Ellis narrowed his eyes. "Do *I* want to know what it means?"

"Probably not," Altaha said with a smirk. "You'll deliver the message?"

"Yes," Luella said before Ellis could think twice.

"Thanks a lot." Altaha tipped her hat. "See you around, lovebirds."

"See you," Ellis said. As she walked off, he opened his mouth.

Luella touched her finger to his lips. "Whatever's to come of it, let it be. He did, for us." She rolled her eyes and added, "Well, eventually."

His smile came slowly but warmly. "Dang. My wife's going to be so much smarter than me."

"Maybe." She held him close as she looked back to find Isla and Ingrid playing tag in the grass with Wolfe and Eveline. "You make up for it by being such a good man and an even better daddy."

"This is all I need in life," he explained, resting his cheek on top of her head so they could both watch. "You. This family. This chance."

"It's more than I ever wished for," she said.

"And I won't ever let it get away from you again."

"I know." She rested her ear to his chest, closed her eyes and listened to his heart.

His voice rumbled through the wall of his chest. "How 'bout we celebrate tonight with some stargazing?"

She grinned freely, running her hands down the long, strong line of his back. "Absolutely."

* * * * *

#2259 COLTON'S YULETIDE MANHUNT
The Coltons of New York • by Kacy Cross

Detective Isaac Donner wants to catch the notorious Landmark Killer in the splashiest way possible—if only to prove to his father he has the goods to do it. But his by-the-books partner, Rory Colton, isn't ready to risk her life for a family feud. Her heart is another matter...

#2260 DANGER ON THE RIVER
Sierra's Web • by Tara Taylor Quinn

Undercover cop Tommy Grainger stumbles upon a web of deceit when he rescues Kacey Ashland, bound and drowning, from the local wild rapids. Could the innocent-looking—yet oh-so tempting—elementary school teacher be tied to an illegal contraband cold case that involves Tommy's own father?

#2261 A DETECTIVE'S DEADLY SECRETS
Honor Bound • by Anna J. Stewart

When Detective Lana Tate comes back into FBI special agent Eamon Quinn's life, he'll do anything for a second chance and to keep the woman he's always loved safe. Soon their investigation threatens not only their lives but also whatever future they might have together.

#2262 WATCHERS OF THE NIGHT
The Night Guardians • by Charlene Parris

Forensics investigator Cynthia Cornwall is brilliant, introverted—and compromised. Her agreement to keep Detective Adam Solberg off his father's murder case has put her life in danger, job in jeopardy and heart in the charismatic, determined cop's crosshairs.

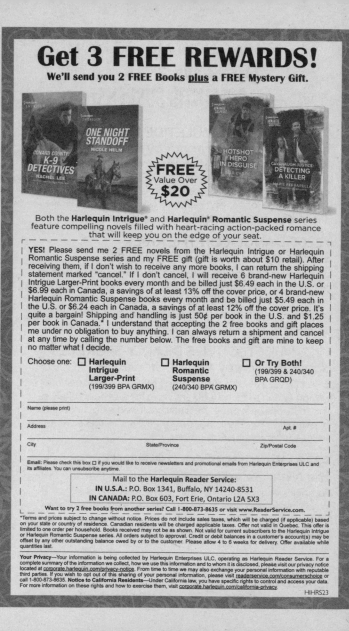

HARLEQUIN
PLUS

Try the best multimedia
subscription service for romance
readers like you!

Read, Watch and Play.

Experience the easiest way to get
the romance content you crave.

Start your **FREE TRIAL** at
www.harlequinplus.com/freetrial.